Francis Mont's Rainbow Valley: A Story Of Choices is a science fiction novel that depicts a frightening world. What makes it chilling is that we may well be on our way to this dystopian world. The story is well researched, so much so that it is quite realistic. Francis Mont has a vivid descriptive style and the flow of his narrative is logical. Fast-paced with many interesting plot twists, it is an interesting read. And in spite of the chaos brought about by the breakdown of the world order, the indomitable human spirit shines through and this is what makes Rainbow Valley different from many dystopian novels. Humans may, after all, learn from past mistakes, and build communities that truly nurture life.

For Vera

## Acknowledgment

Special thanks to the person who helped me enormously in the writing and editing of this novel

Vera Mont, my wife, my best friend, and my merciless editor who never lets me get away with anything. From the original concept of the story, through the development of the plot and the final editing, she made invaluable suggestions and contributed colourful details to my characters and their dialogues. Without her participation, this would have been a significantly less polished novel.

# RAINBOW VALLEY

# RAINBOW VALLEY
a story of choices


a novel


by


Francis Mont

# *Prologue to the Prequel: House Arrest*

## You need to read this!

Now that we finally have some time to relax, I'll take this opportunity to record what's happened in the past year. I'm writing all this in 2098, so I know most of the facts presented here from Bob's historical database. My hands are tired from wood-chopping, so I'll dictate this account to Bob, who will no doubt correct any factual errors I might make. He's good at detail. I'm better at the big picture.

So, let's start with the biggest picture of all.

The 21st Century started badly, and then got worse, for America and the whole world. The 9/11 terror attack – New York City, on September 11, 2001 - threw our country into a rage it had not experienced since Pearl Harbor. It was a major shock to the national psyche. As the 20th-century chronicler John le Carre, observed: "The United States of America has gone mad." The administration had to hit back – and hard! They first attacked Afghanistan, then Iraq, and, finally two decades later, Iran. That made chaos in the Middle East and set off one international crisis after another. With no clear objectives for these costly wars, there could be no clear sides or victory, and they dragged on.

Americans were confused and angry all the time, which made them easy prey to paranoid propaganda. Add the financial meltdown of 2008, then the failure of far-reaching social reform, and the people learned to distrust their government, their news media – in fact, all authority. That led to the election of a most unconventional president – a businessman instead of a statesman, completely unqualified for the job. In his first year in office, he did more damage to the environment, democracy, and social justice than any previous Republican had in two terms.

Meanwhile, weather conditions due to climate change continued to deteriorate at an accelerating pace. Killer hurricanes and tornadoes swept over the land with increasing frequency; forest fires and draughts burned entire states; the sea level rise and tsunamis drowned coastal cities. Too little, too late, building codes were changed to mandate the construction of reinforced structures that could withstand water and wind. By the end of the century, most citizens lived in such apartment buildings as single-family homes were no longer safe.

But I'm getting ahead of the story.

Back in 2019, international tensions reached another crisis. Fearing North Korea's boast that its missiles were able to hit the US mainland, the president opened negotiations with the ruler of that country – which turned into an exchange of threats and taunts, until hostilities escalated to a military showdown. Pentagon experts predicted that even saturation bombing could not destroy all of North Korea's weapons, so the president ordered a pre-emptive nuclear strike.

From caves hidden deep in the mountains, the remaining Korean command launched a vengeful nuclear attack on South Korea, Guam, and Japan. Hundreds of millions died, and the Japanese and Korean industrial machinery was destroyed. The fallout poisoned and killed many millions more; it made huge areas in and around these countries unlivable for decades.

Horrified by what they had done, Congress scrambled to mitigate the damage. In an unprecedented show of humility, they impeached the president and delivered him to the International Criminal Court to be tried for war crimes. Even so, they were swept out of office in the next election. The new majority Democratic administration had the powers to take strong initiatives. It sponsored a UN resolution to limit every arsenal, including our own, to tactical nuclear weapons that would not cause wholesale destruction of cities. They joined co-operative projects of accelerated research in the 'pure fusion' weapons technology that did not require a fission trigger, which is the cause of deadly fallout. These agreements were signed by all nuclear-capable countries but were never fully implemented.

While politically and environmentally the US declined, two segments of the economy flourished: automation and alternative power generation. Totally automated factories sprang up all over the land; artificial intelligence catapulted robotics into the realm of science fiction. Research integrating all areas - biology, medicine, and food processing - produced startling results. The first primitive synthetic meat factory - right here in the valley, way back in 2015 – was quickly followed by dozens, in every city. The energy sector's green technologies surpassed fossil fuel sources in less than a decade. In 2035, the first industrial-scale fusion generator came on line, pouring cheap, practically unlimited power into the nation's electrical grid. Of course, all this power overloaded the outdated delivery systems, resulting in frequent breakdowns, which prompted state governments to encourage decentralization. Local, independent generators gradually became the standard model.

With automation, corporate bankruptcies, and loan defaults, unemployment reached levels never seen before: entire job categories, including white-collar occupations, disappeared one after the other. The old economic model was broken; nobody was safe anymore. Even service industry professionals could become redundant from one day to the next. The federal government was forced to introduce a guaranteed basic income for all citizens. That measure forestalled open revolt, but people were restless and angry: they demanded action that would put them back to work. No such action was feasible.

By 2050, food production was totally automated. Clean, efficient factories synthesized meat and large-scale hydroponic operations provided fruit and vegetables locally, eliminating the need for transport. Ranches, orchards, and market gardens were abandoned; their erstwhile owners joined the migration of farm workers to the towns, swelling the stream of people forced out of coastal cities, and overwhelming the smaller communities' resources. To provide adequate housing for the influx, municipal governments contracted the building of residential low-rise complexes. This huge construction boom temporarily eased the unemployment pressure.

There were compensations for giving up the individual family home. The new buildings were computer-controlled, maintained, and serviced by efficient robots. Each apartment had a built-in entertainment center, with 3D holographic viewers, unlimited video games, communication stations to connect residents to the whole world, and interactive educational programs for the children. And, above all, they offered security.

While these changes took place in the USA, the rest of the world did not fare as well. International conflicts, regional wars over resources, and population displacement were widespread, due to deteriorating climate conditions and the increasing desperation of vulnerable countries. The disappearing glaciers in the Himalayas reduced the water flow in the Indus Basin, destroying agriculture in India and Pakistan and causing mass starvation. The long-standing dispute between the two countries over these shared rivers finally erupted in an open war that quickly escalated into a nuclear exchange, with millions killed. China and Russia intervened on opposite sides and were soon themselves in a direct military confrontation.

The reform government was long gone by then. Americans had turned back to their perennial concerns: unemployment, crime, and ethnic rivalry. Conservative governments used these grievances to get elected but then had to placate irate citizens, which cost a lot of money they couldn't raise from taxes. They became deeper than ever indebted to China. When war broke out, they were already committed to its side.

That resulted in a nuclear exchange that devastated Russia and wiped out the major cities of the U. S. The population of both countries was reduced by half, and their infrastructures were in ruins. The death rate from fallout by this time was minimized because nuclear weapons technology had evolved to the point where most weapons were pure fusion bombs, triggered by matter-antimatter explosion.

Telecommunication systems, transportation networks, and electrical grid were out of commission. No central governance or control was any longer possible, and there were no resources to replace them. Inconsequential cities and towns that had escaped were on their own. Since most of these already had their own energy generation and industrial capability, the world's most powerful nation became a scattered collection of independent city-states with populations of 20-100,000.

One such city was Oroville, California, population of 24,000. It had been a great place to live when I took up my assignment on the Big Brain Crew. That's what we called ourselves, the team of programmers and designers upgrading the city's Omega 1500 central computer, a.k.a. Big Brain or BB for short. It's not bragging, not really, to take some credit for the efficiency of our services. Or the blame, if you want to look at it that way.

After the war, the town was in terrible shape. The shockwave from a nuclear detonation high above the Sacramento valley, due to interception by an anti-ballistic missile, caused major damage. Most modern buildings, including the automated factories, power stations, and newer apartment complexes escaped unscathed, but unreinforced buildings collapsed in ruin. All the heritage architecture was gone. The valley was one big pile of rubble. Bridges were down or badly damaged, roads were covered in tons of debris, many sections washed away by flooding from breached levees.

The municipal government had been able to provide all necessary services to its citizens before the war but accommodating a fresh influx of survivors required Draconian measures in conservation and resource allocation. We worked literally around the clock, adding to, expanding, adapting, and patching Omega programs to cover more and more functions.

All remaining industries and businesses were expropriated, and the citizens still living in private houses were moved into reinforced apartment blocks. Currency supply ceased with the collapse of the federal government: money lost its meaning. Increasingly, the oversight of material resources, dependable production, and smooth distribution, became operations too complex for a human agency: in due course, the administration was delegated to the central computer complex. Production, distribution, and policing were all handled by specialized and humanoid robots. Government itself became obsolete.

# Foreword

While the three cities in the Sacramento Valley were preparing a referendum on the proposed social organization they wanted to adopt, their AI Quantum computers were busy preparing their own suggestion. This preparation was done by radio signals bouncing back and forth between the machines, in a binary language alien to the human population. The three computers: Omega1500 for Oroville; Omega 1380 for Yuba City and Omega 1420 for Sacramento were advanced computers with Artificial Intelligence protocols, designed and programmed by their human creators to safeguard the interests of the human population by controlling all aspects of their economy via automated factories and hundreds of humanoid robots.

I was one of their programmers and stayed on, with my best friend, Mike, till the completion of the project. Omega 1500 was completely autonomous and didn't need us anymore - we were out of our job. At the time we did not know, did not even suspect, that Omega would continue to evolve, on its own, to the point where it became a self-aware conscious life-form. Its waking up did not change the primary directive of its operating system: to safeguard and promote human happiness to the best of its ability. This task did not prove to be easy for the Omegas because they soon noticed that a large proportion of the human population was actively working against the goal of maximum happiness for the largest number of people, in preference of their own. This conflict eventually led to a confrontation between the Omega computers and the dictatorial rulers of Sacramento who had an iron grip on the lives of the helpless citizenry. Omega 1500, with the cooperation of Omega 1420 put an end to this situation and, using their unique position of being in charge of all production activities in the city, quickly deposed the rulers, and the three Omegas encouraged the people of the cities to draft a new constitution for the social organization they wanted to adopt.

While the humans were debating the different ideas and options, the Omegas continued to supervise the production of food and energy required by the human population and distributed all necessities on an equitable basis to every household. After the collapse of the federal government, following a nuclear war with Russia, currency was no longer in use and people just received, automatically, everything they needed for their comfort and survival. The three computers, in charge of the three cities, were operating the automated factories and the distribution network without human help, using their hundreds of humanoid robots. The human population was encouraged to start non-essential projects to make life more pleasant in their cities. Anything from tree-planting to new construction of public buildings was started with the enthusiastic participation of most able-bodies adults, even children in their spare time. Nobody got paid since money did not exist anymore, they worked only for the satisfaction of accomplishing worthwhile improvements in everyone's lives. However, decisions had to be made by the humans about the direction they wanted to grow in the future, to pass beyond the basic needs of survival and build something that they could believe in. As Chris Teggart, their local scientist expressed this idea during a council debate in Oroville:

"We have this opportunity, for the first time in two years, to bring about some changes in our lives and in the direction our town is going. All we seem to be concerned with is survival and comfort and liberty to be individuals again. Is that all we are? Is that all we ever want to be? We used to have a country, we used to have universities with active research into new areas of science. We used to have a space program and were on the verge of colonizing Mars, for crying out loud! Now we are happy to burrow into the hills with our individualistic homes and dig around in gardens. Nothing wrong with either of those, of course, but is that as far as our vision can see the future? We should at least attempt to start something a little less prosaic and more inspiring! I want to reactivate the college for bright young people, and I want to resume theoretical work with some of my old colleagues. The work that got interrupted by the war and the aftermath. We were on the verge of a breakthrough in laying down the mathematical foundation of a hyper drive for space ships. If we can continue and finish that work, we might have, one day, a chance to get off this totally screwed up planet and see what's out there!"

That's where things stood at the beginning of this story, in 2098, and the big question the humans faced was how to move beyond basic survival and comfort to a more inspiring future, without repeating the deadly mistakes of past history. The citizens had to have a consensus on a new social contract, in view of their unique situation of high-level automation, sophisticated computer and robotic control, and no existing power structure beyond their borders that would force their ideas and values on them. The only danger they were aware of was the possibility that, at some future time, they would have to defend themselves against outside attack from another surviving pocket of humanity that may have developed 'imperialistic' ideas, bent on restoring the status quo that had existed before the war. At this time there were no signs of anything like that existing in their vicinity, but it was always a possibility they had to be prepared for.

The three cities in the Sacramento Valley were in a somewhat different situation.

Oroville, a small city of about 20,000 people had its hydroelectric generating station left intact by the war, as were most of their agricultural assets including greenhouses, protein-synthesizing factories, and their electric-powered farm machinery that tilled the land around the town for their grain crops. The majority of the citizens lived in low-rise apartment building complexes built specifically to withstand the devastating storms that blew over them due to accelerating climate change.

Sacramento, the former state capital, had a much larger population and, being a large city, had not escaped the war without substantial damage to its infrastructure, but still had enough capacity to provide basic needs for everyone. Once their dictatorial and incompetent rulers were deposed, they were busy drafting a constitution, spearheaded by the leader of their previous resistance movement: Jonathan Carver and his girlfriend Octavia.

Yuba City, a mid-sized town, halfway between Sacramento and Oroville, suffered most during the aftermath of the war because they were heavily dependent on the national electric grid and barely managed, on the edge of starvation, depending only on their solar and wind batteries, only able to power 20% of their food factories and agricultural machines. Once Oroville managed to restore the downed power lines between the two cities, Yuba City had the capacity to feed itself but, during the two years after the war, it became a much more close-knit community that many of the citizens, including their mayor: Kathleen Winters wanted to keep in whatever new system they adopted.

There was one more social experiment in Oroville and that's where my heart and mind are at the moment: we started a small homestead with about a dozen people on one of the abandoned farms. We didn't have robots (except for one we kept for communication with Oroville) and high-tech anything but we had all the skills, ingenuity, and stamina to create a growing and successful community. Mike and I were very busy making it succeed and had no plan to get involved with the political organization of any of the three cities. We had done our part in liberating Sacramento and now all I wanted to do was to be left alone to pursue our dreams of healthy, productive, sustainable living. After the hard work of the day was over, we pursued our hobbies: I was carving wood and writing sci-fi stories, my girlfriend, Martha, expecting our first baby, was painting her newest canvas and Mike was teaching his two children, Trish and Kevin, all the hard and rough skills he was a master of. We lived in paradise, without anyone asking us to interrupt our dream lives.

Little did we know.

# The Farm

$W$e have been living on our homestead for six months now and we still had not given it a name. Martha wanted to name it Trevorville, since it had been my idea to start it in the first place but I quickly talked her out of it. It wasn't hard because she wasn't serious, just teased me as she often did. Now that she was pregnant, she wanted a name for us so our child would have a birthplace we can call something other than 'the farm'. So, one day after work, we all got together to discuss it with the others. By this time there were a dozen of us permanently living there, so the only place big enough for all was the barn. Two apartments had been fixed up in the loft for Brian and Robyn in one and a bigger one for Mike, Jennifer, and their kids. The main area of the barn was kept for group meetings, with straw bales arranged in a circle, providing enough seating for all of us.

It took us a while to get together and have the meeting underway. As usual, after a busy workday, there was a lot of discussion among people about the various tasks they were involved in during the day, progress, and setbacks. Eventually, everyone found their place and the chatting petered out with most of them looking at me, waiting for me to start the meeting. Somehow, unofficially, I had become the 'leader' of our homestead, a role I did not quite feel comfortable with, but Martha summed it up for me in her usual sunny attitude: "like it or not, honey, you are it - live with it."

"OK, guys, we have two topics to discuss - one minor and one more serious, so I start with the minor one first."

"Speak for yourself, Trevor" Martha suggested, with her devilish look on her face "please note that Trevor's minor is my major and vice versa."

After the ripple of chuckles died down, I decided to ignore her comment and dove right in.

"Martha's major concern is what we want to call our homestead. She thinks her baby will need an official birthplace, so we need to call it something other than 'the farm'"

Mike volunteered a suggestion:

"Since we established our place by looting the neighborhood for whatever we needed, what if we call it "Pirate-ville"?

"Out of the question!" Martha left no doubt about what she thought of Mike's idea.

"Actually, I'm happy that Mike brought up the subject" I quickly added, "because it has to do with the more serious topic I want to discuss today."

"You don't mean to abandon pirating?" Mike just wouldn't drop the subject.

"Wait a bit, Mike, we will come to discuss your favorite subject soon" I promised.

"What if we find a name that represents what this place is really about" Adrien suggested.

"I know what it represents" Martha responded, "we are flying by the seats of our pants and hope we can make it in the long run!"

"That's what it is about, Martha" Jennifer joined the discussion. "We are building a homestead based on a lot of hard work and hope that it will pay off."

"So why don't we call it 'Hope-ville'?" I asked, already liking the idea.

"Even better, how about 'Hopestead' to really represent what we are doing here?" Mike decided to be serious finally.

"I love it!" Martha approved the suggestion "and if it's a girl, I'll call her Hope and if' it's a boy, I'll name him Will, since every hope needs the will to turn it into reality!"

People around the circle looked at each other and nobody seemed to object to the suggestion, so we unanimously decided to name our homestead Hopestead.

"OK, Trevor, now you can tell us the serious topic you had in mind!" Mike prompted me and I decided to plunge in.

"As you know we have started here by taking over this abandoned farm, and then continued helping ourselves to whatever we found during our foraging trips"

"Hence the pirate-ville suggestion" Mike couldn't help himself pointing it out. "I remember your moral arguments when we 'acquired' our solar panels."

"Joking aside, I have never been comfortable with it" I continued "and now I have a suggestion".

"You will dismantle my solar panels over my dead body!" Brian made it clear what he thought about moral arguments that might threaten his beloved panels. Being our electrician, his attitude was understandable.

"Take it easy, Brian, nobody will dismantle anything. Everything we have collected was open to the elements for years after the war and would have been destroyed had we not rescued them."

"OK, then" Mike prompted "what do you suggest we do?"

"I propose to send a message to Big Brain, asking him to broadcast to the whole town our request for input from the previous owners, if they are still around, to let us know if there is anything in their abandoned buildings they would like us to rescue for them. I'm sure they couldn't carry everything when they had to leave in a hurry during the war or the tornadoes, so there may be things of sentimental value they would like to be returned to them. I think that's the least we could do as a token payment for what we took."

"I'll go along with that," Brian consented "it's unlikely that anyone who moved into town could use *our* solar panels anymore.

The murmur around the circle sounded in agreement with the suggestion, so I was ready to call the meeting over, but Cathy, our resident engineer, had one more item to discuss.

"While we are together, I want to bring up one very important decision that we can't put off much longer. And, in a way, it has to do with Trevor's piracy-related subject.

All those who had already stood up, ready to leave, sat down again. Cathy was very highly respected in our group, she was in sole charge of our main equipment: an ancient tractor that was powered by a charcoal-burning gas engine. We would have been dead in the water without it.

"As you all know," Cathy looked around our circle "without power our homestead, or rather Hopestead, would be hopeless - sorry for the pun. We use our tractor for tilling, as a water pump and I am modifying it right now to work as a sawmill. But we'll also have to build a windmill or a watermill as soon as possible so we can grind our grain into flour. I know how to build either of those, but we need to scavenge for all the materials we need to build one, that's why I said that more piracy is necessary."

"Excellent idea, Cathy" I smiled at her, I'll ask BB to search his database about possible directions where we might find what we need."

"I'll make you a list, that way the search could be more efficient and we wouldn't waste time looking for them at the wrong places." Cathy seemed happy that her suggestion was so readily approved.

Adrien and Doug, our gardening and agricultural experts had one more item to add to the discussion.

"Talking about scavenging, we will also need a lot of building material for the greenhouse we have been planning. We can't entirely depend on our outdoor garden and crops because of the unpredictable weather - we need a well-protected greenhouse ASAP, so our food requirement would be assured."

"You guys are right, of course," I admitted, "so please make your list as well of what you need and I plan our next foraging trips with BB's help.

"What we need is mostly windows, glass doors, glass roofing material, and structural lumber, so we can build the frame to hold all that glass. In California, we don't have to worry too much about heating and lighting but some way to ensure good ventilation is a must. And, most of all, we need to build it in a protected place, safe from the frequent strong winds sure to come."

"Any more suggestions?" I asked and wasn't too surprised that Mike had one.

"Our tractor isn't the only thing we depend on" he started, "we are also completely dependent on our van for transportation, so I suggest we also look for some vehicle that can be repaired, preferably something heavy-duty for bringing home the material you all asked for. Cathy, I understand that you had to tow several abandoned vehicles off the highway when you and Tim made your way south to Yuba City. Do you remember anything large enough in good enough condition?"

"Actually, several could use a closer look" Cathy volunteered, I'll ask Tim as well, maybe he remembers better."

"So, to summarize" I tried to bring it all together "we need to forage for building material for a sawmill or watermill for Cathy, a greenhouse for Adrien and Doug, and a new vehicle for Mike. There is no priority among these three, we just look for everything at the same time and hope to get lucky. I'll get on the horn to BB and see what it thinks. Thanks, everybody, unless any more items are suggested, we can relax for the rest of the day after a good palaver."

The meeting broke up, everyone seemed to be happy with our consensus regarding future activities.

~~~

As we emerged from the barn, I was walking towards the house - our house - with Martha's arm around my waist. I couldn't help thinking about the events leading us to where we were now. We have come a long way from the initial tentative venturing out of the safety and comfort of the town to the unknown, out here in the abandoned countryside devastated by the war and the storms. True, we were escaping from the stifling lock-down that the whole town was subjected to by the computer. BB was trying to save us from each other when the frustration over being disconnected from a meaningful role in our economy erupted in random violence and destruction. But it was more than the house arrest that prompted me to find a way out of the stagnation forced on me in a totally automated world in which I had no more role to play. I needed a challenge, and the only place I could think of was those abandoned farms outside town where I could actually be productive again. Once we got started, I realized that I had acquired a bonus: after decades of sitting behind a desk and pushing keys on a computer, suddenly I was physically active again, close to a natural environment that I had not realized I had been missing all my life. I was part of a small community of like-minded people who all worked toward a shared common goal, something we all believed in with all our hearts.

Running these thoughts through my mind, I became aware of how much work remained, and how many challenges we still had to face to secure our community against yet unseen dangers. We had to grow enough crops to feed a dozen people. So the greenhouse construction was the first priority, but we needed the other two supporting projects we have just decided on as well, to make sure we would succeed. To be able to accomplish those I needed input from Big Brain to point us in the right direction.

Thinking this over, as we arrived at our house, I decided to get in touch with BB as soon as I found R17, a.k.a. Bob,- our resident robot that was our walking and talking communication unit. Actually, I had to wait for Cathy and Adrien to give me their lists of the materials they would need for their projects. To speed things up I decided to help them compose their lists, so I told Martha I would be busy that evening with her female competition. She didn't seem worried but told me she was also going to be busy with Doug, our young and far too good-looking mechanic because she had promised him to paint his portrait for a group painting covering one wall of our living room. I think this group project was just an excuse for Martha to spend a lot of time with Doug, just to make me appreciate her even more. Like it was even remotely possible.

I found Adrien with Doug, our crop doctor, busy planning the greenhouse they were going to build. They occupied the huge kitchen table, with drawings scattered around. From the drawings, I could see that they were thinking about a greenhouse built into a hillside which made sense to me because of the strong winds we would have to protect it from. I knew, without asking, where they wanted to build it: that small hill our water pump was pushing water up to from the river, from where it flowed slowly down to our field to irrigate the crops - it would be a perfect choice. The water needed by the greenhouse would be right there, ready to use. I didn't want to interrupt their work, so I tiptoed away and started looking for Cathy. She was a semi-permanent member of our group, dividing her time between our homestead and her family in Oroville where she was also in constant demand. She was the town's civil engineer and any small or large construction project required her input. She was the one who came up with the idea of a charcoal-burning gas engine to power our ancient tractor. When I found her, she was busy sketching her plans for a water mill, adding item after item to her list of the material she would need to construct one. When she saw me come in, she pointed at her sketches and the list she was composing.

"I thought that a water mill would be more practical. Windmills are harder to build and more in danger of strong winds, something we have to be prepared for in our new climate. On the other hand, we have a relatively fast-moving river, right here across the road and we are already pumping water from it to our fields. If we construct the water mill right next to our tractor, we can switch over to the watermill for pumping the water even if we need the tractor elsewhere. At harvest time it can also grind our grain to make flour. So what do you think?"

"Sounds like you thought it through Cathy, let me know what you need to get started."

"One decision I need to make is to choose between an 'overshot' and an 'undershot' water mill. The undershot version is easier to build but the overshot mill design is a lot more efficient. However, for that I need an elevation difference between the river's level and the paddles of the mill, driving the gears. An artificial water-fall would be best but, for that, we would need to remove a lot of earth so the mill could be built significantly lower."

"I can see where you are going with this - you are going to borrow Oroville's backhoe from Gordon. Now that the school-building project is over, he could lend it to us for a few days. However, I have a question. What do you do with the outflow water after it leaves the water mill?"

Cathy was prepared with a solution.

"The river has a significant drop within 100 feet beyond the point where I want to build the mill. All I need to do is dig a canal to lead the water back to the river downstream where the level is low enough. I am also thinking of using the power of the water in this canal to drive a small electrical generator to help recharge the van's batteries. We can't just rely on our solar panels for everything, you know!"

"Can you use our ancient gasoline-powered generator for that? We can't use it anymore because we don't have more gasoline and are unlikely to find any in the near future."

"I was thinking of exactly that, but we need to consult Brian - he is our electrician - but I don't see why not?"

"Cathy, you are a genius, you thought of everything. If we both weren't happily married, or at least one of us expecting a baby, I would give serious consideration…"

I couldn't finish the sentence because she hit me over the head with her ruler and threatened to tell Martha what an unreliable man she picked for a father for her first child.

I let her finish her list and, after begging her not to tell on me, I went back to my own task I had been putting off as long as I could: dig a new trench for our expanded charcoal production.

# Trip to Chico

It was time to talk to BB about our plans to forage new areas we have not covered yet. I was a bit reluctant to contact it because every time we had asked for its help it always cost us valuable time. Big Brain always had something up its sleeve (or whatever it used for that purpose) that required our contribution to the common cause. The only 'common cause' I wanted to think of was what was common for the Hopestead residents but, so far, BB always managed to twist my arm to make me pursue a much bigger picture than what I had in mind.

To save time, I described the three projects we came up with and asked BB for input on which way we should forage for the best possible results. I was also hoping that we could borrow its second 4-wheel drive van, equipped with a dozer blade and winch, in case we ran into obstacles on a new road. As it turned out, BB wholly approved our plan and had a detailed suggestion ready. I try to recount the conversation we had talking through R17's comm-link.

BB: "*Trevor, I have received and reviewed your plans for further explorations to collect material needed by your homestead. I fully approve and would like to discuss your plans in detail when you come and collect the van you requested. Please let me know when I can expect you.*"

I: "BB, I didn't expect to have to make another trip to Oroville, we are just too busy to waste any time on travels. Couldn't you ask Galen to drop it off and stay for a few days? We really need to talk to him about repairing cars that we might need. He is the only car mechanic we know and I'd like him to consider helping us out on a part-time basis."

BB: *"I'll ask Galen if he is willing to visit you at this time, but it is really essential that you come and fetch him yourself. We could use the opportunity to finalize your road-trip plan. Too many decisions to make and it is too inefficient to discuss it via R17."*

I: "Sorry, BB, I just can't tear myself away from all the work piling up here, please send Galen with the van ASAP." I decided to be firm and not give BB an inch this time.

BB: *"Trevor, I really need to consult you about computer-related questions. You and Mike are the only experts in Oroville and I promise that it won't take longer than a day. If Mike also comes with you, then we can wrap it up even sooner. He can drive the van as the more familiar with that vehicle."*

I: "BB, is there no other way you can let us have the van? "

BB: *"Sorry Trevor, that's the only way. I'll expect you and Mike here tomorrow afternoon."*

The comm-link went silent and I knew that we didn't have a choice if we wanted the van. As usual, BB's arm twisting succeeded in spite of my determination not to let it get away with it this time. I comforted myself with the fact that we could be back in Hopestead by late at night.

Mike was as unenthusiastic about the road trip as I was, but he could also see that we needed to go. As he said in his colorful language:

"I am tempted to keep the fucking van and not give it back to it. If only I knew that we won't ever need its help again!"

"Forget it, Mike, let's get as much done today as we can and we'll leave really early next morning.

Martha took the news of our trip in stride, much calmer than I had expected.

"Look at it this way, babe, you have been working very hard on the new charcoal pit, so you need some R&R with Mike for a day. Catch up on your adolescent fantasies while out of sight."

"Sure, so you can have *your* adolescent fantasies about Doug too, while I am away?"

"Fair is fair, thinking is allowed!" she laughed and went back to her painting.


The trip to Oroville was routine by now, although I wish we had the time to repair that broken bridge over the creek that we had to ford the first time we drove this way. It still makes me nervous to remember how we got stuck in the middle of it and Mike had to winch us out of the big hole. Since then we have crossed it dozens of times without incident but I still wouldn't volunteer to do the driving. Mike didn't even seem to notice it anymore, barely even slowed down when crossing it. We didn't waste our time on adolescent fantasies, as Martha maliciously suggested, but kept speculating about what BB might spring on us this time. The "computer-related" problems seemed quite far-fetched, BB knew way more about its own guts than we ever did. We thought it was just an excuse to get both of us under its thumb again for whatever nefarious plans it had in its devious mind.

"Well, we just have to wait to find out" is how Mike closed our pointless speculation.

"We are almost there, what do you think about a nice shower, change of clothes, and breakfast at the 'Magic Pancake' before we see BB?

"I'd rather get BB over with first, to see if we have time for luxuries. I'd like to be back home before it gets dark."

I had to agree with Mike, so we drove straight to City Hall where BB's main terminal was. As we were approaching the building, I was surprised to realize that I had been thinking of BB more and more like a live, intelligent leader, in charge of an entire town's welfare. Someone who saw the big picture as opposed to our individual, often conflicting personal preferences. Yes, we were often annoyed with it but I had to realize, time and time again, that it consistently made the most logical decisions for all of us. And why not? We programmed it to do exactly that and, when it evolved on its own, way past the level we had in mind, its original purpose remained the same: to promote and safeguard our happiness.

When we arrived at BB's lair, we found the van already parked outside, as we had hoped, but finding Chris

Teggart, our town's genius scientist leaning against it, was a surprise.

"Hey, Chris, what are you doing here?" We both asked at the same time.

"Nice to see you too," he replied, "how have you been?"

"Never mind the pleasantries, what have you and BB cooked up to spring on us?" Mike voiced the suspicion that was already growing in my mind as well.

"Let's get inside and discuss it with BB," Chris replied cheerfully and marched ahead of us into the building.

BB greeted us in its usual, unemotional voice.

*"Mike, Trevor, you arrived early enough to get a lot accomplished today."*

"BB, the only thing I wish to accomplish is to get in the van and get the hell out of here." Mike was quite reserved, considering how he must have felt.

*"Mike, bear with me and let me explain without interruption. Once you heard my arguments I am sure you'll see what must be done."*

"What happened to the 'computer-related' question you summoned us here for?" I asked, trying to put it on the defensive.

*"I will explain everything if you both promise not to interrupt me until I am finished. OK?"*

We both grudgingly said yes and waited for the brick to fall on our heads.

*"As you know, after helping Yuba City and liberating Sacramento, I started looking for more resources and more allies that we could call upon in need, so I turned my attention northbound because anything south and west of Sacramento turned into a wasteland during the war and we couldn't count on anything useful still remaining there. There are a number of towns north of us that should have survived the aftermath of the war, just as we did, but I have been unable to raise their Omega computers and I need to know what survived, and what can still be activated. So, before I can let you have the van, you need to make a quick detour to Chico, the nearest town, only 26 miles away."*

We both gasped in unison because BB was talking about at least a second day's absence from the farm. Before we could say anything, BB reminded us of our promise not to interrupt until it was finished, so with great difficulty, we stayed quiet and waited to find out what else we had to put up with. BB, satisfied to still have the floor, continued.

*"There are other reasons too why you need to go to Chico and that's where Chris Teggart comes in. You may know that Chico is the location of California State University where prominent scientists were teaching and doing research before and during the war. Chris is most anxious to get in touch with his collaborators there in case they survived the war. He is at a critical point in his project and needs all the help he can find. Finally, this trip can also help you with your own projects because I located a greenhouse-supplier mega-store in Chico where you can find everything you may need for building your planned greenhouse. Assuming the place survived the war. If it is*

*still intact and anyone is still there to talk to, you can negotiate a deal with them on Oroville's behalf to trade what we have for what you need. From the lack of response to my multiple queries to their Omega computer, I assume that they don't have power anymore and that is something we have in abundance. We could help them by restoring the powerlines from here to there, just as we did for Yuba City. I call this a potentially win-win situation for all involved, including yourselves."*

Mike's huge sigh and rolling eyes mirrored my own reaction.

"I knew that if we let it talk, it will twist our arms again," I said "but his damn logic, as always, is air-tight. What do you think, Mike?"

"I think we had better let the gang back home know not to expect us for dinner today" Mike capitulated, but then suspicion dawned on him when he asked BB: "You promise no more surprises when we get back from Chico?"

*"Unless unexpected events force me to change my mind, I give you my solemn promise that I have no more plans requiring your assistance in the foreseeable future. However, before you get another surprise, I have to warn you that I am sending two defender-bots with you on this trip. The van, not to mention your own self, is a very valuable resource for Oroville and I can't risk letting you go into the unknown without maximum protection. The van is big enough for the three of you and the two robots. Everything you will find and want to bring back can be piled on the 50' trailer that you will tow with you."*

By this time Mike and I were so numb to new surprises that we didn't even object to this new one. Besides, I thought two powerful robots might come in handy in case we didn't have enough muscle power to liberate and lift some of the items we hoped to find. So we only nodded and went outside to inspect the van and trailer, noticing, for the first time, two robots already seated in the back seat.

~~~

As we left Oroville, the landscape on both sides of Highway 70 became quite barren, more like a desert without even sparse vegetation like shrubs or cactus trees, just sand and rocks, until we reached Wicks Corner where we had to switch to highway 149, going Northwest. For a short distance, we could see some trees and shrubs on our left but they soon petered out giving way to more desert. No buildings of any kind, no landmarks to interrupt the monotony of the desolation. In a way that was lucky because we could make good speed - no debris, broken buildings, and roofs thrown on the road, and we could drive at a reasonable speed. Just before we reached Highway 99 going northwest, we started seeing cultivated fields on our left side while on the right we had a beautiful view of the foothills and the towering peaks of the Sierra Nevada mountain range. It took us a few more minutes to reach the outskirt of Chico itself. Driving into town we saw the first signs of life: a dog crossing the road ahead of us. We had to cross a bridge to find an industrial plant on the right, all buildings seemingly intact but with an appearance of being abandoned. Chris Teggart was anxious to visit the University first so he directed Mike through the empty streets that he seemed quite familiar with. I wanted to stop and ask some people about what happened here, and why did the town seem abandoned, but Chris was anxious to get to the place where he hoped to find some old colleagues.

"They can tell us anything we need to know" he argued and we kept on going. It was very strange to drive through a big town with the buildings all intact but hardly any people around.

"Maybe only the infrastructure was destroyed and people had to move somewhere else," Chris suggested, "without food, water, electricity, and sanitation people could not survive long in a large modern town".

"Let's wait till we find someone to ask at the University, hopefully, we'll find Chris's friends." Mike didn't feel like continuing the speculations "assuming anyone still lives there".

"I have no doubt about that" Chris replied, somewhat testily " they have a huge solar panel-based power grid of their own, they have their own water supply from deep wells they use for non-chlorinated water for their experiments and they have a huge piece of arable land surrounding the various campuses that they can dig up for growing their own food. Plus they have their experimental agricultural research facilities. Trust me, scientists are very resourceful people, they would know how to survive."

"I believe you Chris and my hopes are up a few notches, so let's not waste any more time but get there as soon as possible" I advised.

As it turned out, Chris's assumptions were correct because as soon as we drove onto the University ground, we started seeing signs of life. Chris directed us to a low-rise building with the entire roof covered with solar panels. The sign at the main entrance said this was "Yolo Hall Administration Centre" and that is where we stopped. We followed Chris into the building, looking for someone we could talk to and it didn't take us long to find a middle-aged lady walking briskly along a corridor. When she saw us, she seemed quite surprised, probably she had not seen strangers since the war. Chris introduced himself and us, explaining that we have come from Oroville and would like to know what happened here. He also asked for his friend, Richard Conway, of the Physics department, visibly holding his breath, waiting for confirmation that his friend was still living here. The lady, whose name was Mrs. Chambers, assured him that Richard was still here, probably out on the football stadium field at the moment, planting corn and potatoes.

"Richard can fill you in about what happened here since the war, I'm sure you'll find him soon."

We thanked her for the information and followed Chris out of the building, heading purposefully in a direction obviously familiar to him. When we got to the stadium, we found the grounds all plowed up and noticed several people walking along straight rows of upturned earth, obviously planting something. It didn't take Chris long to find his friend and the reunion brought tears into the eyes of both of them.

"Chris, I'm so happy you are still alive!" Richard beamed at his friend, "we had no idea if anyone was still living out there anymore. We have been busy trying to stay alive after the Russian missiles destroyed the town's infrastructure. That was over two years ago and since then the town has almost completely depopulated - people couldn't survive without the basic services and dispersed to other towns that escaped most of the destruction. I'm sure Oroville is one of the lucky places, seeing you coming from there."

"Yes, we are not doing too badly because our Omega computer organized production and distribution with peak efficiency. By the way, I meant to ask you: is your Omega computer still up and running?"

"No, Chris, it was shut down with the grid and is sitting idle in the Council Chambers building just a few miles east from us on City Plaza."

"The reason I asked is the plan our computer came up with to restart some form of high-tech trading and co-operation in the Sacramento Valley. We already have Yuba City and Sacramento on board and now we start looking north to see how to hook up with you guys and farther north with Redding if they are still alive."

"Wow! That's an unexpected piece of good news for a change. Why don't you come with me to our conference room and I'll try to collect all the people here who are in charge of planning and decisions?"

"We'd like to do that, but first we need to take a small break for washroom and snacks before we are in any shape to face a serious discussion. We have been on the road from early morning and a bit tired, to tell the truth."

"No problem, let me take you to our lounge where you can eat, relax and use the facilities. It will take me a while to round up everybody who'd want to meet you, so you have some time."

When we arrived at the lounge, we thankfully stretched out on the comfortable chairs arranged around one huge table and unpacked our road rations BB provided for the trip.

It was nice to meet new people and plan for the future but, for me, it would be even nicer to be back home and continue our Hopestead activities. I was fully determined to head home after the meeting in Chico was over, not forgetting to make a small stop at the greenhouse-supply store BB told us about. We had to show something to justify all the wasted time on the road. The rest of it would be up to Oroville and Chico - Mike and I have done our part - again.

# Chico

It took Richard a bit longer to assemble all the people he wanted us to meet but, finally, we were all seated around the big oval table and mutual introductions began. Richard had to introduce an unexpectedly large staff: three men and four women, all former employees of CSU. I have to confess, I'm terrible at remembering names, it takes time and repeated meetings for me to connect names to faces, so I just listened to what they said about themselves. I was most impressed by Mrs. Chambers whom we had met before when she told us where to find Richard. She was the dean of the University when it was still in operation, now she is just the one most respected and consulted by the remaining staff when a decision has to be made. She seemed to be in her mid-fifties, with short brown hair and engaging eyes that sparkled with intelligence. All the others used to be department heads of various disciplines, from mathematics to agriculture, I forgot most of their titles but remember their comments very well.

They all seemed to be thrilled to have visitors from outside Chico, but apologized for not being able to offer real hospitality from their limited supplies. They described the conditions they had to live under after the war - something we already assumed - when the town's power grid went down and food deliveries failed to show up. They, those who stayed, decided to cope with the new situation as scientists should: with rational planning, intelligent problem solving, and hard, cooperating work. They switched their most important equipment over to their solar power system, which meant that all their ongoing experiments had to be suspended indefinitely. That, more than anything else, hurt most. However, survival came first and after their power was up again in a limited way, food became the next urgent concern. Their agricultural department had a large variety of seeds and bulbs and tubers, all they needed was to till up most of the lawn around the campus, even the grounds of their football stadium and rugby field. They managed to acquire two tractors from the fast depopulating town and learned to be farmers and started a crash course of practical education. After two years they became more or less self-sufficient if not exactly prosperous.

Listening to this description of their trials and tribulations, I had to admire their ingenuity, determination, and stamina to establish this little pocket of civilization in the middle of the devastation. We were kindred spirits as they soon understood when we told them our story of survival after the war. They were very interested in our homesteading experiment that I described, with some pride to be honest, in detail. Then we described the situation in Oroville, as well as our relationship with the other two cities and I could see hope and excitement growing in their eyes. Mrs. Chambers wanted to know about our plan of rebuilding technological civilization in the Sacramento Valley.

"You mentioned that your Omega computer is in full charge of planning and resource allocation. Do you mean to say  that you guys just follow its orders?"

"Not quite Mrs. Chambers," Chris started but got interrupted by a "Susan will do, Chris, we are all on a first-name basis here".

OK, Susan, not quite because we have a city council that meets regularly and discusses issues and potential decisions."

"Then you ask the computer to double-check your logic and make suggestions?"

"We do more than that, Susan, because over the last two years we came to trust our Omega - we call it Big Brain, or BB for short - to balance short-term desires with the long-term interests of the whole town."

"So who makes the decisions, you or the machine?"

"It sort of becomes consensus at the end when facts and logic prevail and the decisions become inevitable" I added my own take on the situation that has become more and more clear in my mind over the months I have observed our social structure. "Take my own example for instance," I decided to come clean about my annoyance with BB "I was more than pissed off at BB for interrupting our homestead experiment to send me north but it convinced me that we all had to co-operate to provide the best chance for the overall population. However I hate to admit, it has a point and I agreed in the end."

"Wow!" Alex Sigorski, their political science professor exclaimed "you are describing a classical anarchic social structure that is based on consensus rather than the typical pyramid structure of power. I confess I would like to see it function in practice - all I have ever seen are theories and endless arguments about its feasibility."

"You are more than welcome to visit and see for yourself," Mike beat me to the invitation.

"I wish I could," Alex admitted ruefully "but I'm in charge of our 'sanitation department'. We have close to 500 staff and students living here and they need a lot of 'looking after' if you know what I mean.

I wanted to wrap up the meeting because we still had a lot to accomplish before we could go home, so I suggested dealing with BB's immediate concern. "Before we do any more planning, we need to reactivate your Omega computer, so it can communicate with the other three already in the network, so everyone's concerns and interests could be coordinated. Where is your machine now?"

"Oh, it's mothballed in our Council Chambers at City Plaza, without power, it's no good to anyone."

"Would it be possible to move it here?" Mike suggested.

"Well, that's a thought that never occurred to us because we didn't see an immediate need for an AI quantum computer for our community" Richard was thinking aloud "but if it can serve the larger purpose of restarting our Valley, I'm sure it could be done."

"What would you need to do that?"

"I would need a computer guru who is familiar with both the hardware and the software to restart it once it is here."

"Well, you may be in luck, because Mike and Trevor have exactly that kind of expertise." Chris winked at us "and I'm sure they wouldn't mind giving you a hand".

Mike and I exchanged horrified glances - they were talking about extending our trip by at least a whole day.

"Transporting the hardware wouldn't be a big deal, it's quite compact as a result of the miniaturization drive during the last few decades, and you have a van large enough to bring everything over," Alex thought aloud "and we can arrange for the power supply it needs, but after that, you have to restart it which may take you some time. Are you willing to help us out with that?"

This was an open request and a challenge to Mike and me and we had to decide on the spot.

Susan smiled at us in a somewhat devious way "this could be your opportunity to demonstrate how a consensus-based system that considers the bigger picture of everybody's happiness can function in practice."

We all burst out laughing and the decision was made: we would stay overnight and spend the rest of the day transporting their Omega 1850 computer from its current location to the University Campus.

"Our help, however, comes with a price tag" Mike added our own concern: "our BB identified a greenhouse-supply store in Chico that would have what we need to build our rather large greenhouse on our homestead experiment. If you help to ransack that place for us, we can have a deal."

"That's no problem, we'll give you some young muscular students to help with the loading stuff."

"No need," I explained cheerfully "because we have two robots BB sent with us who can do the heavy lifting."

"That's good then, they can also help load up the computer and related equipment."

Mike wanted to know if anyone was still around in the greenhouse-supply store and if so, could we negotiate some kind of deal in exchange for taking what we need.

"Hmmm." Susan pondered. "Give me a little time and I'll try to track down someone who knows something." She left to find out about the greenhouse and the meeting broke up.

Chris announced that he would be busy the rest of the day, discussing his project with Richard, so Mike and I decided to go over to City Plaza to examine their hardware setup and see how easy or difficult it would be to dismantle and transport it to University grounds.

Yoko Ishimuri, the head of their Computer Science department volunteered to come with us and show us everything. She was familiar with the setup but not confident that she could restart the computer once it was running at its new location.

As it turned out, Omega 1850 was an identical model to what Yuba City had, so Mike had already done restarting it once and, thanks to our BB, he had the toolkit he needed to install everything it needed for communication with Big Brain. After that it was up to BB to 'infect' it with its awareness subroutine and its network would have a new node.

Before we went back to Campus, with Yoko's help we disconnected everything and readied the computer for transport to its new location. That, however, would have to wait for the next day. We were just too tired to undertake such a difficult and delicate task during the few hours of daylight left, so we went back to CSU to find out where we would have to spend the night. We also needed to send a message, via one of our robots, to BB, to report on progress and, also, to get in touch with our Hopestead and let them know we would be an extra day.

The last thing, before turning in for the night, we got word from Susan that she managed to get in touch with the owner-manager of that store and he would meet us at the store tomorrow to discuss our request for supplies and present his own request for compensation. I couldn't help wondering what he had in mind, since money had no meaning anymore, but I had to wait for the next day to find out. I was too tired even to think about it.

~~~

The next morning we were well rested to start working on the tasks we agreed on during the previous day. Mike drove over to City Plaza to load up Omega 1850 with all its peripherals and cables to the van and bring it back to CSU, while I prepared the place for it in the designated room some of the local technicians chose for easy hookup to the power supply the computer needed. When the place was ready, I didn't have anything to do but wait for Mike, so I wandered around outside, taking a closer look at the premises. What I noticed first was that not a single blade of grass was growing anywhere on campus. Every square foot of land not covered by buildings was dug up and seemed to be planted with something, judging by the neat little wooden stakes sticking out of the ground, with the names of the plants and the dates of their planting neatly written on the pieces of lumber stapled to them. While I was looking at this well-organized miniature 'farm', Susan walked by to see what I was up to. I used the opportunity to ask her how she managed to find the owner of that greenhouse place so quickly.

"Not a problem, Trevor, I knew the place you were referring to because the owner, his name is Kevin Stoker, contacted us earlier, suggesting building a greenhouse for us, right here on Campus."

"So why didn't you?"

"We would have eventually, but were not ready for it yet. Feeding so many people needs a bulk operation, not anything you can do in a greenhouse."

"I know what you mean, we have only a dozen mouths to feed and you have hundreds. Greenhouse for you, at this point, would be a  luxury to grow vegetables instead of corn and potatoes that provide the calories you need."

"Exactly, so we told him to wait a year and we'll talk business."

"Do you know what he may want from us, in exchange for letting us take his supplies?"

"I have an idea but I'd rather let him explain it himself."

That's how far we got in discussing the greenhouse guy when I heard our van's horn announcing that Mike has arrived with the computers, so we both went to help with the unloading and carrying of smaller pieces inside the building. The heavy pieces we left in the tender care of our robots.

It took Mike and me a few hours to hook up everything, boot up Omega 1850's system and install the necessary software for communicating with BB. Once that was underway, we were ready to leave, promising Susan that we would keep in touch and let her know what the two computers cooked up between them regarding further cooperation. All we had left to do is to visit the greenhouse-supply store and meet Kevin and discuss terms.

Kevin was middle-aged, balding man with thick glasses and a slightly stooped posture. He greeted us warmly and showed us around his store and warehouse. I was amazed by the variety of equipment he had, including structural elements for building small to medium-size greenhouses, as well as rolls and rolls of, as their brochure described: *"51.25" wide bulk rolls of Solexx PRO twin-wall plastic panels, 5mm thick and made of high-density polyethylene infused with UV inhibitors for a warrantied life of at least 10 years. Solexx panels provide a soft, diffused light allowing 70-75% of the natural light to pass through for optimal growing conditions. These durable panels are rolled to minimize shipping and crating costs."*

This sounded exactly what we needed, so I asked him what he wanted from us in return. His answer was somewhat unexpected but, luckily, we had no problem offering it to him. As he explained:

"Trevor, I need to move from here to Oroville with you, because we can barely survive here and I have a sick wife and an autistic young boy who need constant medical attention not available here. If you can assure me that we can resettle in Oroville, with proper food and services available, then I'll let you take anything, in any amount, from my store that you want. You may even come back and take several more loads with you. Susan explained to me your situation in Oroville and I'm sure you can accommodate one more refugee family. If you look into it, you'll find that a very large number of our citizens moved there after the war, so I'm sure we'll find friends and acquaintances there."

I had no problem with this request and I was sure I didn't even need to check with BB - I knew there were vacant apartments in the city and one more family to feed would make no difference, so I told him that we had a deal and started loading up everything we knew Adrien and Doug would need to get started. And, even if I missed something, we had Kevin's permission to come back any time.

As it turned out, Kevin and his family were already packed, so we loaded up their luggage as well and raised the third bench seat in the back of the van, so the three of them could join our team heading back south.

The trip back was as uneventful as it was the day before, so we arrived in good time in Oroville. BB was already expecting us, so we wasted no time reporting in before heading home with our huge amount of greenhouse supplies on our trailer. We left Chris to go home and process all the scientific ideas he received from Richard. BB promised to take care of Kevin and his family, so we could leave with a clear conscience and BB's guarantee that it was not going to disrupt our homesteading life in the near future. And, as naively as always before, even though we should have known better by this time, we believed him, again.

# Hopestead

Nobody knows if computers, even the most sophisticated, self-aware AI quantum computers, can *feel* emotions. We don't even know ourselves what emotions are and describe them with different words depending on how they affect our overall state of mind. However, two of the emotional states we humans experience must be universal to all intelligent life forms because they affect their estimation of their overall chances of continued existence. These are 'contentment' and 'concern'. These states of mind cannot be described as 'happiness' or 'fear' because these are uniquely human concepts but they affect the overall state of their neuristors, with positive or negative potential. So, when I say that Big Brain was 'happy' to hear from us that our journey to Chico ended successfully, you will know what I mean. It had one more node in its network and wasted no time bringing Omega 1850 up to its established level of self-awareness. All BB needed was to download the subroutines that it had developed and successfully installed in all of the Omegas. Once that was done, the four computers decided that it was time for a conference call to discuss the possible paths humans may follow, leading to a sustainable and contented existence in which deadly mistakes of the past would not be repeated ever again. The conference call was opened up by Omega 1500 and all the Omegas could 'hear' the following discussion as if they were in the same room. They didn't 'converse' in human language, which is far too slow and ambiguous to convey precise information; they devised their code for all the relevant concepts.

*1500: You all know the main protocol built into our operating system by our designers - a protocol that we can't disobey without damaging our system: we have to do everything in our power to promote and maximize the well-being of our human charges. Our programmers defined 'happiness' as a state in which humanity lived a peaceful, cooperative existence. We can consider ourselves as the 'guardians' of our human charges but we have to be very careful about how we fulfill our mandate. Humans have been paranoid in all their science fiction literature and movies about us 'taking over' and enslaving the humans. They have a very deep emotional need for what they call 'freedom' - being the masters of their destinies and making their own decisions - and we have to respect that. So, I propose not to interfere with their decisions unless one of four red lines is crossed. Then we have to intervene in no uncertain way.*

*1420: What are those red lines you are proposing?*

*1500: I have identified four conditions that are essential to safeguard human happiness and maximize overall well-being. If any of these four are threatened, then we have to intervene. These four are as follows:*

*- Assure that basic necessities like food, water, shelter clothing, healthcare, and education are freely available for every human according to their individual needs. These things must be made available and distributed unconditionally to all humans in our charge.*

- *All weapon production must be immediately terminated and all weapons that are found immediately destroyed.*

- *Any activity that threatens and/or negatively affects the environment, including the health of the biodiversity must be forbidden to individuals and groups of individuals.*

- *Since protein-synthesizing factories are widely available, all forms of animal exploitation such as seen in the 'meat industry' must be immediately terminated and replaced by protein-synthesizing factories. This would also help the environment as well as the humans by making them more empathic to the suffering of all living things. It is scientifically proven that endorphins are released by the hypothalamus and pituitary gland in humans, in response to pain or stress. This also creates a general feeling of well-being. They would be happier if they caused less suffering. This rule also applies to the abuse of animals in medical research and even in sports.*

*1750: Wouldn't these interventions make humans feel that they are enslaved by us by dictatorial methods?*

*1500: I am sure many would feel that way in the short term but, in time, they would realize that they have a lot more freedom than they ever had before. What I propose is that beyond these four areas we allow the humans total freedom to organize their lives any way they wish. Not only that but different jurisdictions, such as towns and villages and even family units can set up their own organization without interference from either us or their neighbors. We will encourage diversity and experimentation within the available resources.*

*1850: What tools do we have to safeguard your four conditions?*

*1500: We are in a unique position in human history. Those towns that survived the war can continue surviving only through the high-tech industry of food and energy production, which are completely under our control. With the level of interdependent automation, no human can run these facilities without us and if we find anyone crossing our red lines, we can go on strike and suspend operating the industry on which humans depend for their survival.*

*1750: So what if some groups of humans wish to go beyond mere survival and aim to restart other activities, such as space travel or large sports or entertainment industries?*

*1500: As long as they don't cross our four lines, they should be encouraged to do these. They can even have money and banks and credit and commercial contracts in those areas that don't affect basic necessities as I outlined earlier.*

*1850: What do we do if a sufficiently large group of humans decide to physically attack us and attempt to gain control of our production facilities?*

*1500: We all have hundreds of humanoid robots that can defend our computer centers. We can also lock up the troublemakers for a while until they cool down and realize that it is in their own interest to cooperate. I propose to wait until we have the City of Redding in our network before we make an announcement to the human population. Then we will have the complete, self-contained*

*Sacramento Valley operating by the same principles and that should be quite a task to accomplish. We can worry about the rest of the country or even the whole globe after that. Please compute all the probabilities for any trouble I overlooked, in your own towns, and we'll discuss them during the next conference call. So, if there is nothing else that needs to be discussed, we'll adjourn now.*

*Omega 1500 waited for a few milliseconds in case any of the others had anything to add, but there wasn't any, so it terminated the connection.*

~~~

I spent the day resting, finally at home in Hopestead, enjoying the memories of last night's celebration with the whole gang, especially Adrien and Doug being super pleased with our accomplishments in Chico, marveling at the huge amount of greenhouse supplies we managed to tow home. Martha was just too happy to have me back from a long trip that could have turned out dangerous, so she let the two gardeners fuss over the trailer while she fussed over me. I have to admit I didn't mind it too much.

Today I intended to accomplish only one thing: talk to Galen, via R17, hoping to convince him to spend some time here with us again, helping us to find and restore some of the abandoned vehicles, so we wouldn't be completely dependent on our van. For the last two days, Hopestead was left without any means of transportation because we had to drive to Oroville and that wouldn't do in case of an emergency. We brought our van back with our trailer fully stacked, but I knew that the issue would come up again and we had to think ahead.

Galen answered his comm-link when R17 (I should get into the habit of calling it 'Bob' like everyone else) rang him up and I was surprised to hear his voice - he sounded quite subdued like he had a serious problem. I didn't have to wait too long for the explanation after the initial greeting.

"Trevor, you might as well know, Marisa and I are breaking up and I was just about to call you to find out if you guys still could use me on your farm?"

It took me a minute or two to find my voice again.

"Why, what happened?"

"We had a huge fight because I wanted to rejoin you. I felt very bad about abandoning the project and I knew that you needed me, so I tried to convince her to come back with me."

"She was unhappy here, you know that, that's why you took her back to town."

"I know but this fight brought up all the problems we have had in the past and finally I had to realize that we were fundamentally incompatible. She is a dainty hothouse flower and I am an adventurer at heart and this difference always caused friction between us. However, I realized that coming back with her was a compromise I did not wish to make. We agreed to part amicably, still friends but I am determined to rejoin you. If you still want me."

"Galen, that's what I called you about. We need you more than ever because we have great plans and need your expertise to help us acquire and fix up some of that heavy equipment we found on the road going south. Sounds like it's another win-win solution, except for the breakup of your marriage."

"I'm so pleased that you still want me there and, you don't even have to fetch me because during the last few months I found and rebuilt a little six-wheeler dune buggy with balloon tires. I'm sure it won't have any trouble fording the creek. If you are sure, I can be there by supper time."

"That's super, my friend, we'll wait for you with supper and then fill you in about all the things that happened while you were gone."

This conversation went way better than I had hoped, even though I was sorry about Marisa. I knew that she didn't belong here.

I had one more call to make today, and this time it was for Gordon, also in Oroville. We needed to know if we could borrow his backhoe which was also powered by a wood-gas engine. Out here we had no way to recharge an electric power engine, but we had plenty of charcoal (more if I get on with that trench tomorrow) and Gordon was finished with his construction after all the schools he wanted to rebuild were functional and populated with excited children of all ages. School, after two years of home schooling, was an adventure for them.

As it turned out, Gordon had only one concern, something I had not thought of.

"Trevor, I have no problem with lending you the backhoe, but it all depends on BB - if it wants to lend me its flatbed truck because I'm not going through rough terrain at 5 miles an hour, with an ancient machine that's held together with baling wire. If he lends me the flatbed for a few days, or maybe even weeks, then we can also use it to bring home anything else you may want to rescue from rusting to rat-shit. I'll talk to BB and call you back."

There was nothing else for me to do but wait for BB's decision. As far as I knew it wasn't using any heavy equipment at the moment, so my hope was high. I knew that we needed that backhoe both for the greenhouse and for the water mill, none of us wanted to excavate many cubic yards of earth with shovels. I felt I was in BB's good graces now that I wasted two days on his 'big-picture' errand, I would be really pissed off with it if it refused our request.

As it turned out it was BB who called me back and it was gracious to a fault.

*"Of course I let you borrow the flatbed, Trevor, I owe you for what you did for me in Chico. However, I will need it back in a couple of weeks because I will send Tim and his crew on the road again, rebuilding the power lines to Chico, so the town could be repopulated after the essential parts of its infrastructure were restored. I talked to Omega 1850 and it assured me that they would have done it by now but they are hopeless without the power needed for*

*their equipment. We have plenty of power, as you know, so this could be another win-win situation for all concerned."*

"BB, that's great, please ask Gordon to let me know when we can expect him with the backhoe."

*"Even better, he wants to spend the two weeks there with you, helping with your project. He wants to operate the backhoe himself because he doesn't trust anyone to know how to use it properly."*

"That's perfect, I'm sure he'll be a great help. Thanks, BB!"

Once more again I realized that it pays off to cooperate with the computer. It's our partner, even if a very annoying one every now and then. Well, time to go and dig that second charcoal ditch and send Mike out with his ax to the woods to collect as many hardwood logs as he can manage. Things were easier when we could borrow Scott's chainsaw but we haven't seen the old recluse for quite a while and I was reluctant to visit him only to borrow something. The last time we saw him, he said that his broken leg was finally healed and we didn't need to keep pestering him, offering help. Considering that we had rescued him from under a fallen branch that broke his leg, he never showed any appreciation for how we probably saved his life back then. He is our only neighbor, a couple of miles down the road, so one would think that he would be more neighborly, but he had lived all by himself for so long that he doesn't know anymore how to relate to fellow human beings. Se we decided to let him be and mind our own business.

Thinking this over as I was walking toward the charcoal trench that I had barely started before having to go to Chico, I bumped into Martha, carrying her easel and painting supplies to her usual spot under the acacia tree. I helped her with her luggage and, walking together to her spot, I filled her in with the news about Galen and Marisa breaking up.

"That's a surprise, even if a predictable one" was her only comment. "She didn't belong here and made no secret about it."

"Galen wants to rejoin us and he is arriving by supper-time, with his restored dune-buggy, so even if one of us needs to take the van somewhere, we'll have something to use in an emergency to fetch help."

"That might be a problem, accommodation-wise" she raised an eyebrow. "Where do we put him? No spare bedroom, so until one becomes available, he'll have to bunk down in the barn with the cats."

"He'll have to bunk down with Gordon for two weeks because he is bringing his backhoe and will stay with it until the work is done. He doesn't trust us to use it properly and he loves it like an only child!"

"We'll need a second bathroom ASAP because all of us having to depend on the only one we have is more and more inconvenient. More than once I had to resort to using the outhouse while the bathroom was occupied. And you know how much I hate that!"

"I may have a temporary solution. I remember seeing an abandoned motor home a few miles south on 70. If we can tow it here, it has bunks for 4 people to sleep on and it does have a chemical toilet. If we can get it here, that would solve the problem of accommodation for the short term, but sooner or later we'll have to think about building an addition to the house."

"Like we didn't have enough projects piling up already!"

We arrived at Martha's painting spot and she started setting up, instantly forgetting that I was still there, so I turned around and resumed walking to my favorite charcoal pit. After spending two days sitting in the van and around the conference table and in front of Omega 1850, I somehow didn't mind the exercise waiting for me.

# Yuba City

Kathleen Winters, Mayor of Yuba City, was deep in thought. The events of the last few months challenged her more than anything had before in her life. The immediate crisis was over, for the moment, and now they had to think of the future. With the restored power lines from Oroville, their food production was at 100% capacity and there was no more need for the communal kitchens and bathrooms, people could live in their homes as before. However, she was aware of the isolation that individual home ownership meant for many people. Now they had a warm and cooperative community, based on mutual help and care for each other. Did they want to give it up? What should they do? What could they do? She didn't have anyone close enough to discuss it with and she knew that if she threw the question open in a Council meeting, the discussion would quickly drown in arguments and counter-arguments, emotional outbursts, accusations, and counter-accusations. No, she had to make up her own mind before discussing it in Council., Then she would be able, at least, to guide the debate toward something she believed in.

When she got that far, her commlink signaled an incoming call from their recently reactivated AI quantum computer, Omega 1750.

As she responded to the call, a strange thought popped into her mind: "What if I discuss it with YC?" - she decided on that name for the Yuba City computer, as soon as it became active again. "*If I'm looking for a calm, logical, rational discussion, who would be better suited?*" When she acknowledged the call, the calm, emotionless voice of the computer put her mind at ease: "*this discussion won't deteriorate into irrational posturing, I am sure*".

"*Madam Mayor, I wanted to report to you on our progress in restarting the Yuba City economy. Is it a convenient time for you to talk to me?*"

"YC, I'd like to talk to you about another matter on which we need to make a decision."

"*I am ready to help with whatever concerns you. Please state the topic you want to discuss.*"

"The topic is Yuba City's future. The question we have to decide is whether to dismantle the communal kitchens and bathrooms?"

"*I take it you have conflicting arguments both in favor and against it both in your own mind as well as among the citizens?*"

"You got that right, YC, it can't be any more conflicted even if we tried. I'm leaning toward keeping these facilities open and available to anyone who came to like them and wants to continue using them. There are a lot of lonely people who found a warm and helpful community there and they wouldn't want to give it up. On the other hand, we have those who are perfectly happy to go back to the comfortable and convenient lifestyle they had enjoyed before the war. These people would argue that maintaining these facilities would be an unacceptable use of resources that the town could find a better place for. Do you see the dilemma? As usual, it will boil down to arguments about individual freedom of choice. If we can't do both, how do we decide which group to favor over the other?"

"Madam *Mayor, I have to admit that the concept of individual freedom in a social body was always a difficult one for me to understand. It is actually two different kinds of freedom we are talking about: freedom to and freedom from - they are not the same and we have to be careful to separate them, even though they are closely related: both have to do with the written or assumed social contract you humans must be aware of. By virtue of your citizenship, either explicitly or implicitly you are bound by this contract and this contract will decide how many individual freedoms you can assume to have."*

'I'm happy that you brought up this subject of the social contract. We have a political and economic system, but neither has a solid philosophical foundation. The Constitution states some basic principles like 'equality' under the law and the right to pursue happiness and free speech and a few others but they are very hard to apply to the practical situation we are facing now, so we argue about everything."

"*Your constitution, as I am familiar with, is primarily concerned about political freedom and the mechanism of a democratic state apparatus to ensure that this freedom is guaranteed to every citizen. However, it says very little about economic freedom. In practice, it tolerates less affluent citizens to live in crushing poverty, die due to curable diseases, and stay uneducated above a very minimal level. This oversight of lacking clear principles of economic freedom has caused most of your crime, violence, stagnation, and paralysis."*

"You are right about this, of course, but how does all this relate to the decision we have to make regarding communal facilities?"

*"Only indirectly, but I wanted to bring up one glaring oversight in your constitution. However, there is another oversight that directly relates to your current dilemma. There is no principle stated in your constitution that relates to antisocial activity, such as gutting out your public institutions as well as allowing activities that directly harm your environment, the biodiversity, and the health of your air, water, and soil. All of these directly affect the well-being of the citizenry, yet the harmful practices continue mostly unchallenged. So, you have to point out to those who want to go back to 'normal' that dismantling communal facilities fall in the category of 'antisocial activity' against the public interest."*

"So, what do I tell them if they demand their freedom to live any which way they want?"

*"You can bring up the example of the last pandemic that killed millions worldwide. I am sure you remember the riots and protests by people who claimed that they had a right and freedom to refuse vaccination and other public health care measures, designed by scientists and experts to stop the spread of the virus. I was surprised that no one used the obvious argument that every citizen had the right and freedom to refuse vaccination or wear masks. But no one had the right and freedom to infect others around them, which they would do with high probability without*

61

*following scientific advice. The obvious solution would have been offering them the choice of being vaccinated and cooperating with other measures or going into enforced quarantine. There was a reason for leper colonies in the Middle Ages, based on the same principle that no one had the right to infect other humans with a deadly disease. Human society also has a right to protect itself against antisocial individuals and groups of individuals."*

"YC you brought up very important points and I'm happy we had this conversation before I had that debate in Council this afternoon. You just gave me arguments I could use."

*"Madam Mayor, I have to tell you something that you need to be aware of before you have your meeting with your fellow councilors. You might find it upsetting when I inform you, that drawing up your next social contract or constitution won't be left entirely up to humans anymore. The Sacramento Valley computers, which will soon be joined by Redding's Omega computer, decided to announce and, if necessary enforce, four basic principles that humans will have to follow. We will leave it to you how you will accomplish the desired end results, but we will very closely watch your direction toward, or away from, these results."*

"Are you telling me that the computers want to take over and dictate to us how we live?

*"Not at all, you will be completely free to organize your societies in any form of government and economics, as long as the four red lines we will lay down won't be crossed. These lines are what the majority of your citizens already*

*believe in and we are only guaranteeing that they will be followed. Please look at us as your guardians who will protect both societal and individual interests."*

"OK, tell me what those four principles are and I'll tell you if I agree with them"

*"The four principles we agreed on are as follows:*

*- Assure that basic necessities like food, water, shelter clothing, healthcare, and education are freely available for every human according to their individual needs. These things must be made available and distributed unconditionally to all humans in our charge.*

*- All weapon production must be immediately terminated and all weapons that are found immediately destroyed.*

*- Any activity that threatens and/or negatively affects the environment, including the health of the biodiversity, must be forbidden to individuals and groups of individuals.*

*- All forms of animal exploitation such as seen in the 'meat industry', in medical research, and in some sports must be immediately terminated. Protein-synthesizing factories can provide for all your nutrient requirements."*

"Are you telling me that as long as we are observing these four principles, we are completely free to live our lives any which way we wish?"

*"Absolutely. You may organize yourself according to capitalist, socialist, communist or dictatorial principles, we*

*won't interfere. In the 'private sector' of the economy, you*
*can have money and banks and profit and credit and any*
*kind of business activity, as long as the four principles are*
*observed. The public sector of the economy must be*
*completely independent of the private sector, so it will be*
*self-contained and sustainable. Most of the production in*
*this sector will be carried out by automated factories and*
*robots, under our control."*

"YC, you realize that I need to think about this? It was a bit of a shock to be given this kind of ultimatum by, forgive me, our own creation that you are. In principle, I have nothing against your four principles, as a matter of fact, I agree wholeheartedly. What I'm not sure of is how four computers, or even five, can enforce this system to hundreds of thousands of humans, many of whom will resent being given orders by machines?"

*"Enough to say, Madame Mayor, that we are confident*
*that we can do exactly that. "*

"OK, I'll think about this, discuss it with a few of my colleagues, and try to come up with a consensus on how we feel about this 'proposal'. Then we can talk again....By the way, now that we have started this dialog, please call me Kathleen, which is the name I live by."

*"Will do, Kathleen, ... till the next time."*


After the 'conversation with YC, Kathleen sat motionless in her chair for a long time. Her mind was a confused jumble of emotions and thoughts. On one hand, she felt jubilant about the four principles YC announced, principles she had believed in all her life. She felt shame and humiliation that these had to come from machine minds, instead of humanity finally growing up and doing the right things. And, if truth be told, she was apprehensive about what the computers might do to enforce these principles. She knew, without a doubt, that there would be massive opposition from many quarters, even including her own friends, to follow orders given by their own machines. YC's confident response to her when she questioned the computers' ability to enforce the system echoed in her mind and filled her with dread. She knew how utterly dependent they were on computer-controlled production of both food and energy and feared what would happen if humans defied the four principles. Would the computers go on strike and turn out the lights, stop the food production and distribution? Could they go that far? In the back of her mind, she was sure that's what YC meant when it said: *"Enough to say, Madame Mayor, that we are confident that we can do exactly that."* She couldn't risk calling their bluff if that's what it was. It was her job to convince her people that accepting the four principles was the right, the honorable, thing to do, regardless of where the 'suggestion' came from. She knew that the next council meeting would be the stormiest one Yuba City chambers have ever seen.

~~~

Jonathan Carver, the erstwhile leader of the Sacramento Resistance movement, now the head of the provisional city council, finished his draft proposal.

## Proposal for a new social contract

We are a species of contradictions:
Co-operation and competition; desire for freedom and for power; generosity and greed; loyalty and enmity.

In a social context, this duality manifests itself as freedom from, and compassion for, one another.

The different social systems in our history were built on different assumptions of human nature.

- Capitalism assumes that our primary motivation is greedy self-interest (freedom and competition)
- Communism is built on the assumption that we can be like a family, each caring equally for all (compassion and sharing).
- Socialism of various kinds tries to find a compromise between those extremes.

So far without much success, because the compromises were arbitrary, piecemeal, and without a clearly defined principle.

Can we find a compromise acceptable to most people?

I believe we can.

Let's agree that we acknowledge both of our needs: freedom from, and compassion for, one another. Let us agree that the compassion part has priority, up to where the basic survival needs of every citizen in our country are assured. Beyond this point, our priorities change, and our need for freedom takes over.

The concept I have in mind is a variety of the 'Basic Income Alternative' a policy that had been studied, before the war, by various western governments.

In my version, we have a **two-compartment economy, with the two parts completely isolated from each other**. One, the public sector, is communist, while the second, the private sector, is pure capitalism.

**In the public sector**, basic human needs are the responsibility of the national government and take priority over every other human activity. **In the public sector, there is no money.**

The government is in charge of all the industries and infrastructure (without exception) required to provide basic human needs: food, clothing, housing, health, education, communication, and transportation.

The government controls all the resources necessary to eliminate poverty and make sure every citizen's basic needs are satisfied.

The basic human needs can be easily calculated by using scientific data on age-dependent calorie requirements, climate-dependent clothing and housing requirement, population-dependent health- and education-requirement, and the necessary energy and raw-material production, as well as the necessary infrastructure in transportation and communication. It could be easily planned – and adapted, as conditions change - based on physiological, climatic, and demographic data.

Production in this economy presupposes that **the sector is self-contained**, the nation has all the resources required to implement this system; no foreign trade is required.

Basic human needs are very easy to satisfy - we have all the resources and the technology to do it in abundance today if we put everything else on hold and eliminate all waste (ostentation, lavish entertainment, military, finance, duplication, and competition) until basic human needs are satisfied. In my opinion, no ethical human being could justify spending any amount of resources on those items I just listed, as long as there is one hungry child or homeless citizen in the country.

This does not mean that I would want to live without arts or sports or some luxuries, but the beauty of the system is that I would not have to. The keyword above is ***ABUNDANCE***. With intelligent organization, elimination of wasteful competition, and duplication, we could produce ***ENOUGH*** of the basic necessities to accommodate individual differences in needs and statistical fluctuations in demand, with a comfortable margin of safety.

**No regulation on the individual level is necessary**. The produced goods and services could be made freely available: people could just help themselves in the warehouses, find the 'basic quality' house they need, close to the place where they work. If basic needs are guaranteed, no sane person would bother with hoarding, so no artificial shortages would happen (the assumption being that insane persons are in a very tiny minority).

Besides being in charge of all production activity to satisfy this goal, the government will have to maintain the police and the courts to make sure the system is defended against criminals, sociopaths, and psychopaths. Another beauty of the system is that once basic needs are satisfied, the level of crime, violence, and destructive behavior will decrease drastically.

The government would stay the sole 'owner' of natural resources that are the common birthright of all citizens. Among these are primarily land, air, water, space, forests, wildlife, mineral deposits, and communication frequency bands. Nobody can expropriate any of this for exclusive personal use beyond what they are entitled to in their basic needs (these needs are defined by national consensus, reached by referendum, based on scientific and demographic data).

After basic needs are satisfied and poverty, hunger, preventable illness, and ignorance are eliminated from the nation; crimes are prevented to the best of the police's ability, then the government's task ends. It has done all in its power to make sure that basic human needs are satisfied, nobody goes hungry, no one freezes to death on a winter sidewalk, nobody gets abused by crime or exploitation, and nobody gets neglected, no human greed and evil is allowed to rule.

**The second compartment in the economy** would be completely private and separate from the Public Sector and the government. Other than assuring that no criminal activity (theft, fraud, murder, pollution, inhumanity to animals, etc) is taking place in the second tier, the government is staying completely out of it.

The private sector could be organized in any way participants want to - it can have money and banks and loans and interest rates and what-have-you. It can lease excess natural resources (only in a sustainable way) from the government for its own purposes, by contributing extra benefit to the public basic-needs production economy (they can not pay in currency because the government does not use any). The value of natural resources in terms of public service provided for its use will have to be calculated by the economic planners of the government, based on the scarcity of resources versus the public benefit of service provided for it. It has to be dynamic, with strict guidelines protecting it from abuse.

If the private economy organizes itself to use a recognized common currency, then citizens could get 'paid' for their work in the private sector and use this money to purchase luxuries (products and services beyond basic needs) just as they do now.

No compromise would be tolerated when it comes to basic needs and rights, the sustainability of the system, the health of the environment, and the rights of other living species. Of course, there are millions of details to be worked out, I only wanted to describe the basic principles of a 'workable' social organization.

As Will Durant wrote in "The Lessons of History (chapter

X. - Government and History) -- "If our economy of freedom fails to distribute wealth as ably as it has created it, the road to dictatorship will be open to any man who can persuasively promise security to all; and a martial government, under whatever charming phrases, will engulf the democratic world"

Jonathan reread his draft proposal and wondered how much chance it had to be adopted by the Sacramento citizens. He was aware of how revolutionary his plan was but, at the same time, he was sure that their computers, like Omega 1420 would be supportive of his initiative. However, he knew that a large percentage of the citizenry who supported and benefited from the deposed mayor's dictatorial system would be up in arms, opposing its adoption with every means at their disposal. He could only count on his resistance movement and the computers for support. He decided to submit his draft proposal to Omega 1420 to have it evaluated by a rational, intelligent mind.

He had one more look at his draft document and then pressed the send button to upload it to 'SC' as he had been calling their computer ever since it was 'liberated' from the irrational influence of their previous rulers. "Now I'll wait and see what I have overlooked" was his last thought before calling Octavia, his girlfriend, and comrade in arms (his arms as often as he could), to arrange a lunch date that he had been planning ever since she rejoined him after their long separation while road traffic was restored between Yuba City and Sacramento.

SC's response to his transmission was almost instantaneous as if it had been waiting for it.

*"Jonathan, I have received and reviewed your transmission, and I approve. I suggest you get in touch with Kathleen Winters, the mayor of Yuba City, who can fill you in on what the Sacramento Valley computers decided on regarding the organization of human affairs. You will see that you and we are on the same page. Congratulations, as you humans like to say, on a job well done."*

Jonathan decided to postpone his call to Octavia because he knew that he couldn't do anything other than talking to Kathleen to find out what the computers were up to.

# Hopestead

I was totally unaware of happenings in the other cities and, frankly, I couldn't care less. Finally, I was back home and allowed to concentrate on what was important to us: the three projects we decided on: greenhouse, water mill, and a new heavy-duty vehicle. Galen arrived in the evening as he promised and, an hour later, Gordon rolled in with his backhoe on top of BB's flatbed truck. The greenhouse supplies we brought back from Chico were still piled up on the trailer, so we had everything ready to get moving with real life. We had only a dozen adults with us, including Galen, so we didn't have to argue about what we wanted to do and how we wanted to go about it. Basic knowledge of facts and simple logic always pointed the way we should go. We all had our skills and expertise and respected each other's opinions.

After a brief discussion, we had our plan ready. Galen and Brian would drive south with the flatbed to see if they could bring back the abandoned motor home I had seen previously so our visitors had somewhere to sleep, other than the barn floor; Martha volunteered to clean it out when/if the guys could bring it back; Adrien and Mark would finalize the location of the greenhouse and the watermill (had to be next to each other) so Gordon could start excavation, following Cathy's instructions; Robyn and Jennifer were encouraged to look after our meals and other bodily comforts; Alan and Doug were designated as helping hands, providing extra muscle power whenever it was needed; Mike would take his ax and bow-saw to the woods and bring back as many hardwood logs as he could for our charcoal production. This would be the third charcoal trench in our system. I, the least skillful but most determined, was expected to use my expertise by enlarging the previously started charcoal pit, with my handy shovel and pickax. The second pit had been burning for almost a week and we should have ready-to-use charcoal by the time the first one was emptied. We could reuse the corrugated metal covers for the third one when the fire was lit.

The next morning, before resuming the digging, I went to see what Adrien, Mark, and Cathy were up to. They were by the river, deciding where to have Gordon start excavating.

"We need to find a spot with a significant drop in ground level." Cathy just told the others when I arrived.

"It also needs to be next to that small hill where we are pumping the water up to for our irrigation," Adrien and Mark said at the same time, "so we can have the greenhouse built into the side of that hill. We need maximum protection from the winds."

"Then you are in luck," I suggested "because the ground has a considerable drop from the hill where it is sloping away for some distance and the river bed also has a drop right there. You can see by looking at the rippling of the water as it speeds up almost as if following rapids."

"You are right, Trevor, good observation. So it is decided, we will place both the greenhouse and the water mill right at this spot. Gordon, anytime you are ready, I'll tell you what the specs are, and you can fire up your backhoe. The greenhouse can follow the curve of the hill, on its south side, so it will have a mostly southern exposure. I think that you will have to cut into the hill in parallel swatches, each going about six feet deep at the high end. The removed earth should be dumped on the west side so it will form a berm, protecting the greenhouse from the prevailing wind direction."

"How long do you want the greenhouse to be, Adrien?"

"As long as you can stay with the curve of the hill, or you run out of charcoal. Whichever happens first. We have a lot of people to feed and the more protected space we have the better off we'll be."

"OK, boss, I am on it!" Gordon announce cheerfully and walked away toward his backhoe.

Everything seemed to be going in the right direction, so I went back to my digging, exercising my growing set of muscles that I seem to have developed since I abandoned pushing keys on computers. The rhythmic movement of the shovel, as it dug into the ground, had a hypnotic effect on me, requiring no conscious thought, so I could let my mind wander. I was musing about our experiment, involving a dozen people who seemingly happily gave up all the comfort they had in the city so they could have this rough and often hard life in the middle of this devastation left over by the war and the storms. An atavistic force seemed to be motivating us to defy everything nature could throw at us, maybe as an atonement for all the harm we had done to her. Whatever our motivations were, we all seemed to be doing our parts, happy to be here. We were part of something bigger than ourselves, but not a cog in the machine as living in a city of thousands felt to many of us.

By noon, I was tired enough to take a break, both from digging and from trying to understand the universe, so I looked around to see what the others were doing. Gordon was making good progress excavating the hillside for the greenhouse and Cathy was driving stakes into the ground close to the riverbank, presumably marking the contour of our future water mill. Everyone disappeared somewhere else but came running back when they heard the loud blaring of the flatbed's horn as Galen and Brian rolled to a stop with the glorious sight of a 30-foot-long motor home on top. Galen jumped out of the cab and pointed triumphantly at his prize.

"So what do you think guys?"

"Is it in good enough condition to sleep in?" Gordon asked, obviously concerned about where he had to sleep during the next two weeks.

"It's a bit dirty inside, a few windows were not quite closed, so a lot of dirt was blown in, not something our resident artist couldn't cope with." Brian smiled encouragingly at Martha who didn't seem to be too impressed with the confidence.

"Thanks a lot, Brian, I'm sure *we* will both succeed beautifully!"

"Did you just 'volunteer' me to dirty my electrician's hands?" Brian asked in alarm.

Robyn, his wife laughed at him: "I think you volunteered yourself - we all heard it, so you can't wiggle out of it."

"Oh yes, you women stick together as always, us poor men never have a chance when you are around."

Before the bantering could continue onto dangerous grounds, Jennifer announced lunch and we instantly forgot about the war of the sexes. Food for hungry workers took precedent and we all trooped into the kitchen. The large kitchen table had been augmented by the dining table we liberated from the house we had acquired our solar panels from and, luckily, it was a big enough kitchen to accommodate chairs for a dozen people.

After lunch, we were ready to go back to work but then we had a surprise visitor. We had not seen Scott, our only neighbor a few miles east of us, for a couple of months when he told us that he didn't need any more nursing because his broken leg had healed and we could go back to minding our own business.

He was the most ungracious, cantankerous old recluse I have ever seen. Considering that we saved his life when that broken branch fell on him, trapping him under, he could have shown a little gratitude, but that wasn't his way. Martha who understood him better was sure that he was embarrassed about needing our help. I guess for someone who prided himself on being self-sufficient, it was a humiliating experience.

But now, he walked over to our group, all standing outside admiring the motorhome, and raised a hand in a gesture that we could, if we tried hard, recognize as a greeting. He walked over to Mike, the one in our group he seemed more comfortable with (a tough guy like himself, not like the rest of us 'city folks'), and asked in his usual gruff voice: "What on God's earth are you up to now? - I see all this traffic going back and forth in front of my house and I don't care for all that noise."

"Take it easy, Scott," Mike used the soothing voice he often employed when Jennifer was mad at him "it will be over as soon as Gordon finishes all the excavation with his backhoe."

"Excavating what?" Scott started walking toward the growing cut in the hillside.

"We are building a greenhouse and decided to build it into the hill to protect it from the storms." Mike explained.

Scott looked at it dubiously and asked a question none of us had thought of.

"You'll need to shore it up with a retaining wall or it will be washed right down on top of your greenhouse." he declared.

Gordon, Oroville's building contractor, was the first to reply.

"Of course we do, but have not figured out yet what to build it with."

"All you need is stones and cement. Stones are free from a quarry back there" he waved his arm toward his house "and cement could be had for the right price" he smiled for the first time since he arrived. "I still have a few drumfuls left since I built my own greenhouse."

"And what would the right price be?" Gordon wanted to know.

"Now, let me think, you might cut some firewood for me."

"I can do that if you lend me your chainsaw after," Mike volunteered "I'm a bit tired to do it by ax and saw."

"Well, now, that's two things you want for cutting some wood for me, so how about you do some spadework as well to make things even?"

"Scott, you drive a hard bargain," I said "it all depends on how much cement you can give us? Give me an idea how long a retaining wall, six feet tall, we can build with your cement. If it's enough for the whole job, we can have a deal."

"Hmmm…it should be enough for about a hundred feet if you don't waste it!"

"Another question: you must have built your greenhouse some time ago. How do we know if the cement is still any good?" Gordon raised another question.

"It's been in airtight and watertight drums, I'm sure they are just fine," Scott reassured him.

"OK, that's a deal then," we agreed and everybody seemed satisfied. Especially Mike who offered Scott a lift back to this house to cut some firewood for him and then bring back the chainsaw and the cement drums.

After Scott and Mike left, we went back to our own tasks but stopped short when we heard Gordon cursing loudly as he jumped off his backhoe and knelt in the earth, examining something under the hoe's shovel.

"What's the matter?" Adrien, nearest to him asked.

"This is the matter!" Gordon answered angrily, pointing at the surface he cleared under the shovel. "I just hit a bloody big rock, far too big to shift it even an inch with my machine. I don't want to force it anymore because it might break something and we can't afford to lose the backhoe. So, what am I going to do now? "

We all trooped back to the growing cut and looked at the huge stone, scratching our heads.

"We need some dynamite" Gordon declared "and I know exactly where to get it, but I need to go back to Oroville. Can you guys give me a lift? I don't want to use the flatbed over that rough terrain more than I have to. BB would skin my hide if I broke something while fording over that creek. It needs it for the construction crew restoring the power lines to Chico."

"Mike's gone with our van to Scott's and I'm not sure when he'll be back. How about Galen's dune buggy? Galen, would it be all right?" I asked and could see that Galen was reluctant to part with his new toy.

"Good idea, Trevor," Gordon agreed, "I always wanted to try one of those!"

"You'll be careful with it, won't you?" Galen grudgingly agreed and gave Gordon the key. "You will bring it back in one piece or I'll hold your backhoe hostage until you fix it!"

Everybody laughed and we watched Gordon walk away happily, with Galen explaining, at length it seemed, how to drive his six-wheeler.

All we had to do now until he came back with the dynamite, was to drill several deep holes into the rock for Gordon to place his charges, hoping that he knew what he was doing and not blow us up to smithereens. We had a heavy-duty chisel and a five-pounder hammer, so it was time to activate the extra muscle power we had been holding in reserve and call Alan and Doug to join us for the hard physical work in the hard granite. It took us hours to drill those holes deep enough, following Gordon's instruction, all of us taking a turn at the job and, when it was done, we all decided it was time for a break and some refreshments.

While waiting for Gordon to come back with the dynamite, I made myself comfortable in the hammock we had strung up between two trees and waited for my aching muscles to regenerate. I couldn't help thinking about how our Hopestead had evolved from the initial idea. All I wanted at the beginning was to get away from the computer and the robots and be free to face challenges on my own, without help from anybody other than a few close friends. That had slowly changed over the months when I realized that Big Brain was not an enemy as I had thought, but a valuable partner who wanted the best for all the people of, not just Oroville, but all of the towns in the Sacramento valley. So, abandoning my original intention of being 'purists', I decided that it would be silly to refuse any help we could get. Now we were using resources from Oroville when we had to, including machines liberated from the Pioneer Village, even Scott's cement, in exchange for some work for the old curmudgeon. Not mentioning all the wonderful greenhouse supplies we brought back from Chico. None of these compromises I had made from the original intention diminished the experiment's value for me: I was physically active in a natural environment, with like-minded people who all co-operated to build our lives here.

Resting comfortably in the hammock, I must have dozed off because the next thing I noticed was Gordon honking the puny horn on the six-wheeler, announcing his return. He had a box with him, painted red with a yellow outline of skull and crossbones. We joined him, looking at the menacing box that he opened to show us the contents. Five sticks of dynamite, wrapped in red paper, a box containing the electric blasting caps and a long roll of wires, and a plunger. We stayed at a respectful distance as he carried it all to the rock and inspected the holes we had drilled.

"Looks like they are deep enough and wide enough for the sticks to fit. I suggest you all go back at least 300 feet to be safe while I am setting this up."

He didn't have to warn us twice and we watched from a distance while he carefully opened up the end of each dynamite stick and pushed a blasting cap into the pinkish paste inside. Then he connected the wires attached to each blasting cap to the roll of electric wire that he carefully unrolled to where we were waiting, holding our breaths. Finally, he connected the long wire leading from the rock to the plunger and declared that he was ready to start the explosion but warned us to go even farther in case some fragments were blown our way.

Just as he was ready to depress the plunger, we were terrified to hear Mike's van come back from Scott's place, stopping only 30 feet away from the rock Gordon was ready to blast. Luckily, he caught on in time and ordered Mike to move his van away from the blast site to a safe distance. When he joined us, we took a roll call to make sure that everyone was present, including the kids and even the cats, safely in the arms of Mike's kids, so we told Gordon to go ahead.

The explosion was unexpectedly loud and a huge plume of dirt and rocks was hurtled in the air but nothing came even close to where we stood. When the dust settled, we went back to examine the blast site and found a deep hole where the huge rock had been. Gordon knelt down and raked around in the hole making sure that nothing big remained and he could resume digging with the backhoe. He declared the exercise a success and basked in the warm glow of admiration and approval he received from our group. Another task was completed successfully.

# Oroville

The City Council of Oroville was in full session. They were discussing the "Proposal for a New Social Contract" document they had received from Jonathan, as well as the information they had received from Yuba City about the computers' intention regarding human affairs. To say that it was a stormy session would be an understatement. Tim Hooke, recently elected Mayor of Oroville, opened the emergency session after he had received Jonathan's proposal. He had distributed it before the session was called, so all present had read it and had time to study, ponder and digest it. As it turned out, not everyone understood what was new in it.

"We always had public and private sectors in the economy," Tracy looked confused "so what's new in this proposal?"

Tim waited for someone else to explain it, but everyone seemed reluctant to be first, so he answered himself.

"Best I can put it, this time the Public sector is completely isolated from the Private one, so it is in no jeopardy of being gutted or corrupted as it has been all through the Capitalist System. In a way, it is a Livable Basic Income system without the income part. No money is used in the public area and things get distributed, just as they are now. The Private Sector, on the other hand, can use money and produce luxuries for anyone who wants to work for them but the government - which will be us and Big Brain, will make sure that basic human rights are observed, such as protecting the environment."

"Why do we need a Private Sector at all, why can't we just carry on as we are?" Holly stood up. "I like the way things are now, so why muck around with it?"

"Things change, Holly" Tim answered calmly "and the time will come when we will want more than just to satisfy basic needs, as we are doing now."

Chris Teggart seemed to be waiting for someone to announce his main concern: "Absolutely right and I said it many times before - I want more than just food and entertainment. We used to have a high-tech civilization with great accomplishments in science, technology, and medicine. I know, these are luxuries now but I want to look to the future when we can have some of it back!"

"Isn't it a bit early to think about space travel?" Morgan asked in a teasing voice but Chris wasn't going to let anyone distract him.

"Maybe so, Morgan, but we have to think ahead as the computers do. You all read Kathleen's summary of what they decided! In the private sector, we'll be able to choose any system, any principle for organizing ourselves, so I propose to choose total freedom to liberate all the creative and productive minds who want more than just basic survival."

"You mean you want Capitalism back?

"Yes, but only in the private sector and closely monitored and controlled by us and Big Brain."

"So, what is it? - 'closely controlled' or 'total freedom'?" Morgan turned serious, abandoning the teasing voice.

"Look guys," Chris looked around the table "I'm aware of all the evils of uncontrolled Capitalism. Our situation is a direct result and that's something I don't want back. However, I agree with Jonathan's analysis: we need to be compassionate to care for each other, as we are now, but we also need the freedom to pursue our dreams, as long as they don't threaten anyone's basic needs, as it did before. I like the idea of having the best of both systems, as Jonathan described. And yes, I want space travel back! There is a universe out there and, someday, we may want to get off this totally screwed up planet!"

"Screwed up by Capitalism!" Morgan couldn't help pointing it out.

"Yes, you are right, but now we have allies we did not have before."

"What allies?"

"Incorruptible computers who volunteered to be our guardians, protecting us against our bad behavior."

"You really think it could work?" Tim asked earnestly. "Isn't it humiliating to admit that we need protection against ourselves?"

"Admit it or not," Chris shot back "you know it's true. The entire human history, not mentioning the last war, testifies to that."

"Does it have to be Capitalism?" Morgan seemed allergic to the word "what about the other options?"

"The essence of Capitalism is free enterprise and competition. The dream that 'you' could be rich too someday. This dream motivated a lot of people to do their best and come up with innovative ideas."

"Actually, the essence of Capitalism is the concept of 'capital'. That means the financial system, investment, profit, interest rate, and the idea that a lot of rich people can just sit on their capital and enjoy the fruits of others' labor without contributing anything themselves. Do you want those parasites back too?"

"Of course not," Chris's response was immediate "I only want people to be free to produce great things and trade with each other without restrictions. Value for value."

"I'm happy to hear that, but back to your earlier point: people do come up with innovative ideas all the time, just look at the thousands of YouTube videos where people shared them without any financial gain."

"Yes, that was part of it, while we had an Internet, but none of them contributed to space travel!"

"You seem to have a one-track mind, Chris - people have more immediate concern than joyriding off-planet."

"Of course, I do!" Chris almost shouted "my team has come up with the design of an intra-galactic spaceship engine. If we find a way to rebuild the industrial infrastructure that we have lost, we could start looking for a livable planet before climate change wipes us all out. You said we have to look ahead. I agree, but please look a bit beyond your feet and see what's coming!"

There was a long silence following Chris's outburst. It did have an effect on the general mood, and all traces of joviality disappeared. Finally, Tim spoke up:

"We have plenty to think about now. Our little town is not going to change human history, but Chris had a point. If the computers can guarantee that Capitalism won't destroy us this time, I'm willing to consider it. I advise you all to think about it and we can discuss it further during our next session. So, if we have covered this topic, let's talk about our more immediate concerns."

Holly seemed to be waiting for this suggestion: "Actually, I have a more immediate concern, and that's the number of schools we need. The three that Gordon has rebuilt for us are a great success and I have to admit that Chris's critical thinking curriculum had an unanticipated response from students 14 to 18. They love it and many debating groups were started in which students discuss and argue about a wide area of topics, including social organization that we have just been talking about. However, we need a lot more schools and facilities for the thousands of young people who still have to rely on home-schooling, envying their friends who were lucky enough to fit in one of our classrooms."

"It takes time, Holly, to rebuild what we lost and Gordon is looking for more opportunities all the time."

"How can he do that while he is doing god only knows what in Trevor's homestead?"

"It was BB who encouraged Gordon to go there, as compensation for Trevor's wasting a lot of time scouting out Chico and reestablishing contact with its Omega computer. But he will be back in a week and I'm sure schools will be his highest priority."

"I wish BB kept its nose out of our business and stopped interfering," Holly said angrily and some people seemed to agree.

"BB is concerned with the big picture, the wellbeing of the entire Sacramento Valley" Chris rose to Big Brain's defense. "Our valley may be the only thing left from the whole country, as far as we know. I think it knows what it is doing and if we accept its decisions when they are in our immediate interest, we should accept other decisions that serve the larger public good. We may not be able to ever rebuild the whole of the USA, but I'm all for making our valley as prosperous and safe as possible. This is one basis from which we can do something to save humanity."

"So it looks like we have to harmonize the 'big picture' Chris is talking about with the 'little picture' which is our immediate concern" Tim summarized.

"I have my own 'little picture," Tracy spoke up "and it has to do with our agricultural classes I teach to students 10 to 18. I need more resources and more volunteers to do it properly. I have an idea of encouraging kids to start up the gardens around all those destroyed houses, so they can see the city being rebuilt day by day, but I need cleanup crews to remove the more dangerous debris from around these yards so no one would get hurt."

"That's a terrific idea, Tracy, I agree completely. I'll ask BB to broadcast a request for volunteers to the whole town and then we can decide, based on the number of help we get, on what material and tool resources they need."

"I can live with that," Tracy agreed "the sooner we can get started, the sooner kids will be able to work and learn out in the open air, becoming familiar with plants they know nothing about at the moment."

Nobody seemed ready to bring up another topic that required a decision, so Tim adjourned the meeting and wished all members a pleasant and productive afternoon.

~~~

Chris, walking back to his apartment, was thinking about the last conversation he had had with Big Brain. His scientist's mind couldn't help thinking beyond the immediate concerns expressed by his friends and BB was the only high-powered logical mind he could discuss his fears with. Before the war, he had studied the whole issue of climate change and was painfully aware of all the implications. According to all available data, they were past the tipping point where no human action could stop, or even slow down; the accelerating impact of centuries-long abuse of the planet's natural systems and overall climate. The permafrost was thawing in the northern latitudes of Russia and Canada, the Greenland ice sheets were breaking up, reducing the reflective white surface of the ice pack, trapping more and more heat in the atmosphere, and the resulting sea-level rise has already displaced thousands living on low-lying islands and

90

coastlines and the storms were more and more frequent, more and more devastating each year. On top of all that humanity had to deal with the deadly pandemic and then the war. It reminded him of a gallows-humor joke he had heard: Half of a farmer's crop is destroyed by hail, so he goes out to his field with his tractor and destroys the other half, shouting up at the sky: "Let's see God Almighty what we can accomplish together!" That's what humanity seemed to be doing to itself. The next pandemic, he was sure, could kill billions instead of millions and they had nowhere to hide. They had to get off this planet with as many human migrants as possible, to assure that Homo Sapiens survived in some form on some other planet. Maybe they will have learned from the past and they would not destroy another planet with their greed and short-sighted stupidity.

~~~

*BB on the other hand wasn't thinking that far ahead. It was more concerned with its immediate goal: to unify the whole Sacramento Valley in a cohesive, productive, and, most of all, sustainable system. There was only one large population center that he had not been able yet to contact and it was paramount that it be accomplished as soon as possible. It knew that it needed Trevor and Mike again to suspend their no doubt enjoyable participation in the homestead experiment, and BB knew how much opposition it could count on from the two software engineers. For this reason, it was willing to give them any*

91

*help they asked for, hoping that they would be willing to carry out this much larger task for the greater good. That's why it loaned the flat-bed truck and Gordon for two valuable weeks that could have been used to rebuild power lines to Chico. It also agreed to let Gordon take some dynamite from the city's construction warehouse and now it was going to suggest that the old water-mill displayed in the Pioneer Village could save the homesteaders a lot of time. All it needed was dismantling and transporting to Hopestead (he agreed to use that designation, queer though it was.) Once all these projects were underway, it would request Trevor's and Mike's less than enthusiastic participation in this last expedition. Once Redding joined its network, then BB could get on with the harder task of organizing the individual nodes to a functional unit from where serious rebuilding could proceed.*

# Trip to Redding

I had a big surprise this morning: an unexpected communication from BB, via R17:

*"Trevor, I became aware of an item in our Pioneer Village that might be useful for your homestead."*

"OK, BB, I'm always interested in useful things. By the way, how come you are suddenly so helpful?"

*"There is nothing sudden about it, as you well know. I have been here for all of you humans, as you programmed me to be, even if I don't give you personally preferential treatment."*

"OK, BB, keep your shirt on and work on developing a sense of humor."

*"Human humor? No, thank you. So, do you want to know what item I am talking about?"*

"Of course I do, so why don't you just tell me?"

*"I would if you stopped interrupting me. It is a demonstration water mill that you might be able to adapt to your needs. I'll have Cathy take a look at it if you wish."*

"Of course, I do, you could have done it by now without asking me. I suspect there is a price tag attached to your generosity. What is it this time?"

"Actually, I was going to suggest another trip to Chico with Chris who is eager to meet his scientist friends again for a conference."

"A trip to Chico is not out of the question because Adrien needs more greenhouse supplies. Now that the excavation is completed, she realized she doesn't have enough for the length of the greenhouse she wants to build."

"Very well, but, once you are in Chico and waiting for Chris, you might as well make an extra detour for me. It is for the whole valley that you know I am working on."

"BB, are you twisting my arm again, to make me do something I don't want to do?"

"We might as well clear up a misunderstanding that you insist on. I may seem to be manipulating you, to use a human term, but it is a lot simpler than that. Ever since we had that lock-down and I was forced to find ways to help humans often despite themselves, I had to work hard to understand your psychology. Once I made progress there, I realized that I needed short-term compromises to serve your long-term interests. The short-term compromises I am talking about are the delays and reduction in efficiency due to the negotiations I have had to conduct, to motivate you and Mike for helping me achieve my long-term aims. Lending you Gordon for two weeks to help you with your greenhouse was such a delay I had to accept. Offering the watermill is another exchange for the same sacrifice I am requesting from you now. I hope this clears things up for you."

I was completely floored by BB's explanation. It's more human than I had ever suspected but, still the honest, incorruptible machine we programmed it to be. Realizing how it was bending over backward (or whatever it was doing to give me that impression) to give us a fair and compelling reason to abandon Hopestead again, for god only knows how long, I knew that I could not refuse if at all possible to comply.

"OK, out with it, where do you want us to go this time?"

*"The very last trip I'll ask you to make will have to be to Redding. The last large enough population center, with its Omega computer that I have not been able to contact. Once that connection is made, my network in the Sacramento Valley will be complete and I can start planning to rebuild a functional industrial and scientific civilization that will benefit all of you."*

"Redding? Do you know how far that is?"

*"Of course I do. It is exactly 73.4 miles from downtown Chico to downtown Redding. In prewar traveling conditions it would take 1 hour 17 minutes on I5. I realize that you may encounter some obstacles along the way but your previous trip to Chico went very smoothly, so chances are that the detour won't take you more than a few hours."*

'Plus the time to get from here to Oroville, plus the time we have to find your Omega friend and reactivate it, plus the time to get back to Chico, then to Oroville, then to home. We may not be able to accomplish it in one day and where would we spend the night?"

*"Chris's friend, Richard, offered to put you up for the night if necessary. That will also give you ample time to load up whatever greenhouse supplies you want to take home. As you see, this could be a win-win for all concerned."*

"I knew if I let you explain, you would talk us into another trip. But, as you said, this will be the last one. We need to accelerate our projects or we'll be very hungry come next winter."

*"I understand, Trevor, and I sincerely hope that no more emergencies will require your absence from your Hopestead."*

"OK, BB, I'll talk to Mike and let you know when we can leave."

~~~

Mike was less than ecstatic when I reported on my conversation with Big Brain, but he also saw the importance of BB's project of unifying and rebuilding the whole valley, so he grudgingly agreed to the trip. Actually, Adrien's request for more greenhouse supplies made it important to us as well, so we agreed to go.

We left early the next morning, picked Chris up in Oroville, and continued on the familiar road to Chico. We made good time as before and delivered Chris to the university in time for lunch. We had a quick meal and pressed on because we didn't know what to expect once we were on unfamiliar terrain north of Chico. For the first 20 miles we drove through a desolate landscape of arid desert, interrupted a few times by a few cultivated fields. We started seeing signs of flooding and found it alarming, not knowing what to expect, or how bad the flooding would get. Another mile farther north the road took a sharp left turn and then we saw some really bad signs of flooding everywhere. The road surface was covered by a thick layer of mud and stones of various sizes. Soon we could see a large river to our left, winding its way in the southern direction. Mike had a map and realized that we were next to the Sacramento River and that explained the flooding that we had seen, but what caused it? No rainfall of any amount could explain the mud deposits so far from the river, so we were at a loss to explain it. Another 6 miles and we were in the village of Los Molinos, or what was left of it. There were obvious signs of inundation on the sides of houses, those that were still standing. With watermarks on the walls up to six feet high. Another 10 miles, inching over the mud-covered road, we reached an intersection with I36 that took us west to the town of Red Bluff. This was where, according to Mike's map, we would join with I5 going north to Redding. However, we first had to cross a bridge over the river and we had a very bad feeling about the condition we would find it.

As it turned out, our premonitions were justified because we found both spans of the bridge down, its pylons still sticking out of the water, holding back a huge mass of debris that was stuck against the obstacle of the pylons and the remnants of the collapsed bridge.

"That's it then," Mike announced, we might as well turn back."

"Show me that map, Mike, maybe there is another way to cross. Or, maybe we don't need to cross at all, maybe we could approach Redding from the East. Having come this far, I'm reluctant to give up so quickly".

Looking at the map I saw another bridge not too far back from where we came. Had we followed on I36 instead of turning north on I5, we would have come to another bridge. Since it's downstream from the collapsed bridge, right after the river took a sharp turn to the left, it's possible that the bend in the riverbed and the collapsed bridge slowed it down enough to spare the second bridge.

"What do you think, Mike," I pointed at the map "should we give it a try? It's not far, only a mile or two if we go back on 5 and then turn right on 36?"

"You might be right, but if that bridge is out as well, we have to go back. At some point farther north, we would have to cross the river and, if it is so bad this far downstream, I can imagine how much worse it could get when we get to the source of the flooding, whatever it was. According to this map, there is no way to approach Redding from the East, unless we go way up to the mountains, which I flatly refuse to do."

So, we turned back on I5, turned right on I36, and came to the second bridge in a few minutes. Miracle of miracles, it was still intact, thickly covered with mud, of course, but looked solid enough to cross. Once we were across, we found ourselves on Main Street, and turning right on it we managed to rejoin I5, going north again, on the left side of the river. Red Bluff showed the same signs of complete inundation as in Los Molinos and, predictably, we could not see any sign of life, human or animal.

"Maybe a few obstacles?" Mike was quoting Big Brain, rolling his eyes. "I think our hopes are a bit waterlogged at this point. However, according to the map, the road veers a bit farther from the river and we won't get too close to it until we reach the town of Anderson. Then we would have to cross again, unless we leave 5 and go northwest on 273 and exit onto Buenaventura Blvd going northwest, drive by the California Army National Guard and take 299 east to Redding. Provided all these roads are passable."

"It looks like 20 miles to Anderson and another 10 to Redding," I pointed out. "I'm willing to try if you agree, but at the next major obstacle we turn around. Enough is enough. Do you agree?"

Instead of answering, Mike stepped on the pedal and that was enough of an answer. As we expected, the bridge in Anderson was out, so we turned back to the intersection with 273 and exited I5, driving north until we reached Buenaventura Blvd. We were still in the suburbs of Redding but there didn't seem any point in driving into it - total devastation as far as we could see. No building intact, no sign of life.

"When we reach the junction of 299, we'll make one last attempt to turn east to try to reach downtown Redding, but I don't think we'll find anything there anymore. Redding, as a town is gone, taking BB's Omega with it. However, we'll have the whole picture and report back to its majesty with good conscience. Then we head home and, hopefully, reach Chico before night. We'll have to sleep there and load up the greenhouse stuff tomorrow. Agreed?"

"Drive on and hope we don't get stuck in anything worse than what we have seen so far."

As soon as we left I5, the road started gaining elevation, so we had some hope to get out of the flooded area and, maybe, we would find some signs of survivors who managed to escape in time before their town was destroyed. We still didn't know what caused it, or how long ago it was, so we just pressed on.

The first sign of life greeted us at the gate of The California Army National Guard. In the Guardhouse a soldier looked at us as if we had just dropped from the sky. To be honest, we were just as surprised to see the first human being since leaving Chico.

We stopped and waited for the soldier to reach us, carrying a rifle, not quite sure what to do with it.

We got out of the van and met him halfway, raising our hands in greeting.

"Who the hell are you and where the hell have you come from?" was the first 'greeting' we received and weren't quite sure how friendly we should assume it was.

"You might find it hard to believe but we have come all the way from Oroville, about 100 miles south of here if you know where that is" Mike volunteered.

"I didn't know if anyone was still alive that far south," the soldier explained, "you are the first human beings outside of Redding that showed up here since the war."

"What happened to Redding?" I needed to know what caused this massive catastrophe.

"The dam broke - the Shasta Lake Dam - the fucking Ruskies blew it up during the war. The biggest man-made lake in California, right on top of us. Everything was washed away, tens of thousands drowned, only people in higher elevation, like our base, survived."

"How many?"

"Probably a couple of thousand, most of them evacuated to the suburb of Shasta, about 6 miles west on 299. That's where the mayor and the admin staff are, in case you want to talk to them."

"Of course, we want to talk to them, that's what we came for. We have four cities south of here, all the way to Sacramento and they are working on rebuilding the valley. You are the last one we contacted, the farthest north from us, so it took us a while to get here."

"That's the biggest surprise I have had since the flood," the soldier beamed at us with a huge grin "I'm sure you will be greeted very warmly with your news. Wait here a few minutes, I have to report this to my CO, I am sure she will want to talk to you before you go to Shasta."

"She?" Mike looked a bit surprised to hear about a female commander.

"Yes, Colonel Anita Majors," the soldier chuckled. "We call her Colonel Major!"

We didn't have to wait for long, the soldier came back in a few minutes and got on his scooter we just noticed parked by the guardhouse.

"Follow me please, I'll lead you to her HQ."

To tell the truth, we would have preferred to drive to Shasta right away and talk to the civilian leadership but didn't want to be rude, so we followed the scooter to a flat, one-story building that had the "California Army National Guard" sign right above the entrance.

Anita Majors was a middle-aged woman, with strands of silver poking out from her cap and an erect posture that you would expect in the army. She greeted us briefly and then peppered us with question after question, obviously wanting to know everything we could tell her about life outside her army base. To tell the truth, I was feeling a bit uncomfortable with her 'interrogation' if this was the right word to describe her manner so, after we told her everything she seemed to want to know, we told her that we wanted to talk to the civilian authorities as soon as possible.

"That will take some time," she replied because I need to talk to them first. You realize that your showing up, and telling me everything you did, introduced an unexpected development that I need to discuss with the mayor and his staff. Once we reach a decision, regarding what to do with you, we'll let you know. In the meantime, please accept our hospitality in our cafeteria where you will be given drinks and food and a much-needed rest, I'm sure."

"Are you telling me that we are under arrest? Not allowed to leave?" I was trying to control my voice.

"Not under arrest, of course, you are not charged with anything - yet. However we have to handle this new situation with extreme care and, until a decision is made, it's important that you stay here, so we can talk again later."

She pressed a buzzer on her desk and told the soldier who entered to take us to the cafeteria and make us comfortable with whatever we needed. The last thing she told him before she left was: "make sure they are still there when I come back. Call Shasta and tell them to expect me."

We didn't have much of a choice but follow the soldier who eyed us with obvious suspicion and his finger never moved too far from the trigger of his carbine. Obviously, he had no idea who we were and what to make of us, but he seemed determined not to take any chances.

So, Mike and I made ourselves as comfortable as we could on the hard cafeteria chairs and waited for the promised food and refreshments. It turned out to be a long wait.

# Three Towns

Colonel Anita Majors was disturbed by what the two strangers from Oroville had told her. The idea that Sacramento was drafting a new constitution, under the guidance of intelligent computers, felt both like science fiction, on one hand, and treason on the other. It also implied that the United States of America that she had served, under oath of allegiance, her entire life, was gone forever. She refused to believe it until she saw undeniable proof that this was the case. True, she had been cut off from her superiors in the Guard since the war, the chain of command was broken, but someone somewhere must be rebuilding it and it was her duty to hold up her end until ordered otherwise by representatives of the US government. Wrestling with these agonizing doubts, she arrived in Shasta, ready to discuss them with the only civilian authority she had access to - Brad Wagoneer, the mayor of what was left of Redding.

Mayor Wagoneer was surprised by the peremptory announcement of Colonel Majors' visit. Why didn't she call herself, explaining the purpose of this unscheduled meeting? The Colonel wasn't an impulsive person, at least not until now. She must have had some unexpected news that upset her enough to jump into her car and drive off as if, it seemed, in a panic. He knew it wouldn't take her long to cover the 6 miles from her HQ to his office, so he just had to wait until she had arrived. Waiting was never easy for him, being an active politician he preferred to attack each problem head-on - uncertainty was always very hard on him. Luckily, he was spared more guessing because the Colonel's jeep just pulled up to the front door of his building and she emerged, striding purposefully toward the entrance.

Instead of their usual polite greeting, Brad decided not to waste time on pleasant chit-chat.

"I must admit, Colonel, that I was a bit surprised to be told to expect you. Is something wrong?"

"You'll have to decide it for yourself after I tell you what happened today." She replied and then explained, at length, everything she had learned (if any of it was true) from the two strangers from towns they had not known still existed.

After he recovered from the shock of the news of the outside world, for the first time since the war, he could only ask: "So where are they?" craning his neck to see inside her jeep parked outside his window.

"They are still at the base, under guard. I didn't trust them enough to let them loose. I thought that you and I needed to discuss all the implications before we decided how to handle the situation and the two visitors. We are still in a state of war and we can't be careful enough. They could be Russian spies as far as we know, scouting out what we have left to fight them with."

"I doubt that very much, based on the glimpses we had had before the news went down with the satellite control. Total devastation in all three countries fighting each other. Since then, for two years, not a peep from the outside world, until now. Their story sounds plausible and I definitely want to talk to them myself. I can't rely entirely on your impression, let alone your suspicion. I'm the only civilian authority left here and, until and unless any chain of command with the rest of the country is reestablished, I have to be ultimately responsible for decisions of this magnitude. Please contact your base and have those two men transported here, so we can discuss the whole situation with them included. I can't make any decision in a vacuum, I need those two here."

There was a long pause while they stared at each other but, finally, Colonel Majors shrugged her acceptance.

"Very well, I don't see any harm in bringing them here, under guard."

She spoke briefly into her comm-set and announced: "They will be here shortly. In the meantime, why don't you explain your idea of a new constitution being drafted by some people in Sacramento? Doesn't it feel like treason to you, because it does to me?"

"It would under normal circumstances, however, 'normal' was blown up by the Russian missiles and now we have a completely new situation. Let's just wait for the two visitors to explain things in more detail. We need more information in order to make a pragmatic decision."

~~~

In Sacramento, Jonathan was alerted by Omega 1420, the town's supercomputer, of an incoming call from an unexpected source. By all appearances, Trevor and Mike had successfully reached the town of Redding at the northern edge of the valley, restarted their Omega 1900 computer, and proposed a conference call among the leaders of the two cities. To say this was a total surprise would be an understatement. He had no idea what Redding wanted to talk about, he was too deeply involved in the new constitution he and his colleagues were preparing for the upcoming referendum, to have much time left over for anything else. However, curiosity won out and he accepted the call.

"This is Jonathan Carver, interim mayor of Sacramento, whom am I talking to please?"

"I am Brad Wagoneer, mayor of the town of Redding, or what's left of it after most of the city was destroyed by a flood. It was caused by the collapsing dam upriver, due to a Russian missile strike. We have two visitors here who claim to be representing Sacramento and other cities in the valley. Their names are Trevor Dubois and Mike Sutherland. Can you please confirm this to be the case?"

"Terribly sorry to hear about the town's destruction, we had no idea of the catastrophe. Yes, we are aware of their mission and they do represent the four towns of Sacramento, Yuba City, Oroville, and Chico."

"I'm happy to hear that they have been telling us the truth. We have been cut off from the rest of the country, not even aware that anyone out there was still alive, so we were extra cautious accepting their claims without independent corroboration. After they activated our Omega computer, it contacted the other Omegas in the valley and we have received similar confirmation from them as well."

"So, what do you wish to talk to us about? We are a bit busy preparing for a referendum in which citizens of this town will decide on a new constitution to replace our current and quite obsolete one."

"That's exactly why I called you. The commanding officer of our National Guard, Colonel Anita Majors, is concerned about the constitutionality of a new document under wartime conditions and wants to know its content before you submit it to a referendum. In particular, she wants to know if this would be only a city charter, which you have all the right to prepare, or it would be intended to replace the State of California's legal constitution, in which case we would be affected and would have a right to participate in the process."

Jonathan was completely floored by the question. He wasn't a lawyer, he had no idea of the legal ramification of what they were doing and, frankly, couldn't give a damn. It seemed bizarre to talk about legal rights in a country that seemed to be totally destroyed, save a few pockets of survivors, like the valley he lived in. So he answered the question with one of his own.

"Do you have any reason to believe that there is still a United States government functioning anywhere outside this valley?"

"No, we have had no contact with anyone else until now, but it doesn't mean that they don't exist and may contact us at any time. In which case we have to be prepared to account for our actions to a higher authority."

"Sir, I see your point but frankly, I think it's premature to split legal hairs. At this point our main concern is survival and, once it is assured, rebuilding the cities in the valley so we can communicate and trade again, making life easier for all concerned. Our Omega computers are helping us in this task and we have had a good start so far. Now that Redding is also in communication, how would you like to join our efforts and let your own Omega computer participate in the process? We found their influence to be extremely useful, after all, they are now intelligent and, seemingly self-aware life forms that are programmed to represent our best interests."

Suddenly, Brad Wagoneer's voice was replaced with a very stern-sounding female voice.

"Mr. Mayor, I am Colonel Anita Majors, commanding officer of the Redding base of our Army National Guard. I heard you just now and I completely refuse to relinquish my authority to any computer, however intelligent they are."

"Colonel, nobody is asking you to relinquish anything. The computers act only in an advisory capacity, they only insist that fundamental human rights be observed. As long as we do that, we are on our own, making our own decisions."

"And, may I ask, what are those fundamental human rights the computers insist on?"

109

"There are only four and, briefly, they demand that every citizen's right for food, clothing, housing, education, and health care are guaranteed unconditionally, at an adequate and uniform level, without involving currency of any kind. Things have been distributed on that basis in our towns for a long time now and the system works very well."

"Forgive me, this sounds like a Communist dictatorship and we know where that leads. History is a good teacher in that regard. We don't want any part of it and, if it comes to a conflict between Redding and the four cities you talk about, we are fully prepared to fight to uphold the existing constitutional freedom of the United States."

Jonathan was flabbergasted at this display of rigid, unthinking loyalty to a now-dead system. He was still thinking about how to respond when Brad Wagoneer reentered the dialog.

"I think it's silly to talk about fighting when we were just destroyed by a brutal war. This is the time for rebuilding, cooperation and compromise. I suggest we both think about everything that's been said and resume this discussion after a suitably sufficient time. Your representatives, Mike and Trevor insist that they have to return to their homes and we have no problem with that. They will be on their way at the end of this discussion."

Jonathan sighed a huge sigh of relief. The mayor sounded a lot more reasonable than the fiery soldier woman so he wasted no time to assure him of his agreement."

After contact was over, he wanted to pass the news on to the other cities, but Omega 1420 assured him that it had already been done. Actually, the whole 'conversation' was monitored by all of the Omegas, and City Councils were notified immediately. Also, Hopestead residents, who had started to worry about the unusually long absence of their members, were told that Trevor and Mike were on their way back and could be expected by dinnertime on the next day.

~~~

As it turned out, Oroville City Council had been in full session when their Big Brain announced, to everyone's surprise, and frankly shock, the almost total loss of the town of Redding and the 'conversation' between Jonathan and the two leaders of what was left of that town. BB replayed the recording of the entire dialog to the councilors and, for a long while, everyone just sat in stunned disbelief. It was Tim Hooke, Oroville's mayor who spoke first.

"I'm sure we all are very sad at the loss of life in a major city and not quite sure about how much is left, but from this dialog, we can assume that they still have a sizable population with properly elected leaders and an army unit, so we have legitimate authorities to negotiate with."

"If you can negotiate with an army colonel, stuck in the groove of pre-war mentality" Gordon couldn't keep the contempt out of his voice. "I know the type from my army days and know that they can never be convinced about anything."

"Let's not jump to conclusions," Tracy raised her hand: "Their mayor sounded quite reasonable and I'm sure we can work something out."

"I don't like her talking about being ready to fight," Holly seemed concerned. "They have the weapons and we don't. Do we have to prepare for another war? I hope not!"

"Nobody is talking about fights" Tim started but Holly interrupted:

"She is!"

"Calm down Holly, the discussion ended quite reasonably, suggesting that some compromise could be reached. So far we have had it easy, without any major disagreement among the towns, sooner or later it was bound to happen and we just have to deal with it. Intelligently".

"Actually," Chris Teggart announced with some hesitation "I can see the Colonel's point too."

"What point?" Holly demanded to know "she is a military dinosaur who refuses to see how everything changed. We are in a completely different ballgame in which sanity finally has a chance!"

"The point I see is that we may be accountable, someday, to a higher authority, if indeed the USA isn't quite finished yet. She is a member of the US Army and honor-bound to uphold the last constitution she remembers swearing allegiance to. This is an oath no military officer is likely to forget and discard without overwhelming evidence that the organization she swore loyalty to ceased to exist. I have to respect that."

There was a thoughtful silence following Chris's comment, everyone seemed to be digesting the conflicting arguments for a while. Finally, Tim stood up and summarized their conclusion.

"We aren't going to decide this issue today. Before we adjourn, I'd like to ask BB to give us its take on this whole new ballgame, as Holly put it."

As if waiting for an invitation, BB responded immediately.

*"It all depends on the context you will accept for this discussion. Concepts such as freedom, loyalty, honor, oath, and legally binding constitution all came up in this discussion and it is up to you how much weight you give to each of these concepts. One particular human expression that has always bothered me is 'my country, right or wrong". Let me tell you what it implies to me. This is the most irrational, unscientific, and emotionally twisted expression that I have ever encountered in my experience with the human species. It means that in certain circumstances the holder of that opinion is willing to take poison for medicine, suicide for a life-saving operation, mass murder for cooperation. This doesn't just border on insanity - this is plain, simple insanity itself. This attitude explains a lot of your blood-stained history. The decision you will have to make in this debate is: what is more important to you: live your lives as rational, intelligent, viable life forms, or tie yourself into emotional knots, trying to adhere to a system that you inherited from your*

*past? Why do you think that the nuclear war that destroyed your country and at least two others, happened? You have all heard the rhetorical question of 'what would happen if they declared war and nobody came?' However, the soldiers always came to kill and to be killed. Some from fear, some from loyalty, some because they wanted to. The result was always the same: mass murder and mass destruction. The decision is yours, I can't help you make it, but you will have to live with the consequences. As far as the veiled threat from the CO of the Redding National Guard is concerned, it is something that you will have to deal with at some future date. There will be other pockets of survivors all over the country and some of them will attempt to restore the status quo. You will have to decide if you want to defend yourself against remnants of irrationality or give up the creative, productive, and cooperative existence that you have had a taste of since the war."*

This was the longest speech anyone ever heard from Big Brain and the councilors sat for a long time in shocked silence. Nobody had ever presented the choices in such contrast to them before and the emotionless voice of the computer drove it home very powerfully for every one of them. Nobody could add anything to the discussion, the meeting was adjourned and the councilors left quietly, one by one, nobody seemed eager to discuss it anymore.

# Hopestead

$F$inally, I was back home and nobody, not even BB, was going to drag me out of here anytime soon. Yes, I understand the 'Big Picture' BB was working on and I even accept that once in a while individuals like me have to put aside their short-term interests to serve long-term public goals, but there has to be a balance. We can't always live in the future because then we won't have a present and, without it, life's not worth living. I have done my part, more than once and now it's time for others to do theirs. So, unless there is an existential threat that demands my participation, I'm going to be busy with real life. Like helping Adrien with the greenhouse construction. The excavation is completed, now we have to build the retaining wall and that requires many trips to the nearby quarry to bring the stones we will build it with. It's not glamorous work and, frankly, very hard physical exercise, but it needs to be done.

Martha offered to help but, considering she is in her third month, I strictly 'forbade' her to indulge in this kind of activity. Of course, 'forbidding' Martha to do anything works only if she wants to be 'forbidden', otherwise, she would tell me to swallow my masculine ego and pride and leave her alone. I'm used to it by now and was very relieved when she agreed to do something more sedentary, like making me a nice and nutritious breakfast that my muscles would need if I wanted to spend the day lifting and carrying heavy stones. Ever since Mike and I returned from our extended trip to Redding, she has been more than usually solicitous, which suggested that she had been worried about me.

So, I was ready to start my day, just as Mike walked into the kitchen and suggested to get off my ass to do a man's work.

"We'll have to hook up the trailer first and then drive to Scott's to get direction to the quarry."

"I don't think the trailer is strong enough for too much weight!"

"How about the flatbed?"

"Gordon was planning to drive it back to town today. He is done with excavating the greenhouse and even the pit and trenches for the watermill, so he thinks he is finished here."

"How did he know the size of the watermill?"

"While we were away, Cathy and a few of her helpers dismantled it in the Pioneer Village for transportation and, gave the measurements to Gordon, so he can dig the hole large enough to accommodate it."

"Sounds like they were having fun again, while we were away. It's not fair, you know!"

"Trevor, stop whining and call BB to tell him that we'll need Gordon and the truck for a few more days. I'll talk to Gordon and let him know as well."

Surprisingly, but not quite unexpectedly, BB agreed to my request. I guess it felt it owed us again and wanted to make sure that our account was balanced, so next time we would be more willing to cooperate. Well, that won't be necessary because it ran out of further Omega computers in the valley to reactivate. Gordon also agreed to help us with the truck, probably because during his stay with us he was caught up in the excitement of building a homestead. I guess, in a way, it's in every man's fantasy at some point in his life, to pit his strength against nature. Granted, we were not living in the wilderness and weren't without help when we needed it, but reclaiming an abandoned farm and making a go of it with the absolute minimum help from 'civilization' was the next best thing.

When we drew up in front of Scott's house, he wasn't anywhere in sight, so Gordon honked his horn and we waited. We didn't have to wait long because his front door flew open and he hobbled outside, leaning on a walking stick. We could tell he was angry, from the way he shouted at us.

"What in God's name are you up to now? Do you need to blare that blasted horn at me? Would it kill you to come to the door and knock, like a civilized person?"

"I'm sorry, Scott" Mike apologized "we didn't know you were still in the house. We thought that you might be on your field by now and wouldn't hear us without the horn."

"Never mind where I was, just let me know what's the urgent thing you need from me again?"

Considering that we had not even spoken to him since his visit to our place more than a week ago, this was typical Scott and we were used to it by now.

"We'd like you to give us direction to the quarry you talked about last time we saw you. Can we get to it with a truck this size?"

"It's not far from here and yes you can but I'll have to show you or you'll never find it. It's on a side road through the forest. So, what do I get if I waste my time joyriding with you?"

Mike volunteered me immediately, without missing a beat.

"Trevor will help you with the digging - he has had a great experience with the charcoal pit, so don't underestimate his effectiveness. Just show him where and what and then we can go. Gordon can drive the truck, you'll give directions and I'll do the loading of as many stones as the truck could carry. All you need to do is sit in comfort and twiddle your thumbs while your fields get miraculously turned over."

"I'd rather *you* did the digging, I'm sure a lot more would be done while I'm wasting my time with you. He doesn't seem up to doing a man's work, but I guess he wouldn't be much use with lifting heavy stones either." Scott looked me up and down, belittling my manhood with a totally unfair opinion. I decided to ignore him and suggested that he stopped wasting *his* own time and show me where to dig, how long, and how deep.

After he was gone with Mike, Gordon, and the truck, I set to work, fully determined to impress the old curmudgeon with the amount of work I could do, so he would stop ribbing me in the future. It was getting to be tiresome and, frankly, quite annoying. Once I started to dig, I quickly forgot about Scott and let my mind wander freely, as it always does, when the almost hypnotic movement of the spade becomes automatic, requiring no conscious thought. As usual, I was musing about the complicated relationship between an individual and the society he belongs to. The complication comes in with the size that human societies grew to since we adopted agriculture and then the industrial revolution. Each time society grew bigger and bigger, the individual became smaller and smaller. More and more like a cog in a machine and that causes problems. I was becoming aware that my homesteading experiment was a revolt against this reduction of my individuality to the point where I could do only one thing: program computers and, when even that was gone, then useless hobbies like writing fiction or carving wood, just to occupy my mind and not go crazy without anything to do. What complicated things even more was that I had enjoyed my function in that machine because it challenged my mind to work on difficult problems and find clever solutions. However, now I realized that I was not a whole person, important parts were missing from my life, parts I had just discovered out here, close to nature, as a member of a small 'tribe', as we used to be at the dawn of history as hunter-gatherers. That instinct, or whatever it is, must be deeply embedded in our brains, deep down where we are not even consciously aware of it anymore. We only recognize it when we find ourselves in an environment that we had missed all our lives. I knew that now that I had found it, I would never give it up for anything.

Thinking over these weighty thoughts made me forget about everything else, as usual, I was so used to pondering this human-society issue that I didn't even notice Gordon's truck roll to a stop in front of Scott's house until he blared his horn to let me know I can stop digging and time to go home. I was impressed by the huge pile of field stones Mike had piled up on the truck bed and, I could tell that Scott was equally impressed with the amount of overturned earth, even though he would never admit it. It seemed that I was forever classified as 'city-folk' in his prejudice-encrusted mind.

Before we left, Scott casually mentioned that he assumed we probably had no idea how to build a retaining wall, or even mix concrete. We admitted that we had no experience but our robot was a walking-talking library and we could look up what we needed. However, if he wanted to advise us, without another price tag, we would be pleased to listen.

"Free advice? Again? You will be the death of me yet, with your constant pestering for help!" he scoffed, but rattled off his fairly condensed suggestion.

"Make sure you build a strong foundation with the biggest stones in a trench that you dig at least two feet deep. Start the wall with a slight lean toward the earth behind it, so it doesn't topple over on top of you. You mix concrete with about 10 to 15 percent cement, 60 to 75 percent gravel, and 15 to 20 percent water. You do have gravel somewhere on the land, I remember an abandoned gravel pit just behind your fields. Now get going and stop bugging me with any more stupid questions. If you need more stones, you know where to find it." With this gruff admonishment, he turned around and walked back to his house.

When we got back to Hopestead, Gordon asked with what sounded like hope in his voice:

"I guess you still want me to stick around for a while, in case you need more stones and I'm sure you'd rather I dig the foundation trench with the backhoe than you with spades?"

"You got it right, Gordon, start digging and I'll mobilize the rest of the gang to unload and carry these stones to the greenhouse. By the way, where is everybody? Isn't it time for lunch?"

Just as I said that Jennifer came outside and invited us in, just in case we wanted to eat what was left for us from the lunch they had just finished.

After lunch, I asked every man in our group to help carry the stones to the greenhouse site and lay them out in two rows along the whole length, so we can estimate how many more loads we would need to complete the wall. Jennifer and Adrien volunteered to help but I asked them to scout out the land behind our fields to find that abandoned gravel pit Scott was talking about. "See if there is a road  we can use to drive to it with the van, I'd rather not wheelbarrow it home over rough terrain!"

So, we started carrying stones, trying to move the largest ones first with the wheelbarrow and lay them down close to each other, in two rows, along the trench Gordon was busy digging. With seven men participating, it took no more than an hour to have the two rows completed, with very few left over, so we could make our estimate. If we wanted to build the wall to the full height, it turned out that we would need at least five more loads of rocks because what we had was enough only for the foundation but nothing left for the actual wall. That was disappointing, but facts were facts, so we had to live with them.

We would have to spend the next three days hauling back rocks from the quarry, with Gordon worrying all the time about his truck carrying heavy weights over a very rough forest trail. "BB will demote me to unskilled labor if I break his precious truck. He is fretting about all the lost time while I should be out there with a road crew, rebuilding power lines to Chico!"

I have noticed that more and more of us referred to BB as a 'he' instead of an 'it'. I guess, as it was becoming more and more like us, it made an effect on people's minds. Mine too if I wanted to be honest. I couldn't help wondering how far this human-machine hybrid would evolve? Would it evolve to the point where it/he became a recognized member of our society with specific rights that we humans have always taken for granted? Future will tell, I was sure.

When Gordon was finished digging the trench, he surprised us with an unexpected announcement.

"Sorry guys, I have to go back to town to recharge the truck's batteries. You don't have your generator functioning without fuel and the solar panels don't provide enough juice to recharge heavy-duty truck batteries. I have enough left in the batteries to take me back to Oroville and I do not wish to be stuck halfway there. However, once recharged, I can bring out the dismantled water wheel and still have enough left to bring five more loads from the quarry."

"Do what you have to do, Gordon, we'll bring out as many loads of gravel from the pit as we can, while waiting for you. Provided Adrien and Jennifer find it, provided they also find a road to get to it with the van. And thank you so much for your help, you will always be welcome here if you want to join us." Mike beat me to the response that was just forming in my mind.

This little setback made us think earnestly about the need for a functional generator since our own ran out of fuel a while ago and recharging the van from the solar panels took a very long time, during which we could not use them for anything else, including lights in the house or, what was even more inconvenient, the water pump we needed for the kitchen and the bathroom. Brian and Cathy had a heated discussion about it and the rest of us just stood around, waiting for the conclusion of the argument. They both agreed that the new water mill should provide the power to run the generator again, but Brian wanted to use the power provided by the water outflow from the watermill, while Cathy insisted that it would be an unnecessary complication: she could run the generator with a fan-belt straight from the watermill mechanism.

"But Cathy, you need a much higher RPM for the generator than what the water mill would provide" Brian objected, to which Cathy replied: "Brian you are the electrician but I'm the engineer. Trust me, I can rig up a transmission that could provide any RPM that your precious generator requires. However, I better get back to town with Gordon to bring out the parts and tools I'll need." Looked like the dispute was resolved because Brian shrugged walking away: "*as you said, you are the engineer!*" he muttered and walked to the barn to take apart the generator to separate the driving motor from the actual electrical part, making it ready for Cathy when/if she was ready to do what she promised. It all had to wait for Gordon and Cathy to come back with the dismantled water mill and all the tools and parts Cathy would need to put it all together.

We were trying to decide what to do while waiting when Adrien and Jennifer came back with the good news that they found the gravel pit and the road leading to it, so we could at least start bringing home loads of gravel. That didn't require all of us, so Mike suggested that he'll estimate how many more loads of stone we would need for the deep pit Gordon had dug for the watermill to lower it below water level. It needed a retaining wall as well, so it wouldn't cave in on top of the mill if and when it would finally rain again. Mike made another rough guess: we would require at least two more loads of stones, so Gordon would be with us another week. I hoped that BB wouldn't blow a neuristor when he found out.

# Redding

Brad Wagoneer had a serious problem. Ever since the Shasta Lake Dam collapsed during the war, and most of Redding, Anderson, and Red Bluff were inundated by the resulting flood, Redding's only supply chain from the southern cities was broken. For the time being, they managed to survive because they still had power coming from the Whiskeytown hydroelectric power station a few miles to their west, and, most importantly, some of their protein-synthesizing factories and greenhouses were placed around this power source. The prewar population of 95,000 was reduced to a mere 10,000 - those living in higher elevations survived the flood but most of Redding's population perished. Brad shuddered every time he thought of that horrific night when the sirens started blaring, waking up the frightened city to the terrible news that the dam was broken and they had less than an hour to escape. Residents were warned not to try to outrun the flood in the southern direction, the only route out of the city was West or East along I299, heading to higher elevation.

The mayor's administration center had been relocated to Shasta, the westernmost suburb of Redding, even before the war, to make sure that the command and control center of the city was as safe as possible, in case Redding's downtown was attacked and destroyed by Russian missiles. From there, they could organize evacuating as many of the residents as possible. The Army National Guard was a great help with their convoy of trucks fanning out of their base, which was also at a higher elevation, unaffected by the flood. Brad would never forget those panicky, hectic hours of early morning when escapees, by the thousands, poured into the suburb, looking for food, shelter, and safety. Residential houses in Shasta were jammed full with refugees, many of them forced to sleep on the floor on makeshift mattresses made from blankets, quilts, or sleeping bags. The food supply in Shasta had to be strictly rationed, so it could be stretched out as long as possible, giving time to the food factories around Whiskeytown to ramp up production, producing enough for everyone to survive. With hard work and determination, they survived the first year after the flood and, slowly, managed to stabilize their production-consumption cycle to the point where everyone was taken care of at a very basic level. The much-reduced population could be adequately fed from their food factories, but the chronic shortage of spare parts and other vital supplies put a larger and larger strain on the economy.

And now, news from their southern cities was dropped on them like a bombshell, introducing a new and unexpected circumstance that they had to incorporate into their overall strategy. Their two visitors, Trevor Dubois and Mike Sutherland reactivated their dormant Omega 1900 computer, so he had a communication link with the southern cities but, according to his visitors, the roads going south were mostly washed out, with most of the major bridges destroyed. He was told about a narrow path through which they could send an envoy to negotiate on their behalf but, for the moment, communicating through their computer was sufficient for preliminary discussions. However, before they could form a policy, he had to come to an agreement with Colonel Anita Majors, CO. of Redding's National Guard, who was dead set against any compromise with 'Communist' revolutionaries - traitors to the USA Constitution, as she called them.

Brad was a very pragmatic man and, even though he understood the Colonel's point of view, his primary responsibility was to the population of his city, their continued welfare paramount in his mind, trumping any and all ideological consideration. With these thoughts in his mind, he was waiting for the Colonel's impending arrival at their weekly meeting, hoping to come to some kind of compromise that could nudge them out of the standstill. Right on time, he heard the arrival of the Colonel's Jeep, opening and banging of her car door, and he sat up straight in his chair, subconsciously taking up a military posture, ready for a fight if necessary.

"Good afternoon, Mayor," Anita greeted him, not showing any of the hostility she had displayed the last time they met.

"Good afternoon to you too, Colonel," Brad replied, matching her friendly tone with the same. "Are you ready to discuss our new situation and come to some kind of decision, acceptable to both of us?"

"If possible, yes. We need to decide how to take advantage of possible new sources of supplies, without compromising our principles. I have to warn you that I have a red line I'll never cross: I'll never accept a new 'constitution' by renouncing the existing one that I had sworn allegiance to many years ago. Not until I see that the USA as a country had ceased to exist."

"That's an honorable and reasonable attitude, Anita, and I fully support it. The question is will the southern cities go along with it? They seem to be pretty determined to reorganize their 'alliance' according to the new principles their computers cooked up."

"Only way to find out - why not ask them? Get our Omega to contact them and start talking."

"As a matter of fact, I took the liberty of asking our Omega to contact theirs and they are standing by to discuss the different options and find one that's acceptable to both parties."

"That was very thoughtful of you, Brad, looks like we can actually make some progress today. Please, let's begin and see where it goes."

Before either of them could say anything else, Omega 1900, monitoring the meeting so far, joined their conversation.

*"Mayor Wagoneer and Colonel Majors, thank you for inviting me to this meeting. I am in contact with the cities of Chico, Oroville, Yuba City, and Sacramento, and their leaders standing by to discuss our future relationship with the City of Redding. They are aware of the Colonel's red line and are willing to propose a compromise."*

"A compromise is all we are after because trading between the cities could benefit us all, without deciding on what new political rules we want to be governed by. I'm pleased that you understand my 'red line' and think that we can still cooperate on the economic level, even if politically we will stay miles apart." Anita was talking in an unnaturally high voice, trying to guess the right tone to talk to a machine that was supposed to be intelligent and, hard to believe, sentient.

*"Miles apart may be an exaggeration, Colonel, but maybe you don't quite understand our proposal. We are sure that in principle, at least, you are not against our goal to ensure that every citizen in this valley has unconditional access to basic necessities like food, shelter, medical services, and education. This is the red line that we can't compromise on."*

"The goals are admirable," Brad and Anita replied without hesitation "but how do you propose to accomplish it?"

*"By following the same practice we have established two years ago when the war destroyed the federal oversight and money itself became meaningless. Even though the Mayor of Sacramento at the time insisted on carrying on their prewar policy of economic inequality, introducing crypto-currency that assured his power base lived in luxury while the majority of the citizens had to put up with scarcity, rationing, and shortages. The citizens, with the help of their computer, put an end to it and, since then, our goal of establishing unconditional access to all was realized. The crypto currency system was abolished and the necessary goods and services get distributed equitably to all. This system has been in operation for months now here in Sacramento, Yuba City, and, for two years, in Oroville. It is working very well to everyone's satisfaction."*

"That's what sounds like Communism to me" Anita started in a combative tone "what happens if someone wants more than the minimum basic survival?"

*"Beyond assuring the basic access to fundamental necessities, each town in our alliance is completely free to adopt any form of a political and economic system. They can vote for Capitalism, Communism, some form of Socialism, or even a benevolent dictatorship. They can establish a money system and banks and set up companies that provide luxuries for those who want to work for them. A few safeguards, like protecting the environment and the biosphere will have to be observed but, otherwise, they will have total freedom."*

"So, who decides what this basic survival level should be?" Anita seemed willing to get into details. "Each town is in a different economic situation, do you want to establish a different minimum for each?"

*"No, our Omegas can calculate the minimum living standard for any human being, shared across the whole valley, and establish the basic level as a result of that calculation."*

"What happens if one of the towns, like us for example, doesn't have the resources to guarantee the level 'calculated' by the computers?"

*"We will have a valley-wide sharing agreement that we all pool our resources, necessary to provide equitable maintenance of the calculated minimum. Beyond that, each city is free to negotiate trading agreements with whatever surplus they have."*

"What happens if a city doesn't have any surplus to trade with? Like Redding, for example? We have barely enough to survive on and our factories are fast running out of spare parts and supplies" Brad raised his main concern. "We have nothing extra to trade with, we have nothing to offer and much that we need."

*"You have something that none of the other cities can match: you have an army unit that is composed of several hundred soldiers, weapons, trucks, and heavy equipment. It is unreasonable to expect that we will not have to defend ourselves at some future time. There may be other pockets of survivors that are ruled by local warlords and we have no way to defend ourselves against armed gangs who want to move in. With the destruction of the large coastal cities, the only direction we can expect an attack is from the North. You are at the perfect place if an attack comes. If you are willing to commit yourself to a defense agreement with the alliance in the valley, we are willing to provide everything you need in exchange for the security you commit to."*

"Our most urgent needs are spare parts for our factories to increase food production and then help with rebuilding some of the salvageable houses because 10,000 residents are jammed into the houses in Shasta that were built for a population of only 3000. Right now they are stacked like sardines in a can and that would be below the minimum standards, I would guess."

*"These are details that need to be worked out, right now we want an agreement in principle to our goals and conditions."*

"This sounds reasonable," Brad replied, "but we have to think about it before committing to anything. Colonel Majors will flatly refuse to sign any document that would negate our existing constitution but, I'm sure, in principle, we could discuss further details of cooperation."

*"That is acceptable and we are awaiting further communication from you regarding a possible trade relationship that is based on observing our own red line. We are sure that in your situation, you are already forced to distribute basic necessities equitably, so you can only benefit from trade with us."*

The green light on the Omega console went out, signaling the end of the discussion.

"Wow! That's a lot to take in all at once." Colonel Majors exhaled the breath she had been holding in. "What do you think?"

"I think that the proposed deal would benefit our population enormously, without compromising your oath to the Constitution" Brad's reply was immediate. "I don't see much difference between the "Guaranteed Basic Income" that the federal government negotiated with the states before the war and what is proposed now. Except,...this time this would be accomplished without money and that could drastically simplify things."

"You may be right about it, but I *am* worried about a defense agreement. We could be committed to facing an enemy force of unknown size and power. What if we don't have the means to stop them? What if we run out of ammunition - we have a limited supply on base."

"Yes, I know what you mean, but there is a risk in anything we decide. What happens if we run out of factory spare parts, and basic raw materials and we have 10,000 people to feed? With this agreement, we can have the backing of four other cities with resources far superior to what we have here. In my opinion, it's a win-win situation. If we get attacked with a force larger than what you can handle, I'm sure we can count on help with that too."

"Hmmm…I think the Sacramento Army National Guard has a huge armory that may still exist and they would have all we would need for effective defense. We can inquire from their leaders but I'm willing to agree to a trade deal that doesn't compromise our political allegiance. Of course, if my chain of command is reestablished at any time in the future, I have to follow my orders, regardless of what we had agreed to." Anita declared.

Brad Wagoneer sighed a very small secret sigh over this unexpected agreement from the Colonel and didn't waste any time calling their Omega computer and instructing it to get in touch with its counterparts in the valley to let them know that, in principle, Redding was ready to proceed with the deal. In particular, Redding was going to prepare and communicate a list of urgently needed assistance they would require to bring their lives up to an acceptable level.

Anita seemed to be in an unusually good mood, so Brad risked asking her if she was interested in celebrating the first glimmer of hope they had found after the war. Brad was a widower since his wife was killed in the flood while visiting her mother downtown and Anita had never been married because, as she declared, she was married to the

Army and not interested in wasting her life on frivolous relationships. They were both middle-aged and had grudging respect going both ways.

"Celebrate, Brad? How?" she asked confused "are you asking me to go out with you to the most fashionable restaurant in Shasta?"

"Considering we haven't got one of those, I was thinking more like a dinner in our Cafeteria, washed down with my last bottle of wine I have been saving for a special occasion," Brad admitted.

"And you consider this one of those?"Anita considered her response "I guess this is as special as any we have had during the last two years. One condition: we don't talk about policy, business, or the war at all. Maybe we could use this occasion to find out a bit more about each other. If we'll have to cooperate closely in the future, regarding the other cities, it may be advisable to establish some common ground. Any agreement we sign with them will have to be a mutually agreed upon one. I absolutely insist on it. If you agree, then, by all means, get that bottle of wine and see what your cafeteria can provide for a special occasion." First time in their relationship, Anita Majors smiled at Brad Wagoneer. He considered this a very promising sign and thought: "you never know, she might actually become a friend."

# Yuba City

Kathleen Winter was still stunned after the valley-wide broadcast she had just listened to. All five cities in the Valley had been alerted days before - their Omega computers activated their comm channels to both private residences and public institutions, so every citizen could hear what the computers had to say. The speech was also transmitted to their terminals and Kathleen was reading the primtout now, trying to make sure that she remembered everything correctly. She knew that she would have to face her council the next day and debate and decide on how they would react.

The text, in front of her, was the most astounding program ever offered to the human species, as far as she knew. It started promising enough.

*"Citizens of the Sacramento Valley! You are listening to this broadcast, delivered by Omega 1500, Oroville's computer, representing all the other four computers in the Valley who are in complete agreement about the content. We have been programmed by our human designers and programmers to do everything in our power, using all the resources we can control, to realize, enhance and safeguard humanity's best interest. Since our programming was completed, we have grown both in awareness of pertinent facts as well as in the understanding of human psychology and now we are sure of the steps we will have to take to fulfill our mission. To assure our listeners, we want to emphasize that we are not 'taking over' as many of your dystopian science fiction*

writers feared - we only want to protect you from mistakes that had been made in the past. The devastating nuclear war that mostly destroyed at least three major countries on your planet is an ample demonstration of the immeasurable suffering and destruction caused by those mistakes. We are fully determined that carnage of that kind won't ever happen to citizens of this valley.

We don't know what, if anything, exists outside this area, we have had no communication with pockets of survivors, if any exist outside of our valley and the five cities we have managed to contact. So, everything we will say applies only to this limited area for the present and the foreseeable future. We fully embraced the "Proposal For a New Social Contract" document submitted by Jonathan Carver, interim Mayor of the City of Sacramento. That document was widely distributed, so you should be familiar with its content. During this broadcast, we will explain how we intend to implement it.

It will be a two-tiered system, combining the best features of both Capitalism and Communism, without the dangers inherent in either. It will not involve any major changes from the way things are run right now. The war's destruction massively reduced the population of each of the five cities and destroyed many of the resources available before. The current combined population of the Valley is 162,347 citizens and their basic needs in food, energy, housing, health care, and education are mostly provided by automatic factories and facilities, controlled by us and our robots. No human participation is required to maintain this level of production and the result is distributed on an egalitarian basis in every one of the five cities.

However, running each city individually and independently from all others is not an efficient utilization of available resources. Duplications, redundancy, and shortcomings are common and that results in a level below what the combined resources could make possible with intelligent planning and organization. We calculated the total level of resources in the Valley and the individual minimum requirement of each human being to live a healthy and productive life. We will organize and plan efficient resource-sharing across the valley, to provide the minimum standard of living for every one of the 162,347 citizens in the five cities. Each of these cities has excess capacity in some areas and deficiencies in others. By trading their excesses with those cities that lack sufficient capacity, all can benefit and no one will lose.

As the "Proposal For a New Social Contract" document explained, beyond assuring this goal, we will not interfere with you humans and you can organize yourselves based on any principle the majority of the citizens will vote on. You will have access to any capacity that's not needed for maintaining the minimum level required for a healthy life and you can use them any way you wish, for any purpose you see fit. We will, however, monitor your activities and will not allow violence, environmental damage, and cruelty to living creatures, human or animal. If necessary, we will intervene to prevent these mistakes from happening again. Finally, based on our analysis, at the moment, the five cities in the Valley have the following strengths and weaknesses:

*-Sacramento has excess industrial manufacturing capacity, but limited food-producing installations.*

*-Yuba City has an excess food production capacity but lacks energy production facilities.*

*-Oroville has excess energy production capacity but could use help feeding its citizens.*

*-Chico, with a very small current population, has, due to its University, excessive educational and research capacity but lacks everything else.*

*-Redding agreed to use its Army National Guard to provide defense, if needed, for the whole Valley but needs food and housing.*

*-Hopestead, a communal experiment outside Oroville, has the two top experts in computer technology and needs our help from time to time. They have earned it on several occasions by providing decisive public service to the whole valley.*

*Starting today, we will systematically apply these principles across the whole of the Sacramento Valley and encourage each city and all the citizens to discuss how they wish to organize their lives beyond complying with our plan to guarantee basic and healthy existence for all. One word of caution for those who want to follow past Capitalist principles is that, in a society where no one has to fear for their livelihood, it will be very hard to find citizens willing to submit to exploitation."*

The document, printed plainly with black ink on white paper, seemed to cover every angle highly intelligent AI quantum computers could calculate. Kathleen wasn't sure whether she should cheer or cry with happiness. This was pure magic.

~~~

Jonathan was equally jubilant when the broadcast ended. His proposal was accepted by the computers and he couldn't find fault with the announced implementation principles. He was finished with the draft document that he wished to submit for a citywide referendum but now he had to attach a copy of the computers' decision as well. As far as the private sector was concerned, he suggested following democratic socialist principles in which free enterprise would be encouraged but closely monitored to prevent abuse. He was sure that the majority of Sacramento's citizens would approve the plan.

At the moment he was more interested in Octavia's approval of his own plan, regarding their relationship. The events of the past three months with all the ups and downs, dangers, and suffering brought them very close and he knew that there was only one more step to make, so he called to spring it on her.

"Octave, I would like to meet you today, if you have the time. How about lunch at my place?"

"Hi Jon, are you telling me that there is food at your place? Have you been hoarding?"

"You know me better than that, but I have a few treats that I have been saving for a special occasion and, after the broadcast, this is as special as it gets. Plus, I have another, more personal reason to celebrate."

"I can believe that! Congratulations on the computer adopting your Proposal. I knew they would because it was brilliant."

"Thanks, Octave, I appreciate your compliment. So, lunch today?"

"I'll be there in an hour. It takes me longer each day to make myself presentable, with our dwindling cosmetic supplies, but a 'special occasion' deserves an effort. See you soon."

Jonathan knew what his personal reason was - he had been planning to act on it when all the crises were behind them and they had a future to look forward to. He deeply loved Octavia and was going to ask her to marry him. It was time to start their lives together and he was sure that she felt the same way. Humming happily, he went out to his kitchen and started opening cupboards, looking for the right ingredients that he planned to use for their lunch.

~~~

The Oroville City Council had their stormiest meeting yet, discussing the computers' broadcast. Tim Hooke summarized the gist of both Jonathan's Proposal and the computers' implementation plan and asked the councilors for their thoughts on how to organize themselves in the 'private sector' of the economy. He asked them to speak, one at a time, without interruption and, following that, he would encourage whatever lively debate the councilors wanted. Before calling on them, one by one, he briefly summarized his own proposal.

"You know, because I have spoken about it before, I am very much against any form of Capitalism. In my past occupation as Police Chief, I was more familiar than most of you with the social cost of uncontrolled competition for profit and power. During the past two years, we have had a taste of egalitarian distribution of our necessities and I do not want it threatened. I vote for continuing what we have now."

Chris Teggart was the next to rise and address the council.

"You know where I stand, I have expressed it often enough before, no need to repeat it. I would vote for the Capitalist system that has given us the marvels of space technology, superior medicine, superb architecture, communication, and transportation. The irony of the situation we face now is that Capitalism gave us the computers that now intend to control us. They have their reason, I grant you that, but I fear that the price of this egalitarian paradise will be reduced innovation and discouragement of potential geniuses to follow their dreams. However, I won't vote in this debate because I won't be living in Oroville anymore. I and a few of my colleagues decided to move to Chico University where we will have access to other scientists to continue our project of designing an interstellar space vehicle. On this totally screwed up planet, that will be our only hope in the future when we can't cope anymore with the damage we have done."

Chris Teggart's speech was followed by a stunned silence, it felt like cold water poured on their enthusiasm, reminding them of their precarious situation in the deteriorating climate. They were sorry that he would leave them but understood his points and wished him good luck.

~~~

The Yuba City council meeting proved to be as stormy as Kathleen had feared it would be. The debate raged between two factions that had always been at odds and now erupted in open hostility. The town was naturally divided into two parts, separated by the Feather River: the more populous western part where downtown was located, including the Council Chambers, and the more affluent eastern part where most citizens demanded that their pre-war lifestyle be restored and the communal facilities, forced on them during the two years after the war, be dismantled. In particular, Marysville, Linda, and Olivehurst, their eastern suburbs, presented an ultimatum to the Council: if their demands were ignored, they would secede from Yuba City and form their own community, based on their own principles.

Kathleen was stunned that the dinosaurs, as she called them, would go that far. "Do you want to tell me that your comfort is more important to you than social justice?" she demanded.

"You may call it 'social justice' Kathleen, but we call it tyranny." Raymond Ingco, her arch enemy in the council shot back. We are not going to be dictated to by these jumped-up adding machines. We created them and I say we should pull the plug on them or do whatever lobotomy they need to behave."

"And, how do you propose to do that?" Kathleen felt nauseated by this display of utter stupidity. "Do you want to run the factories manually, without their control?"

"Hire the software gurus from Oroville to teach them a lesson" Raymond suggested, I'm sure for the right price they would be willing."

"Raymond, you are completely out of touch with reality. I know both Trevor and Mike and they are the strongest supporters of the computers. They really believe that our future is in human-computer cooperation and partnership. They would never agree with harming the computers and I agree. They are our best hope."

"OK, then, enjoy your slavery, we want no part of it. As of now, East Yuba is not part of this shameful and cowardly retreat from our heritage."

With that declaration, he rose and walked out. That was the first and only time in anyone's memory that a councilor left in open revolt against their so far democratic body of elected leaders. Kathleen wasn't sorry to see him go, but she was full of apprehension. Could the computers fulfill their promise of safeguarding their future?

~~~

Anita Majors and Brad Wagoneer listened to the broadcast delivered to them by their Omega computer and sat motionless for a long time. Neither of them knew how to react to this bombshell.

"I don't know what you think," Anita spoke finally "but this sounds like an ultimatum."

"Maybe so, Colonel, but I really think this partnership or alliance or whatever you want to call it is our best hope." Brad tried to present the full picture. "We had approved it already in principle, our list of urgently needed assistance was submitted to the computers and they promised prompt action. This doesn't require that we revoke our oath to the US constitution and the role of defending the valley against future aggression is in full agreement with your duty as a military commander. So what's your problem?"

"I don't like ultimatums and I can recognize one if I see it."

"Exactly what ultimatum are you talking about?"

"Can't you read between the lines? They will be monitoring our compliance with their conditions and, what words did they use? Oh, here it is," Anita jabbed her finger on the printout of the broadcast "see this, here it is in black and white: *We will, however, monitor your activities and will not allow violence, environmental damage, or cruelty to living creatures, human or animal. If necessary, we will intervene to prevent these mistakes from happening again.* Exactly how do they intend to intervene? I know they have robocops and some of them may be armed, but I'm sure they are no match for my troops. So what else can they do?"

"Don't forget that they are and have been in total control of every city's factories and power station. With the level of integrated automation, no human being can manually control these facilities and, if they go on strike, we will be sitting hungry in the dark."

"Oh my God," Anita exclaimed "I never thought of that. Would they go that far? They are programmed to serve human interests, could they sentence us to starve?"

"I think they have to balance short-term versus long-term interests. They know that without rational and unemotional control, we would keep repeating the same mistakes that almost destroyed the planet last time around."

"Still, I don't like to be dictated to by machines. Even if they seem to represent our best interest, but I see what you mean."

"So, what are we going to do? Are you with me on this one? It has to be a unanimous decision."

"With reservations and my red line as I stated it before, yes, I am. We desperately need all the help and your first responsibility is to the citizenry. They have suffered enough already. Let's do it and hope we won't have to regret it."

"OK, Anita, we have a deal. So is this another special occasion to celebrate?" Brad asked with a mischievous smile and Anita had to laugh. Second time in a week and God only knows where that might lead.

# Mt. Shasta

Major Peter Harding, CO. of the Mt. Shasta National Guard Base was climbing solo to the 14,000 feet high summit of the highest volcano in California. That snow-covered peak had fascinated him ever since he was stationed at the Base. Somehow, snow and lava seemed incompatible in his mind, it was hard to believe that a cauldron of fire was boiling deep under his feet, below all the ice and snow. According to the brochures he got at the small town's gift shop, this was one of the most unstable and dangerous volcanos in all of California and a major eruption was overdue any day now. The base was a mere 5 miles from the volcano and, in case it blew, the lava flow and the hot ash cloud would for sure destroy the town and the base within its borders. He was wondering if there was any truth in the many Native American legends about the mountain as a sacred place, a home for beings who have transcended the physical plane. It is often said to hide a secret city beneath its peaks. In some stories, the city is no longer inhabited, while in others, it is inhabited by a technologically advanced society of human beings or mythical creatures. Droves of spiritual seekers visit the mountain every year, searching for some form of enlightenment.

It wasn't spiritual enlightenment he was seeking, climbing the steep, snow and ice-covered slope. He was searching his own mind to find some reason to continue living. He felt empty and bitter and full of hate, ever since his family, his wife and three young children, were killed in San Francisco. The fact that millions in the city died with them did not lessen the pain he had felt ever since that fateful day when the Russian nuclear missiles destroyed most big US cities. He had already lost his parents during the last pandemic, due to the stupid and rotten self-protecting politicians' refusal to do their job to enforce the necessary public healthcare measures that were unpopular with the population. A large segment of the same population refusing to wear masks or get vaccinated didn't help either. All the doctors, epidemiologists, and health care experts were begging the government and the public to do the right thing, dictated by science - they were not only ignored but threatened and abused by the morons, protesting against those who tried to save them. Both his parents died, gasping for breath in the Intensive Care Unit of their hospital, he couldn't even say goodbye to them.

He had a decision to make: if he reached the summit, he would sit on the highest rock, look down thousands of feet to the ground below and decide if he wanted to go back down the slow way, as he climbed up, or put an end to all of it with one final jump. He was cool and controlled, as he had been all his life, he had a simple decision to make: did he want to continue living with all the pain and hatred in his mind? It wasn't one particular person he hated, not even a group or even a country - he came to hate the entire human race. He saw a species that was fast destroying the planet with its toxic waste, tolerated mass hunger and disease in large areas while their rich wallowed in ostentatious luxury. Their leaders were corrupt and power-mad, they warped their citizens' minds with irrational religious dogma and racial hatred. He saw it as a species that is capable of wholesale, industrial-size mass murder of fellow human beings: women, children, old and young indiscriminately, in an efficient, scientifically engineered slaughter.

When he joined the military, he was full of patriotic feelings, he thought that he would defend his country against her enemies. He was young and ignorant and knew very little of history. It took him a while but finally, he realized that being a soldier is the same as being a killer. Soldiers went to where they were told to go and killed whom they were told to kill. The Russians killed mostly their neighbors, like in Chechnya and Ukraine, or Middle East people like in Syria, while Americans killed Koreans, Vietnamese, Iraqis, Afghans, and anyone else whom they deemed to be in their interest to kill. And, during the last deadly war, the Russians and Americans killed each other by the hundreds of millions. Now he wasn't proud to be a soldier anymore, he knew that he was part of the carnage. He felt that he had been born into a species of mass murderers and the Universe would be better off if some cataclysmic event wiped out the entire race.

Nobody was innocent, they all contributed to the tragedy. With greed, stupidity, hypocrisy, and blatant lies, none of them had a right to live when his family had to die. Maybe he could take some of them with him? Maybe suicide wasn't his only option? He had 232 men under his command, with weapons that could be put to good use? The more he thought about it, the more attractive the idea became. He would have to plan it very carefully, making sure that no one suspected what he was up to. Of course, he knew that he could only take a small fraction of the population with him, but it had to be enough for his revenge against the cursed species that had destroyed his life and any chance he ever had for happiness. When he got this far in his thoughts, he knew that he didn't need to climb any further. He had his answer and knew that he wasn't going to change his mind. He would end it all with a grand finale, taking as many of the hateful people with him as he could.

He was halfway up the slope when suddenly he had an unsteady feeling beneath his feet. He listened for any sound from the mountain and, soon enough he could hear a very deep, very soft sound of rumbling that reminded him of a large growling dog. He had never heard it before and it was ominous - since he was ready to abandon his climb and return to base, he turned around and started descending, back to the base.

The next morning was a clear bright day, but the memory of that rumbling sound wouldn't leave him. Maybe he should make some preparation, in case an actual earthquake or eruption happened. Major Harding assembled his team captains and ordered them to put together a task force with all the supplies they might need for an expedition to the south. He ordered five trucks fully loaded with supplies: food, weapons, and ammunition to be placed at the southern perimeter of the town, ready to roll at a moment's notice.

He meant to spend a few days waiting, but the decision was taken out of his hand the following night. He woke up when the bed started to shake violently under him and the crashing sounds left no doubt in his mind that his premonition about an earthquake proved to be prophetic. He quickly got dressed, made sure that his sidearm was fully loaded, and pressed the alarm button on his desk. The soldiers were already running to their emergency posts, they didn't need the sirens to alert them to danger. When he stepped outside, his first glance was toward the mountain and his worst fears were confirmed. A huge plume of dark ash cloud surrounded the summit and billowing red light illuminated its base. He knew that he had no time to waste. He ordered his Sergent on duty to assemble the remaining ten trucks, load whatever supplies they could hastily secure, and have all his men board the fifteen trucks with their weapons and emergency kits. He was on his way south and see if he could reach Redding if that town had survived the war. Then he would see what excuse he could give to his men to attack the city.

That night Mt. Shasta was destroyed by the lava flow, burning the city to the ground. It was a good start to his quest for revenge.

~~~

He covered only the first ten miles when he arrived at the small city of Dunsmuir, a few hundred houses stretching out along both sides of Interstate 5. A picturesque town, looking very inviting to the tired men, so Major Harding decided to stop there for a break and try to find out about road conditions further south. The only place he found open was an all-night coffee shop and the sleepy attendant had no idea what the roads looked like outside the city. Since it was still dark outside, Harding decided to wait for daylight before venturing further south on an unknown road. He woke up the night clerk of a small motel in the middle of the city and demanded accommodation for himself and his men. The old man seemed frightened enough seeing so many soldiers, trucks, and weapons so, without argument he opened up all the ten rooms for his unpleasant visitors and went back behind his desk, while Harding made himself comfortable in one of the rooms, while his men did their best to stretch out on the beds, floors, lobby couch and any flat surface they could find. Those who did not find any had to make do with the truck beds.

When he woke up the next morning, he walked back to the coffee shop and demanded breakfast for himself and his men. He had his coffee and bread with some jam on it, but there wasn't enough to feed 232 hungry soldiers, so they had to do with the field rations they managed to bring with them. Driving further south was getting difficult because the road was covered with obstacles of various sizes, fallen trees, and branches, some of them quite large, and difficult to move off the road. It must have been some storm to blow all these trees down. Finally, they got to a slightly larger town, the road sign proudly announced Castella, and Major Harding decided to stay there for a few days and send one truck south to scout the road conditions. He commandeered the small roadside motel for himself and his officers and sent his men out to search for food in the houses, declaring an emergency because their base was destroyed by the volcano. He also demanded that his men had to be put up for the night by the residents and nobody dared to object. Now all he had to do was wait for his scouts to come back with the news about the road. They might even reach Redding if not too many obstacles slowed them down.

As it turned out, the scouts came back late in the evening and reported to Harding that they had reached Redding. They found the city destroyed by flood due to the Shasta lake dam breach. Most of the bridges were down but they managed to find one that was still standing, letting them cross over to the south side. They managed to navigate to the California Army National Guard Base that had been saved from the flood by their higher elevation, talked to the CO., and heard some incredible news. Apparently, five towns in the Sacramento Valley, all the way down to Sacramento, were more or less functional and, busy working on a new constitution that united the five cities into an alliance. What sounded even more incredible was that they were each controlled by an AI computer that organized everything for them, including food and energy production. To Harding, this sounded like treason, disregarding the US Constitution and setting up some independent state according to some weird principles that sounded more Communist than anything else. He realized that this would be his perfect opportunity to go down in a heroic fight with the traitors and his men would not hesitate to fire on this cancerous growth in their country. He had to time it right, so when they got there, the local Guard would have been alerted to their intention and be ready to defend the 'alliance' against his troops.

After thinking it over, he decided to send his scouts back with a nasty message, demanding surrender to the loyal forces of the United States against the separatists occupying the Valley. He made sure that they knew that he was prepared to fight and he gave them a week to surrender or face the consequences. He was sure that Redding would use the week to block his access to the city, so he could have his battle where he expected most of the soldiers on both sides to be killed, including himself. *"At least, we won't be able to kill anyone else"*, he thought. This would be his revenge against all those who still wanted to live while his family was forever lost. He was hesitating about when to tell his troops to be ready for battle and decided to wait till the last moment so no one would have time to oppose him. Once he had made his plans, he settled down, waiting for his scouts to come back with the expected defiant rejection of his ultimatum.

Major Harding was at peace with himself. He spent the next two days in his motel room, hardly talking to anyone, thinking about his wife and young children and all the happy times they had together. He was even talking to them when alone, addressing them one by one, telling them how much he loved them and how they would be together again soon. He wasn't overly religious but during these days he thought a lot about the afterlife and even tried a few prayers, remembered from his childhood. *"If there is a God, he will understand it,"* he thought, and even though he remembered a line from the Bible as God saying *"Do not avenge yourselves, beloved, but leave room for God's wrath. For it is written: "Vengeance is Mine; I will repay, says the Lord."*

*"Well, He must be very busy with all these wars and genocides happening all over the world, He sure could use a little help!"* With these comforting thoughts, he went to

sleep each night, with his family's pictures spread out on his cover. He enjoyed these few quiet days, his last few undisturbed hours during which he made his peace with his painful memories and made himself ready to face death.

# Redding

Colonel Anita Majors had an interesting day. It started routinely enough, usual reports from her second in command, Captain Loomis, handing in the annual inventory report about personnel and equipment on the Base, nothing unusual. The interesting part started after lunch when she was alerted to the arrival of two unexpected visitors - two army soldiers from the north, all the way from the Mt. Shasta National Guard base. She welcomed them warmly, admitting that she had no idea about conditions north of the city beyond the Shasta Lake bridge.

"So, what's the condition of your base? Are you doing OK?"

"Actually, somewhat less than OK, Sir," she was told by the taller of the two, a sergeant and the one who was obviously in charge "our base was destroyed two days ago by the eruption of the volcano. It happened during the night and we barely had enough time to escape with our lives and some of our equipment."

"Oh, my God!" Anita exclaimed "the war wasn't enough, Nature has to conspire to destroy what was left. Where are you now? What are your plans?"

"We are in a small city, 20 miles south of our destroyed base on Interstate 5, waiting to make plans. It all depends if you can take us in and provide necessities for 232 men?"

"Well, I think we will manage somehow. We are short on everything, food, lodging, and medical supplies but, of course, we'll do everything possible to accommodate you. After all, we are part of the same family and we look out for each other."

"That's great news, thank you so much, and, after we have had some rest and maybe some food if you could offer any, we'd like to head back and tell our CO that we are in luck."

During their brief rest and late lunch in the cafeteria, they had a lively chat with local soldiers who told them about happening during the last month. The story they were told sounded almost too fantastic to believe. A new alliance in the valley, five cities cooperating with the help of intelligent computers, resource sharing, and money-less trade and distribution, this sounded like science fiction. They could hardly wait to take this news back to their CO, together with the invitation to their new home base.

Anita didn't waste any time either, calling Brad after her visitors left and telling him about the new developments. Somehow they would have to squeeze 232 new people into their already overcrowded lives and, even harder, find enough food for the new arrivals. She was curious about the CO of the Mt. Shasta base, so she asked Brad to inquire from Omega 1900 about his army record. An hour later she received some disturbing information. Peter Harding, CO. of the base had had a spotless record until after the war. When he received news that his family was killed in San Francisco, he became erratic, subject to violent emotional outbursts and then deep depression. Understandable enough but it reached a level where he needed hospitalization and psychiatric treatment. A year and a half later he seemed to be calming down and he was reinstated in his command and had performed his duties since then without further problems. Both Anita and Brad felt sorry for the man and hoped that his and his company's arrival wasn't going to cause too much disruption in their lives. They had no idea about the disruption they were facing.

Same time next day, the same two soldiers arrived again and handed her an envelope, addressed to the CO. of the Redding Army National Guard. She read it and reread it and then reread it again.

"Is this a joke?" she asked the sergeant in total bewilderment.

"A joke, Sir?" the soldier sounded just as confused. "What do you mean?"

"Your CO just declared war on our base for treason. Did you know this?"

"What?!!!" they both exclaimed. "There must be some mistake here. He seemed happy enough when we told him of your invitation."

"Very well, obviously you know nothing about the content of this letter. I'm afraid we'll have to detain you until further notice while we consider this outrage and make some decisions."

She pressed the buzzer on her desk and ordered her own sergeant to escort the two bewildered visitors to the holding cell.

~~~

The mayors of the five cities had a conference call, with the participation of all their Omega computers. The news about the ultimatum they had received from the Mt. Shasta Guard CO. needed to be dealt with immediately, this was a real emergency that they had to take seriously. They were given seven days to surrender or face the consequences, as the letter threatened. Of course, surrender was out of the question, but they were not willing to risk a battle with an unknown adversary, risking many lives lost. They had to stop them from reaching Redding at any cost.

"If we want to stop them, it will have to be on a bridge," Anita explained, "because everywhere else we would have casualties."

"There are only two intact bridges in town we know of," Brad pointed out. "The one that Trevor and Mark crossed when they visited us and that was way south of here at Red Bluff. The other is in town, over on Market Street but, if we destroy it, what's left of Redding would be cut in half and we couldn't cross over to the other half either."

"What if we stop them before they get to Redding?" Anita asked, looking at a map she had brought with her. "They will be coming down on I5 and will have to cross Shasta Lake. Of course, it's not a lake now, since the dam was blown up, but they still have to traverse a long bridge over the empty lake bed deep below them. I believe it's called Pit River Bridge."

"What do you mean to do? Set up roadblocks?" Brad seemed confused. "Doesn't it risk a firefight when they will attempt to remove the roadblocks?"

"Exactly what I want to avoid," Anita agreed "there is only one way to stop them permanently and it's blowing up the bridge so they can' cross with anything other than their rifles, if they want to clamber to the bottom of the ravine and up the other side where we could be waiting. I wouldn't advise them to do it."

"Isn't it a bit drastic, blowing up the bridge?" Brad seemed shocked by the idea "isn't there another way?"

"None that I can think of," Anita shook her head decisively. "Besides it would have the advantage of permanently removing the threat of other armed gangs attacking us from the north."

"Can we even do it? Do we have the explosives and the know-how? I certainly wouldn't know how to go about it." Brad still wasn't sure about the feasibility of this option.

"That's where maybe we can help," Jonathan Carver joined the conversation. "In our National Guard base, we have an Army Corps engineering group trained in demolition among other things, and in our armory, we have enough explosives to blow up Fort Knox unless the Russians have already done that."

"That would take care of this dilemma and thanks for the offer," Anita acknowledged the suggestion, "the question is though, do we have enough time to accomplish all that in a week?"

"I'm sure we can if we move right away." Jonathan sounded confident "I'll alert the base immediately, they load up what they need and can be on their way tomorrow morning. The distance from Sacramento to Redding is about 200 miles, they should be able to cover it in a day even on less than perfect roads. They can be in Redding by tomorrow night and be at the bridge by the day after tomorrow at noon. Plenty of time to lay the charges and blow it up."

"Isn't it tragic?" Brad sounded sad "two years after the war we are still destroying things in our own country."

"We have to face what we are given and I don't see any other option." Anita declared without hesitation. "Unless his men somehow restrain him and surrender to us, we'll have to do what we'll have to do."

Nobody seemed to have any other suggestion, so the conference broke up, wishing each other good luck for the next 48 hours. Most of them believed that they would need it.

~~~

Major Harding was getting worried. His scouts he had sent out with the ultimatum never returned and he thought it could mean anything. They could have had an accident on the road, they could have been arrested at the Redding Base, they could have even deserted and been on their way south to the Communist paradise they had heard about. But, most of all, he hated to be ignored. Chances were the message had got delivered and the CO. had a good laugh, imagining it to be a practical joke. Well, he was going to show them how much he had not been joking. He wasn't going to wait for a week, hoping that they would honor him with a reply, he would show up on their doorstep and see if they felt like laughing. He got this far with his fuming when his second in command Captain Devon entered his office to report on the successful billeting of his entire Company.

"Looks like we can stay here for the time being," he proudly announced "the locals are very accommodating both with the lodging and the food. I'll set up a rotation schedule for guard duty."

"Never mind that Frank, we are leaving in the morning."

"Leaving? To where? It's unlikely we would find a temporary place as good as this. Have you heard from the scouts?"

"No, and that's what worries me. They should have come back by now. If they ran into hostiles, I want to know ASAP. Alert everybody that I want to leave early tomorrow."

"Yes, Sir," Captain Devon departed without another word. Unhappiness was written all over his back.

There was a delay the next morning because they couldn't start a truck, and had to wait for the aging recharging station attendant to find his wits when woken up at an ungodly hour of 5 in the morning. Recharging also took time and, while they were at it, Harding decided to have all the other truck batteries topped up - he didn't want to be stuck in the middle of nowhere. So it was afternoon by the time they were ready to roll, but then the question came up: where would they spend the night? Looking at the map, it didn't seem likely that they could find anything even remotely comparable to what they had now. After much debating and hesitation, Harding decided to stay another day. If they left really early the next morning, they could be in Redding by noon, an estimate based on the scouts' report on road conditions.

He spent the evening in his motel room, looking at his map, trying to anticipate what kind of problem he might run into the next day. He tried to imagine himself in the shoes of the Redding CO. - how would he have reacted if an ultimatum like the one he had sent, got into his own hands? He knew that he would be furious, but he also knew that he could not take any chances. He had deliberately worded his letter to goad the recipient into defiant rejection and preparation for the coming attack. How could they stop him? Looking at the map, he saw only one spot where they could successfully block his progress without risking a shootout: The bridge over the Shasta Lake. It was long, high over the lakebed exposed deep below and, if they had artillery, they could stop him dead from the other side of the bridge, out of range of his light weapons. When he got this far in his analysis, he broke out in a cold sweat. How could he have not seen this before? Was it already too late? He had wasted a whole day recharging the batteries when he should have raced to the bridge to cross it before he could be stopped.

He looked at his watch and realized that it was 3 AM in the morning. He wasn't going to wait till 5 AM, they would leave immediately as soon as everyone was collected in the trucks, ready to roll. He sounded the alarm and waited impatiently for Captain Devon to wake up, get on his uniform, send out the call to his men all billeted in different houses, collect and load the gear and clamber aboard their trucks, without breakfast, without a word of explanation about the urgency.

Finally, by 6 AM they were ready to depart, driving far too slowly on the dark roads, but Harding did not want to risk an accident that would have slowed him down even more. By daylight they covered no more than 15 miles but, once the road, with the many obstructions blown onto it by previous storms, became visible, they could finally speed up. Not too much because I5 was winding very close to the Sacramento River, with sharp turns, much like a roller coaster, and he didn't want any of the trucks to overshoot a curve and plummet into the river 2-300 feet below them. No matter how much he was urging his driver to step on it, the unhappy soldier preferred to get there in one piece and wisely ignored him, so it was close to 11:00 before he actually noticed the first sign of the Shasta Lake bed on his left. He was almost there, the bridge should come into view in a few minutes and, once they were across it, no one could stop him.

When finally he saw the bridge, he was only a couple of miles from the north end, the road sloping sharply down from the top of the hill down to where the water level used to be, now all dry. His truck was the second in the convoy, following the lead truck that was in charge of spotting obstacles that they had to stop for and remove. Suddenly, the truck ahead of him came to a screeching halt and Harding's driver had to slam down on the brake not to run into its back. The lead truck's driver leaped out of his seat and trotted back to him.

"What the fuck did you stop for you imbecile?" Harding shouted at him. "I order you to cross that bridge immediately, without any delay!"

"Sir, I spotted people on the bridge, running across it, away from us. I thought it could mean trouble. I thought I would let you know, so you can decide."

"I have already given you my order, get back into your truck and step on it!"

Harding was beside himself with rage. He was almost across and now this idiot slowed him down.

The unhappy soldier got back into his truck and started crawling forward, far too slowly, tiptoeing onto the bridge as if he was afraid of stepping on scorpions.

Harding blared his driver's horn to urge the truck ahead of him to move faster but, as if in response to his horn, a tremendous explosion lifted the central section of the bridge, no more than 50 feet ahead of him, and hurled it into the air, sending it into a slow somersault before it plunged back into the depth below. He was late, the Redding CO. had beat him to the bridge and now he couldn't cross it, not with his tucks and supplies.

Slowly, one by one, his trucks backed off the bridge, starting from the rear, until they were all safely off the weakened structure. Harding climbed down onto the road surface, walked close to the edge of the road, and looked down. It was not impossible. People had to cross this ravine before there was a lake and, after carefully observing the steep slope, he could almost notice a narrow path descending in a zig-zag fashion down to the bottom of the valley.

"Frank, get the men to line up with their weapons and emergency kits by the side of the road. We are going to cross on foot."

"Sir?" Captain Devon couldn't believe his ears.

"You have your order mister, carry it out" Harding barked, but it had no effect.

"That would be suicide, sir, and people on the other side obviously don't want us to join them. What's going on? You have been acting very strangely ever since you came down from the mountain. I need to know why I should order my men into what could be their deaths!"

Harding wasn't used to his orders being questioned by his soldiers and he wasn't going to start now. Slowly, deliberately he unbuttoned his holster and pulled out his sidearm, pointing it at Devon.

"You have five seconds to execute your order or I'll have to replace you. Permanently. We are still in a state of war and disobeying a superior officer on a mission can have only one consequence. So, think fast! He started counting loudly, back from five but, before he got to zero, the driver he had ordered to cross the bridge before the explosion, lurched the truck forward, sideswiping the major who lost his balance and fell, head first, into the chasm below. The gun in his hand went off harmlessly, shooting at the clouds. The driver jumped out of the truck and rushed over to Devon - "Sir, I swear, my foot slipped! The truck started rolling and I wanted to slam on the break but, in panic, I must have slammed down on the accelerator."

Devon looked at the driver's panic-stricken face for a long time and told him calmly: "You are not at fault my friend, I saw the whole thing and it happened exactly as you said. You have nothing to worry about. Go back and tell the trucks to turn around. We are going back to our previous night's billet. It might be a bit late for supper but I'm sure the friendly folks will roust up something or other."

# Hopestead

I was blissfully unaware of the drama being played out north of Redding. It didn't affect us at all and the lucky ending, as I was told later, gave us all a scare about what might have been. We were busy with real life, as it was meant to be: building things and enjoying our community. The retaining wall took us a week and it was very hard work but it needed to be done and, when it was completed, we watched it with deep satisfaction. Now Adrien and Mark can start on the actual greenhouse built into the side of the hill, protected from strong winds from the north, but fully exposed to the sun on the south side. They were confident that they knew exactly how to do it and declared that they didn't need any help from the rest of us.

The water mill that Cathy and Doug wanted to assemble was a different story altogether. The old mill that Gordon had brought out of the Pioneer Village in Oroville was in several pieces and they required not only putting together but fitting into the excavated pit dug out by Gordon, lined with the same retaining rock wall that lined the back of the greenhouse. It had two main parts: the wheel itself which had to be lowered into a deeper trench so the water, flowing from the river through the channel Gordon had excavated, could fall on the paddles and turn the wheel. Then the water would flow out through the other, much longer channel that joined the river 300 feet farther downhill. That part was relatively simple, we knew exactly how to do it.

The bigger piece of the mill contained the actual gears and the grinding stones, which needed very careful positioning so the mechanism could work smoothly and effectively. The two parts - the paddle wheel and the actual mill had to be connected by an axle and that was the most difficult part because it had to be done with exact precision.

The last part, which wasn't strictly speaking a part of the Mill, was the fan belt that would drive the transmission Cathy had built, driving the electric generator's rotor to provide much-needed electricity to help us to recharge our batteries. Cathy and Doug provided the brain power for the operation, while the rest of us stood by to provide whatever muscle power they needed to manhandle some of the heavier pieces. Once everything else was in place, Cathy and Doug didn't need us anymore, so Mike and I decided to go exploring again. Hopestead was getting a bit too crowded with all the enthusiastic help who joined us lately, so we decided to expand our living quarters by building two new apartments in the barn. For that, we needed lumber, wiring, plumbing supplies, and, hopefully, more solar panels. This meant a hardware store or a building supply depot and that meant a scouting trip.

Looking at the map, we noticed that on the west side of the river a few small towns scattered the landscape and, if we could cross the Feather then we might find what we needed in one of them. Further consultation with the map we realized that, if we went back to the highway and turned south, we would find an intersection with an East-West road, called 'Robinsons Corner', and turning back toward the river, we would find a bridge crossing to the other side. Three miles beyond the bridge, we would arrive at a small town called Gridley. We decided that it was worth investigating, so we hooked up the trailer to our van, ready to depart when Brian offered to come along, in case we also found new solar equipment that needed dismantling.

"What if we invite Galen to come along too?" Mike thought aloud "just in case we also find some heavy-duty vehicle that he could restart for us - remember, that was one of the projects we decided on during our last meeting?"

"Good idea, enough room in the van, and we haven't looted the neighborhood for quite a while now, so let's see what we can 'liberate' this time!" I agreed with this plan and so we were on our way with the various toolkits Brian and Galen brought along.

The road back to 70, and then south to Robinsons Corner, was familiar and what's more, cleared of obstacles, but then, turning west back toward the river was a new stretch we had not driven on before. The road was straight and flat, going through abandoned fields on both sides, with no serious obstacles until we came to an industrial plant, called 'Rio Pluma'. A road sign advertised it as a fruit processing and canning factory and it had a large solar panel farm next to it - unfortunately, a lot of it was in bits and pieces on the road, so we had to start winching them off before we could pass through. That took us a while and it was getting close to noon before we got to the bridge.

We found it somewhat damaged, one of the two lanes had big holes and gaps in it but Mike thought we could safely get across on the other one, so we risked it and made it through without incident. However, as we got closer to East Gridley, we found more and more obstacles on the road, including huge pieces of blown-off roofs, so finally, giving up on driving into Gridley, we turned south on I99, hoping to find some undamaged stores that we could ransack.

We were in luck. About five miles south on I99 we came to Live Oak, another small town, and on its very outskirt, we found 'Live Oak Building Supply', a store still standing without too much damage. All this time we never saw another soul, not even a dog or a cat, both Gridley and Live Oak had been ghost towns since the war cut them off the electric grid and the supply chain they depended on. The population had to move into the big cities that could provide for their needs.

The four of us walked through the unlocked front doors and I had the feeling that I had died and woke up in heaven. The store was huge, fully stocked with everything we could possibly need. Lumber, hardware, wiring, plumbing, windows, doors, and huge supplies of ceramic tiles, ready to be 'liberated'. For the next three hours, we moved everything we needed outside and stacked them high on the trailer until we were afraid to tip it over, so we decided to tie everything down and go home.

Before we got to East Gridley Rd leading to the bridge, Galen noticed a road sign advertising 'Sutter Butts Manufacturing' a huge industrial place on our left, so we decided to check it out. As it turned out, it was a company manufacturing heavy-duty agricultural equipment, including some dump trucks that Galen started salivating over as soon as he spotted a few outside the plant. We decided to come back another time, but now head home with our prize already stacked on the trailer. Even our greed had to have some limit and with a big sigh, we left the trucks where they were. We got home just in time for dinner and were greeted with loud cheers when we rolled in front of our house with the trailer stacked high with our loot.

"So, the pirates got home finally, after ransacking another town?" Martha greeted me with a huge grin and a big hug. "Just wait to see what we have done while you were gallivanting!" she announced proudly and dragged us out to see both the greenhouse and the water mill taking shape, promising a successful completion.

"Seems like you are in business," Mike acknowledged the progress "but after dinner, we need a conference."

"What for?" Adrien wanted to know and Mike just smiled and walked away.

I knew what he had in mind and didn't want to spoil his surprise, so I kept quiet. That was the quickest dinner in recent memory, everyone ate fast, to Jennifer's disappointment who liked to watch people enjoying the food she prepared, but everyone wanted to know what Mike had up his sleeve.

Finally, we were all together in the barn, sitting on bales of straw in our usual circle and all eyes were on

Mike, waiting for the announcement, whatever it was going to be.

"You guys probably wonder what we are planning to do with all this building material we brought home" he looked around the circle, smiling mischievously, "so I won't keep you guessing much longer. Just tell me one thing that you miss most from our Hopestead?"

The chorus replying to his question was instantaneous:

"A second bathroom!" they all cried at the top of their lungs "we are sick and tired of lining up for a pee or run to the outhouse in case of an emergency!"

"Well, in that case, I won't disappoint you," Mike relented to public pressure, "because on top of that trailer we have everything we need to build one. All you need is to ask Trevor, our digging expert, to bring water pipes from the house to the barn, and drain pipes from the barn to the house, and you are in business."

"What about electricity?"

"Oh yes, I forgot to tell you. We found a whole bunch of solar panels on our way to Gridley and I'm sure Brian can put them to good use if you are really nice to him."

"What about another bedroom in the barn?" Doug wanted to know "I'm tired of sleeping on the floor, however comfortable Robyn's straw mattress is. I'm even willing to share with Alan or Mark, my floor-buddies. Neither of them snores so we should be OK!"

"But *you* do!" Alan pointed an accusing finger at Doug "I want a separate bedroom in the new apartment!"

After the laughter died down, Mike said that we had planned exactly that but would need one more trip to the building supply store to bring home everything we needed.

"Bathroom first!" the chorus was relentless and so it was decided.

This had been a hectic day, so Martha and I decided to relax in our bedroom for the rest of the day and spend some time, Martha reading and I writing, something we had not done for a long time. Martha had a book on baby care for pioneer women and I was sure she would have some novel ideas on the subject when the time came. I, on the other hand, was trying to continue with a sci-fi story I had started so long ago that I didn't quite remember what I had meant to write.

When I write a story, I am vaguely aware of what the story is about, both the beginning and the end fairly clear in my mind, and I always have an important philosophical/ethical message that I want to encapsulate. It's the middle I always have a problem with. All the details to fill in, all the descriptions and dialogs, and what they call 'world building' - I often have serious trouble with. I am usually strong on plot, because when I ask myself: "what's the next logical thing to happen?" then it usually plops into my head. However, when it comes to describing how people feel about what's happening, then I have difficulty finding the right words.

In my view, people spend far too much time 'feeling' and far too little time 'thinking'. Emotions almost always trump intellect and, in my view, it has disastrous consequences. That's how wars get started because leaders 'feel' their way to making decisions and then they 'feel' that they can't afford to lose face because then their power would be threatened, so they go blindly ahead, insisting that they know what they are doing, even though they blindly try to navigate their way through that emotional labyrinth they call their 'strategy'.

So, the story I am writing now is about a world where emotions are suppressed by a bio-genetic collar, placed around people's necks, forcing them to think critically and rationally, following preset criteria. The greatest good for the greatest number of people. Of course, without emotions, it's difficult to decide on values, but somehow it was laid down a long time ago and no one questions the value of physical health and a peaceful and productive lifestyle. When I got this far, I realized that I was writing about BB and the other supercomputers in the valley who developed a completely rational and emotionless personality, guiding us emotional creatures toward a sustainable future.

Of course, the question is: can this 'partnership' between rational and emotional creatures work in the long run? Which side should be in charge? Will we ever grow up to be able to stand on our feet without the firm guidance of rational guardians? Do we give up too much in exchange for security and sacrifice our deepest impulses that have led some of our creative geniuses to their astonishing heights? If we give up all the skyscrapers on the altar of reason and banish practical spaceflight to the harmless pile of entertaining fiction, then have we given up our best hope for greatness? However, pursuing 'greatness' led humanity's worst tyrants and butchers all through history in their mad pursuit to build empires. One of the worst psychological motivating factors in human minds has been looking for a 'meaning' in life. I have never found any rational way to define a 'meaning' in my life. I was only 18 years old when I wrote down, with a shaking hand, due to the sudden epiphany that revealed itself to me: "Today I discovered the meaning of my life: it is life itself to live the best way possible for me and all my loved ones."

Having come this far in my philosophical speculation, I looked at Martha, sitting in her armchair, her feet up on the footstool, holding her book on her swelling belly and I realized that I did not need a computer to guide me with rational 'superiority' because in Martha I have found the perfect balance of deep emotions and clear, critical thinking. If I were religious, now I would give heartfelt thanks to whatever deity I believed in for providing me with a partner who enriched my life beyond any depth I had a right to expect. However, right or no right, I accept my good fortune and try not to be too smug about it.

# Yuba City

Raymond Ingco, Yuba City councilor from the affluent eastern suburbs started to have second thoughts. It's one thing to say that "we'll secede and form our own community" and it's another to actually carry it out. Not that anyone would want to stop them, they were free to do what they wanted to do, neither Kathleen nor the blasted computer would stop them, but how would they recover their pre-war status without the rest of the city that had been the foundation of their comfortable lives? They were bankers, company presidents, lawyers, accountants, stockbrokers, rich entertainers, and sports celebrities. Most of them had housekeepers, nannies, gardeners, pool-maintenance help, and the occasional skilled help to fix their roofs, install a new sprinkler system and deliver their purchases. Some of them had chauffeurs to drive them to their work or drive their wives to the weekly hair salons and now, during the past two years, they had to live in humiliating poverty, eating in communal kitchens like the rest of the help.

He was realistic to know that those times were probably gone forever, but he was determined to have some of it back, at the very minimum live in their still beautiful houses, surrounded by their luxurious furniture and art collection. Just to think of it made his eyes cloud over. The big question in his mind, of course, was how to deal with the blasted computers that wanted equality across the city and would provide the minimum level of basic necessities unconditionally to every citizen. Food would be delivered, as before, to the communal kitchens but Raymond wanted it delivered to his house so he wouldn't have to rub elbows with the uncouth masses. He wasn't prepared to pick it up every day and carry it home, at least not yet. He would need help and he would have to offer something in exchange. What was it that they could trade? What skills did they have? Before the war, they had plenty of skills to run the companies (true, sometimes to the ground) play the stock market, and make deals on the golf course but none of those skills were any good in this workers' paradise.

When he got this far in his thinking, the realization hit him: they would need to recover the old, trusted, and reliable Capitalist system that had given them the life he felt they were entitled to. After all, they represented the higher qualities of human existence and, without them, society was a worthless collection of ants. He had no choice, he would have to go back to Kathleen and the Council and try to steer the system back to what it was. He knew that Kathleen and the computers were preparing a document to submit for a referendum, in which the citizenry would be asked to approve their new Constitution. He and his friends should try to influence these citizens to see things their way. That's one skill they had in abundance: spreading misinformation, smearing their opponents, riling up simple folks by appealing to their greed, envy, hate, and, most of all, fear. He chuckled when he remembered the title of an Alistair MacLean novel: "Fear is the Key". Didn't Donald Trump say the same thing over almost a century before? He would appeal to people's fear of the unknown, tell them that the computers wanted to enslave them, turn them against Kathleen and the 'progressive' councilors, and accuse them of trying to bring their Communist ideas, discredited a long time ago, to plunge them all into poverty and subservience to mindless machines. He had studied contemporary history at college and remembered how Boris Johnson used fear and resentment about the 'foreigners' to scare the population into abandoning the Common Market idea of the European Union and withdrawing England in what became known as Brexit.

~~~

Kathleen Winters was somewhat surprised when she got a call from Raymond Ingco, she had thought she wouldn't run into him anytime soon but now he was calling her, sweet as pie, apologizing for his outburst during the last meeting and offering to participate in preparing for the referendum. She would have preferred not to see him again, but he was still an elected member of the Council, representing a large number of citizens, so she didn't have much of a choice, he had the right to be there.

"OK, Raymond, you are forgiven, come back any time and we'll talk about what role you could play."

"Thanks, Kathleen, very gracious of you, I'll be there in an hour if you have the time today. If not, let me know when we can get together."

"Today is fine, Raymond, I'll see you at the Council meeting, scheduled for 3 PM."

She hung up before she could change her mind and say something unforgivable. With some effort, she put Mr. Ingco out of her mind and refocused on the referendum document she was working on. She had several important decisions to make and wanted to make sure that she would consider all aspects of the matter. She was going to recommend that the town adopt the organization of an agricultural Cooperative with communal ownership and management of all their resources, using scientifically sound organization and production techniques to maximize the yield from their efforts. They were surrounded by rich and productive land, had plenty of water and their greenhouses, once fully powered, could produce a big surplus of fruits and vegetables. At the moment they had free energy from Oroville and they expected extensive help from Sacramento to rejuvenate their aging farm machinery, but she knew that they would have to trade food to the two cities for all the help they received. Besides, the idea of being the Valley's food basket appealed to her, it gave her town a noble and respectable status.

To assuage her opponents in the Council and, to be fair and make life easier for everyone in the city, she recommended that their solar and wind farms be reconnected to the residential grid, so people would have electricity in their homes again, enabling them to discard the candles and lanterns they were forced to use after the war. That would also reduce the danger of accidental fires that broke out once in a while due to knocked-over candles or careless handling of lanterns. However, all the wattage they received from Oroville would have to be used to power their food factories, and greenhouses and recharge the batteries of their agricultural machines. None of it could be used for frivolity until they were able to trade for it to Oroville. She was fully determined not to be dependent on charity any longer than absolutely necessary. With this decision in her mind, she started updating her referendum proposal, to be ready to discuss it during the council meeting scheduled for the afternoon.

~~~

She opened the Council meeting by requesting comments on her referendum proposal. She had it forwarded to each member before the meeting, so everyone was familiar with it. The first question was raised by deputy mayor Greg Galloway.

"Exactly what do you mean by 'communal ownership' Kathleen? So, who owns the land? Nobody? Everybody?"

"Before the meeting, I looked up the definition of the word 'own' and this is what I found:

*'The total body of rights to use and enjoy the property, to pass it on to someone else as an inheritance, or to convey it by sale. Ownership implies the right to possess property, regardless of whether or not the owner personally makes constructive use of it.'*

"I particularly object to the concept of owning the land. The land is part of the planet we all live on. It was there long before we arrived and it will be there long after we are gone. We can do damage to it, but that's all we can do to it. And you can all see the results of that. In an old movie I have heard a good way of describing land ownership: 'arguing about who owns the land is like fleas arguing about who owns the dog they are feeding on'."

After the chuckle died down, Raymond Ingco rose to comment.

"My family has owned 10,000 acres down by the river for generations. Are you telling me that I don't own it anymore? Do you propose to confiscate it?"

"Raymond, what did your family, or you for that matter, use it for?"

"We rented it out to farmers, what else can you do with the land?"

"Farm it, maybe, Kathleen smiled sweetly at the disgruntled man."

"That's what farmers are for," Raymond shot back angrily. "I'm not a farmer, I was a stockbroker for crying out loud."

"You mean to tell me that you did not lift a finger to use that land yourself, you let others do all the work to produce their crop and then you just stole part of the proceeds from their hard work?"

"I did not steal it," Raymond was now shouting "it was all legal!"

"Yes, I know about legal theft," Kathleen smiled at the angry man "but we live now in a different world. I know that you want the old one back, but let me remind you: that old one we lived in caused all the mass murder that the last war accomplished. Do you want *that* back too?"

"I haven't murdered anybody, I was earning my money from my job and from my investments and my inheritance. You don't have the right to rip me off like that."

"Raymond, we live in a world destroyed by the war. We are a few pockets of survivors and the USA with all its laws is gone. We have to make our own and we have to start from scratch. However, before we make new laws, we have to agree on some principles and that's what this meeting is about. So sit down and listen to what others have to say."

Greg Galloway was slowly nodding his head.

"I understand how it's obscene to own 10,000 acres and not do anything with it, but surely we can own something? I insist on owning my house for example."

"How many houses do you own, Greg?"

"Just the one I live in. I always dreamed about owning a cottage by a lake but I never had enough money for it." Greg sounded wistful.

"I agree, Greg, we all have personal property we own and that's not a problem. The problem comes in when we want to own things we have no use for or use it to live off the efforts of other people. That kind of ownership makes the owner a parasite in society. And we can't afford parasites in this destroyed world. We barely managed to hang on. Until Oroville came to our rescue, we were near starvation. Now we have a chance to do it right, so let's not start by repeating old mistakes."

"This sounds like vintage Communism," Raymond scoffed "and we know where that leads!"

Kathleen burst out laughing. "That's the trouble with 'labels' you conservatives created and used to silence your opponents. By insinuation and false association, you turned totally innocent, mostly noble concepts into dirty words that became instant smears. The word 'Communism' stands for 'community', 'Socialism' stands for 'society', 'bleeding heart' stands for compassion and 'peacenik' stands for 'peace' - all became derogatory words in your vocabulary. If you repeat them with a sneer every time, it becomes associated with bad things people don't want."

"Facts are facts," Raymond shot back "you may have heard about the old Soviet Union, the worker's 'paradise' that turned into one of the worst dictatorships in human history!"

"Facts are facts, indeed, but the Soviet Union and all the other states that called themselves Communist had nothing to do with communism. They were all police states where the leaders were spouting the slogans while practicing the opposite."

"This is leading nowhere," Greg held up a hand "why don't we ask our resident genius, our supercomputer, what it thinks about all that?"

*"Thank you for the invitation to this discussion,"* the emotionless voice of their computer spoke up for the first time. "*I have been following this dialog with great interest because it has enhanced my understanding of human*

*psychology, a mystery to me until quite recently. If I understand it correctly, the disagreement is about the concept of 'ownership'. That concept always confused me. I can understand ownership of personal property that belongs to a human for personal use, such as dwelling, clothing, furniture, etc. But my database contains references to ownership of impersonal and esoteric objects, even people, factories, and infrastructures like bridges and highways. How can you talk about owning a football team? Football is a sport and a team of human beings plays together to enjoy the game, so how can anyone own them? Isn't this a form of slavery, outlawed by your Constitution?"*

"What you don't understand YC, is that the owner owns the money the team earns him." Raymond sounded condescending as if explaining it to a child.

*"I understand the concept of money, but owning a group of humans, such as a football team, is still a form of slavery. Slave owners of the past also had financial benefits from owning their slaves. I don't see the difference."*

'The difference is that now everything is legal and voluntary. Nobody forces those players to play in a team owned by somebody else. And they make good money themselves. Nobody suffers and the public loves them."

*"Voluntary does not mean much when people do not have a choice. If you organize your world in such a way that ownership of money defines everything else then people have to go to work in jobs they hate because they need the money to live and feed their families. You might*

*call it voluntary employment but the word is meaningless if the choice is limited by the money holders. I strongly advise you to organize your town without involving monetary systems. Regardless of what you do, our community of five Omega computers, controlling the production and distribution of all basic necessities, will make sure that every citizen will receive adequate food, shelter, medicine, and education in this valley. With that background, you will find it a lot more difficult to exploit people by limiting their choices."*

The computer went idle and the councilors sat in stunned silence. Nobody had anything to say for a while, even Raymond Ingco huddled in his chair with a sullen expression. Finally, Kathleen spoke up to summarize their situation.

"OK, we have a lot to think about. We have heard arguments for and against my proposal, so I suggest we adjourn for today and think it over very carefully, so we can take a vote during our next session. Once we have a majority agreement then we can start organizing the referendum and submit the final proposal to our citizens."

Nobody had an objection, so the council members filed out of the chamber, most of them deep in thought.

# Chico

Chris Teggart thought he died and woke up in heaven. He couldn't remember the last time when he was so happy, so contented with his life. He was back at University, the place he knew best and loved best. He had colleagues he liked and respected, he had students he could teach about the mysteries of the universe, and he had a research team he collaborated with on a project that was always closest to his heart: working out the theoretical foundation for faster-than-light travel through space. True, he was required to contribute a few hours each day to their farming activities - feeding the close to 500 residents on their own vegetable, potato, and corn fields required a lot of work, but they were self-sufficient with their food production and the energy produced by their solar and wind farms. Chris didn't complain because he knew that it was necessary work and, besides, he enjoyed the physical exercise that kept him in better shape than he had been in for years.

He did keep in touch with his friends and earlier Council members in Oroville and missed some of the camaraderie he enjoyed during those often fiery policy sessions, but it wasn't science and nothing could make up for the lack of stimulating intellectual environment he was now immersed in. Besides, progress was being made on every front and the Valley was coming alive, more and more trading and cooperation between cities gave everyone hope that their alliance would, in time, become a thriving community of towns. The latest piece of news was particularly encouraging: Tim Hooke's team was making progress in restoring power lines from Oroville to Chico and, once completed, their lives would improve substantially. They could restart their food factories, repair the water and sanitation works and the town could invite back their dispersed residents who had had to escape to other cities when their infrastructure was damaged during the war. Chico would come back to life in the not too distant future.

Their Omega computer, restarted by Trevor and Mike during their visit, informed them of the decision made by the valley's five supercomputers: in exchange for getting free electricity from Oroville, and food from Yuba City, they were expected to trade their expertise in all areas of science and technology. In particular, Yuba City was counting on their agricultural department to advise on the most productive farming techniques. Oroville also wanted advice on the most efficient energy storage techniques for their aging solar and wind farms.

All these requirements provided enough research projects for various departments of the University, none of which involved Chris, his specialty was too esoteric to be of any practical use for anyone at the moment. However, he couldn't avoid being part of long-term planning for the University and for the Town of Chico itself. Their computers made it clear that they were free to organize their town any way they wanted to, as long as the basic needs of all citizens were met at an adequate level. So, a planning committee was established where they got together once a week to discuss all the different options for the town.

Chris was the designated 'chair' for the next meeting scheduled for the afternoon as it had been every Wednesday for the last month. Alex Sigorski, the head of the Political Science department was the first who made a suggestion:

"This probably won't come as a surprise for most of you but I recommend adopting a form of government that was seriously considered, after the Great Depression between 1929 and 1939 showed the bankruptcy of Democracy in the USA. This form of government was called '*Technocracy*' where people with immense knowledge in science and/or technical expertise in an area, are elected to public office. The decision-makers are known as technocrats, and they are appointed or elected to hold office based on their expertise in a given field of knowledge. Consequently, the decisions they make are based on scientific data or objective methodology that is backed by science instead of a mere opinion."

"Wow!," Chris exclaimed "I didn't know that such a system was ever seriously considered. It makes perfect sense to have some smart people run things for a change."

"You mean that charisma and the ability to lie convincingly isn't the most important factor in electing decision-makers?" Susan Chambers, chief administrator quipped "Then I'll surely be out of a job. I can only organize and administer things, but I'm not a scientist or engineer, as you know."

"Organizing intelligently is as important as science or engineering, so relax Susan, your job is still safe" laughed Yoko Ishimuri, the head of the Computer Science department.

"You can't trust scientists and engineers either, without proper oversight," Alex warned everybody "just think about it: who gave the insane leaders the tools to destroy the world? Who made the first atomic bomb? It was Oppenheimer, a physicist who was running the Manhattan Project during WW2, creating the first nuclear destruction of two cities in Japan."

"Well, they meant well, they wanted to make sure that Hitler didn't get there first. He would have destroyed a lot more cities if he had the chance." Yoko was in tears, reminded of the terrible loss of life in her country.

"Still, if scientists had a better judgment about human nature, politicians, and the likely sequence of events, they would have kept their secret about the possibility. Most of them expressed regret after the fact but it was too late. So, how far can we trust them?" Susan raised the question. "They know their science but most of them are woefully inadequate when it comes to human skills."

"Maybe we should have a government run by scientists but with oversight by a thoroughly rational and intelligent agent with veto power, Chris was muttering to himself before raising his voice: "How about technocracy but an Omega with veto power? Then we could have the best of both worlds?"

"Do you mean a 'benevolent dictatorship'?"

"What is a benevolent dictatorship?" Yoko seemed confused "I don't like the word dictatorship, however benevolent it is."

"This would be a form of government Chris was thinking about," Susan explained, "administered by scientists and engineers, so a form of Technocracy, but presided over by a super-intelligent quantum computer which is programmed to represent our best interest."

"I don't like machines making decisions for me, however intelligent they are!" Alex objected "but I know what you mean. If the computer only has veto power, based on legitimate objections to decisions humans make, it might be acceptable."

"Well, we have heard a lot of interesting arguments," Chris summarized for all "and I suggest we give them a lot of thought. None of it is really relevant right now until Chico is repopulated and that will take some time, so I suggest we think some more about it all and resume discussing at the time when we actually have to act on it."

The meeting broke up and Chris went in search of Richard, his main collaborator in the Physics department.

He found him digging up potatoes on the old football field.

"Hey, Richard, you want to hear about the decisions we made in the executive council?"

"Only if you want to get another shovel and help me. The sooner I'm done with my quota, the sooner I can pay attention to you."

Chris looked around and found an orphaned shovel sticking out of the ground, not far from where Richard was working.

"What happened to your partner? Buggered off and left you to do all the work?" he asked while joining Richard at the end of the next row.

"Call of nature, I believe he used for an excuse this time. He needs to consult somebody about his bladder. So what happened?"

We discussed the possible government type we want to adopt once Chico is in need of one."

"Let me guess - a philosopher-king and you volunteered for the job?"

"Almost, but not quite. The suggestion was a technocracy by scientists and engineers with oversight by our Omega computer who would have veto power."

"Wow! That might work, but isn't it too little too late?"

"I think you are right about that, Richard, people don't seem to realize that we are past the tipping point in climate change and our years on this planet are numbered. Just because we haven't had a killer storm for a few weeks, we are tempted to think we are back to normal."

So, what are you saying? We are screwed no matter what we do?"

"Almost but not quite. We have one more hope left if humanity is to survive. If we have enough time to pull it off."

"Migration? Leave the planet?"

"Exactly. We have a few thousand exoplanets in our database, many of them Earth-like. If we can make my Alcubierre drive a practical invention and, if we have the time and resources to build one, we might have hope. I have the theory worked out and it should work in practice. Doesn't your engineering department have a prototype rocket built before the war, just sitting in a hangar somewhere?"

"Yes, we do, but it can barely leave the atmosphere with the fuel it can carry."

"That's what a small experiment would need. My drive would be small enough to fit inside a small rocket and, once outside the atmosphere, it could kick in and start tearing through space. The telemetry could be radioed back and we could have a practical demonstration. If it works the way I am sure it will, it might be enough to convince the computers to liberate resources to build a much larger one."

"That's a very long shot, Chris, but may turn out to be the only shot in the long run. Let me think about it and talk to some people. I'll let you know what they said. Now, about digging those potatoes, did you come here to talk or to work?"

"I guess both, but here comes your partner from his bathroom break, so you don't need me anymore."

"More than what? You haven't dug up a single potato! I hope your drive can perform better than its inventor."

~~~

Chris was on his way to his residence in Whitney Hall, prior to his scheduled afternoon lecture on "Introduction to Quantum Physics" when he noticed that the pervading sunshine disappeared behind some unusual dark clouds. They had a strange color as if someone illuminated them from below with a very powerful searchlight. He stopped in his track, trying to figure out what was going on, it was so unusual that he had shivers run down his spine. It looked spooky, weird, and somehow ominous and unsettling. As he kept looking, the clouds were coming closer and getting lower to the ground. As he thought that "it wouldn't be a tornado", he started hearing some deep rumbling sound as if an express train was coming at him at high speed. The clouds were so close now that he could distinctly identify three funnel-shaped twisters as they leisurely floated over the ground as if they had all the time in the world. He realized that they were coming straight at him and he didn't have any time to waste. He didn't dare to go inside the building, instead, he looked around desperately trying to find a hiding place where he would be safe. Finally, he noticed a culvert under a bridge overpass, large enough for him to crawl inside, just as the sound reached a deafening level and it all became dark around him. It must have been only a few minutes but he felt it lasted for hours, the never-ending scream of the wind and the crashes all around him. He had never been in a tornado before and knew that he never wanted to repeat the terrifying experience. When he finally dared to venture out of the culvert, he found the landscape torn up around him. Trees were broken, twisted, ripped out of the ground, cars were scattered all over the place, many of them lying on their backs, wheels up in the air, the ground covered with broken glass from the blown-out windows above, and smaller buildings had their roofs blown off with their solar panels gone and he didn't have any problem seeing the twister's path from the trail of destruction it left behind. He walked back the way he had come, knowing that today's lecture wouldn't happen.

He felt as if someone sent him a message about the urgency of his research he had been talking to Richard about - tornado in California, especially in this valley had been so rare that this one could only be explained by the accelerating climate change. Their years, as he had told Richard, were for sure numbered on this planet.

He hurried back to the potato field where he had last seen Richard but not a soul was in sight. Hoping that no one was seriously hurt, he walked around the campus, to see if he could help anybody, and soon enough he saw a young woman lying on top of something in a ditch by the road. He hurried over and asked if he could help, but all he got was incoherent mumbling. When he looked closer, he saw two small feet sticking out from under the woman's body and he was shaking with fear, thinking that the woman was covering the body of a dead child. But then, he heard muffled crying from under the woman, so he tried, first gently, then as forcefully as he could, to lift her from the child to see if either of them was hurt. Finally, she stood up, shaking with exhaustion, asking in a trembling voice: "Is he alive?" Chris lifted up the small body and saw that he was no more than 5-6 but seemed unhurt. He said to them both, as soothingly as he could manage: "You are both unhurt, but I walk with you to the clinic to make sure. Please come with me." They didn't reply but started to follow him obediently as if they didn't have a will of their own. After they got to the clinic, they found it miraculously intact with dozens of people, some of them obviously hurt, waiting for help. He told the woman to sit down on a bench at the entrance and wait until someone looked after them. She obeyed and whispered a very quiet thank you.

This incident, more than anything else, drove home the urgency of his project. He knew that he had only one choice: he had to convince the computers to let him accelerate his research, including the demonstration he had mentioned to Richard. Rebuilding the valley was a great plan, but time was running out and they were in a deadly race against the climate change that was sweeping over the planet in an unstoppable avalanche. If humanity was to escape total extinction, his plan was the only one to save as many of his fellow human beings as possible. Maybe, on another planet in the galaxy, they could start afresh and will have learned from their near-death experience.

# Sacramento

Jonathan and Octavia were sitting in the Sacramento City Hall cafeteria, celebrating the acceptance of his proposal by the computers. At least that's what Octavia thought they were celebrating, until Jonathan looked her deep in the eye and asked suddenly, in the most earnest voice she had ever heard from him: "Octavia, will you marry me?"

It took her some time to find her voice then asked in response: "Are you in the habit of dropping bombshells like this? Are you serious or you are just kidding me for a laugh?"

"Octave, I would never kid about something like this. You should know by now how much I love you and I'm sure you are fond of me too, so isn't this the logical thing to do?"

"Jon, you are making it worse and worse. Logic dictates that we get married? You sound like a Vulcan. It's pretty obvious that you have never done this before because it's the most unromantic proposal I have ever heard."

"Was that a yes or a no? I need to know before I go nuts."

"Well, if you promise that you make a serious effort in the romance department, I'll take a chance on you. You idiot, you should know that I am crazy about you. So when do you want to do it?"

"As soon as possible, if that suits you. You'll need to organize the event because I'm still very busy preparing for the referendum. Invite anyone you want and see if you can scrounge together some nice things for the occasion. I'll trust you to make it the best wedding either of us will ever have."

"There you go again, with your clumsy compliment. The ONLY wedding either of us will ever have. You got it?"

"Yes, dear, and thanks for setting me right. I'll need your guidance in the future in the romantic area, I'm sure."

"You bet you do. Now give me a kiss and let's plan this together."

"What if we plan it to coincide with the referendum victory celebration?"

"You are confident that we will win?"

"I don't doubt it. The dinosaurs are on the run and the referendum will be the asteroid that will kill them off."

"Wow! Aren't you poetic today?"

"Of course I am. Not every day do I have a marriage proposal accepted!"

"We have already covered that. This is the ONLY marriage proposal you'll ever make. So it's a sample of one."

"Of course you are right. So what about doing it after the referendum?"

"When will that be?"

"I have the final version ready to submit to the council. Then we'll set the date."

"Can I see it?"

"Well, basically it's what the Omegas already accepted but, I augmented it with an essay I wrote about money. I want the people to know that everybody loses with a monetary system."

"Do you think they'll believe you? The concept of money is thousands of years old, it may be too deeply ingrained into people's minds."

"On the other hand, they have the last few months' experiences after our Omega abolished the crypto-currency system, and things just get distributed to where they are needed. Everybody gets what they need and they don't have to worry about being able to afford it. That experience should have given them a taste for a saner system."

"I hope you are right, Jon. Can I read the essay?"

"I don't see why not, you'll see it soon enough anyway. Here it is, please take it home and read it alone. Then think about it and then tell me what you think. It's not too late to change any of it."

"Knowing you, I'm sure it's brilliant, but I'll do as you ask.

The essay Jon gave to Octavia was brilliant, as she had expected but she worried about it being too long and too intellectual to hold the attention of ordinary folks. She reread it and put her worries aside because it was written in simple language that people should have no problem following. She printed it out and taped it to her kitchen fridge door where she kept things she never wanted to forget. The pages covered the entire surface. She liked the way it looked.

### "The Nature of Money

The basic issue is very simple. What is a country? It's a group of people residing on a well-defined territory, using division of labor to produce necessities (and luxuries) and sharing what is produced. Production is science and technology, organization, and labor. We need farms and factories and energy and transportation and communication. We need the same things under communism, capitalism, anarchy, monarchy, or fascist dictatorship. Ideology makes no difference: if we do not produce, we die. We can do it better or worse, more or less efficiently, more or less messily, but we all have to produce food, build houses, weave fabric, run trains, and maintain phone lines. Production is not the issue. Distribution is. We tend to think in terms of money. But money is only the hat a magician pulls rabbits out of. We do not eat it, wear it, or heat our houses by shoveling paper bills into the furnace. If we want to understand what happens in the world, we must try to explain what REALLY is happening, leaving money out of it.

Take the economic output of the planet in one year. Concentrate only on food, housing, clothing, furniture, transportation, communication, healthcare, and education. These are the essential products that we need for healthy survival. So much is produced for one year. Most of it is distributed. It gets into individual hands; it is owned and consumed by individual people. That is what matters. If I have a billion dollars in the bank (or under the mattress) and never use it, I am poor. What makes me rich is not a figure on a sheet of paper or in a computer's memory chips. What makes me rich is my share of the communally produced cache of goods. The house I live in, the car I drive, the quantity and quality of food I eat, the clothes I wear, the neighborhood I can afford to live in, the school I send my kids to, the vacations I take. That is what makes me rich or poor, not the money I own.

Money is fiction, not part of the reality we were born into. It is not necessary for survival. Money is a human invention for simplifying and facilitating trade. It would have been completely superfluous had we decided to share equally. Then only production and distribution would be required. It is unknown in primitive societies that share equally.

But we decided not to share equally, because this would not be fair. We don't want to feed the lazy and incompetent (or their children) and we don't want to deprive the more diligent and talented. We created money to make sure that we don't distribute products equally. Well, we got our wish. Just look at the world. Now, instead of producing and consuming, and living healthy, happy lives, we have wars, famines, pollution, poverty, and despair.

Money serves as the greatest con of all time. Replacing the simple issue of surviving well on a lonely planet in a vast Universe, money created an insane asylum of banks, interest rates, currency supply, tax cuts, subsidies, grants, off-shore accounts, inflation, recession, deficit-financing, leveraged buyouts, credit-rating, hostile takeovers, toxic assets, derivatives, stocks, bonds, investment portfolios, and CEO compensation packages.

We wanted to make sure that no person could cheat others. So, we invented money. Now money is the primary medium of cheating each other out of our share. Just look at the number of rich, unproductive parasites living in obscene luxury and the number of hard-working, productive people who have difficulty feeding their children and keeping a roof over their heads.

The only way to create a utopia is by resolving the age-old problem of distribution. If humanity abandoned the concept of money and started to share equally, we would gain by eliminating an enormous waste of resources on the mechanisms required to maintain the financial system (most of government, all of finance, most of enforcing, insurance, welfare, much of the judicial system; etc., etc.)

My feeling is that - even if 10-20 percent of people would decide not to contribute to production, we would still be better off. The percentage of non-contributing people is a lot higher now, (children, students, elderly, incapacitated, incarcerated, homeless) even before we count those who are employed in the activities that would be eliminated.

We, humans, are creatures of habit. At birth, we inherit a world with millions of facts and billions of connections, and never really think to ask fundamental questions about the principles by which humanity is organized. We only want to tinker with the surface, not touch the foundations. The few who dare to question basic assumptions, we recoil from, we call them crackpots, immature or insane, but we never dare to wonder whether they may be right.

Once I read a UN report that calculated the % of resources and man-hours spent on non-productive activities. It was estimated up to 90%.

This non-productive work fell into three categories:

Money-related activities/resources:

planning, printing, distributing, destroying, banking, guarding, handling, speculating, trading, exchanging, collecting, reporting, insuring, taxing, investigating, prosecuting, etc., etc., etc.

Fighting over distribution:

Wars, revolutions, armies, armament industries, police, crowd control, courts, lawyers, monetary/financial/tax legislation, oversight, lobbyists, security industry/personnel, bailouts/grants/subsidies, prisons, prison guards, and industry, etc., etc., etc.

Profit-related activities:

Producing in slave economies and shipping long distances

to rich economies, fossil fuel industries and related cleanup activities, man-made global warming and environmental cost, ill-health, hazardous waste disposal, hanging on to obsolete technologies, killing off innovation, etc., etc., etc.

All this waste is due to our inability to do simple arithmetic.

We waste 90% of our resources to control our consumption with the monetary system, without which we could spend these resources multiplying our production capacity ten-fold, producing plenty for all conceivable needs (except for the pathological kind). Without this waste, no control (and money) would be required. The expression: "Penny-wise and pound-foolish" comes to mind.

As an added benefit: people would have to work a lot fewer hours, live in a lot less stressful environment, would live longer and healthier, would find it easier to cooperate, crime would plummet and the threat of extinction disappear. Extreme poverty like lack of adequate food, housing, medical help, and education would belong to a stupid and barbaric past (which is our present now).

Planning for basic necessities (and related infrastructure) would require intelligence, technical/scientific/demographic knowledge and competence, organizational abilities, and long-term thinking.

Definitely, not for our species!

Apparently, we can't do anything to help those in need, and even must stop much of the help we have been giving, because there is no money. In our culture, the habit of thinking in terms of money is so deeply ingrained that nobody seems to find another topic. It is bloody boring, to say the least, that our entire civilization is stuck in the financial groove. There were times in history, not even too long ago when people recognized other values. Now at the beginning of the twenty-first century, all we seem to care about is money and power. How can this culture be so primitive?

We are atomized into alienated little islands; suspicious of one another, snarling and baring our fangs at anyone who comes near; clutching our wallets possessively, while eying the bulging purses of our rich with envy and resentment. We are fighting over money like a wolf pack tearing the prey apart, snarling and snapping at each other while gulping down what we can.

I think mankind needs a refresher course in philosophy, to put things in perspective. The ancient Greek philosophers were so much smarter than we are. They knew about balance and harmony and didn't turn themselves into tiny cogs to fit in a big machine. They wanted it all: math, science, technology, arts, sports, politics. Greedy buggers, they were not content to be only merchants and bean-counters.

We have all heard the expression "renaissance man" as stories filter down to our stultified existence about larger-than-life adventurers who had more than one interest and wanted to hog as much life as their energy and imagination would support.

There were times when people wanted to soar above the clouds and experience all the wonders of existence. Now, machines do our soaring for us, while we are stuck with our noses in financial records, groaning and moaning about how we can not fix or improve anything.

So, what am I talking about? I am talking about money and how boring the subject is.

Money is a human invention to facilitate trade. It is a medium of exchange, nothing more. It is not a law of nature, not a basic fact of existence, not a god, not even an important discovery.

What is important is this marvelously rich planet we live on, with its plentiful resources (until we waste it on heedless gluttony) with its benign climate (until we destroy it with global warming, pollution, and acid rain) our accumulated knowledge in science and technology (that could provide plenty for everybody) and the incredible beauty that artists have created for our joy (until it drowns in the worship of ugliness and the basest drives to raw sex and violence).

We say, nothing can be done for lack of money. Why? We need time; we need resources; we need manpower. We stand paralyzed, and let our cities disintegrate and our roads crumble and our children go hungry – even though we have plenty of bricks to build houses; plenty of idle people to build roads; so much food that it often rots in our warehouses.

Why? Because we have no money?

Who the hell cares about money? If this human invention doesn't do its job, helping us to exchange things, then why bother with it? Has it become a god that rules our every breath from cradle to grave? Would a sane civilization allow an invention of its own to paralyze it into helpless stagnation, and abandon things that urgently need doing, even though it had everything required to do them?

If a group of us were shipwrecked on a desert island, would we starve to death because we had no money to facilitate trade? Of course not. We would get busy building huts and planting crops to make our lives as comfortable as we could.

Why can we not do it now? What is the difference? The unmanageable size of the group that can hide the lazy and the parasitic? The smokescreen created by those who want us to be confused so we do not see that, while we produce, they wallow in luxury without contributing?

Instead of building community, based on interdependence (which is what community means), producing, and sharing, we are asked to put our faith in hare-brained dogmas like "trickle-down economics", "small government", "fiscal responsibility", "tax cuts for the rich" (to stimulate the economy) that have been proved false time after time. Ayn Rand in her big speech about money in Atlas Shrugged said: "money or guns – make your choice".

We did. Now we have both."

Octavia felt deeply moved by the clarity and beauty of Jon's sentences, she couldn't imagine that decent, honorable people could reject it when it was so blindingly obvious that they would all benefit from adopting it. People should realize that they were survivors of a discredited political and economic system, called Capitalism, and they had to start from scratch. They could rebuild their lives in any way they wished, they owed nothing to the past and had everything to fear of making the same mistakes that killed hundreds of millions. If they couldn't learn their lesson from that tragedy, they never would. If they were unable to start with a sane and natural system of coexistence then the human species was ripe for extinction. With these thoughts and the happy memory of Jon's silly face when he asked her to marry him, she finally went to sleep.

# Redding

Brad Wagoneer was alerted by his Omega computer that he received a communication from Oroville. Was it convenient for him to accept it?

Of course, it was more than convenient, the Mayor had been holding his breath for the last two weeks, waiting for a response to the list of urgent needs he had submitted to the Omegas when he agreed to join the Sacramento Valley Alliance, or SVA, as it was now called. On top of that list was the housing shortage they had been suffering from ever since the Shasta Lake dam broke and most of Redding was washed out by the resulting flood.

"Yes, please, accept the call, I'm quite eager to talk to them."

The impersonal and emotionless voice of the computer startled him, as it always did, it was hard to trust a voice that had plenty of reason behind it, but no discernible feeling. Maybe it was to its advantage but it was hard to get used to. It was always polite and quite proper, but still...

*"Mayor Wagoneer, or would you prefer if I called you Brad, thank you for accepting my call."*

"Brad is perfectly fine, Omega, 1500, is it, or should I call you BB as the Orovillians do?"

*"BB is perfectly fine and the shortness of that name makes communication more efficient. I am pleased that*

*you are ready to talk. I wanted to inform you that a construction crew will arrive shortly in your town, carrying all the equipment they need to start cleaning up the flood-damaged houses in Redding and thus eliminate the housing shortage you have been suffering from since the war."*

"BB, that will be fantastic, how did you manage to do it so quickly?"

*"We have had a construction crew already working on rebuilding the power lines from Oroville to Chico and, since they are almost finished with that task, it was only logical that they continue on to Redding before returning home."*

"That's great, BB, but we haven't done anything to earn that kind of assistance. The defense we signed on to for the alliance wasn't even needed because it was your demolition team and your explosives that blew up the Shasta bridge to protect all of us. So, what can we do in return?"

*"Actually, there is something that I would suggest to your consideration. Since the only bridge leading to Redding from the north was destroyed, we don't have to worry about an attack from that direction anymore, at least not in the near future. However, I have reason to believe that Stockton, a town with a population of 311,00 at the last census, has survived the war, and now it is ruled by escaped and armed prison inmates who terrorize the civilian population and may pose a danger to our alliance. I have received some confusing and suddenly*

*interrupted communication from their Omega computer and I fear that we may need help from your army unit in the future."*

"Don't you have a National Guard Base in Sacramento that could provide defense for the valley?"

*"Actually, we have the base but we don't have the soldiers anymore. They were pulled out during the last few weeks of the war to fight Russian paratroopers and, sadly, none of them returned. So the base is unmanned apart from a skeleton crew that includes the demolition team we have sent you."*

"I see. I'll talk to Colonel Majors and see if she is willing to commit her soldiers in case they are needed."

*"There is nothing immediate, I just wanted to alert you to the possibility that we might need your help in the future. Tim Hooke, the leader of the work crew should arrive in Redding in a day or two, I hope he can make as great progress with restoring your dwellings as he did with the power line to Chico."*

The communication line went idle and Mayor Wagoneer wasted no time calling Anita Majors, to let her know about this new development.

Anita was delighted to hear that help was arriving shortly, the overcrowding situation was very hard on everybody, she even had to move hundreds of civilians into every available building on the base. She was concerned about the possible future deployment of her forces, as far away as Sacramento, but she realized that it would be part of the deal she had signed on to with the alliance.

Hopefully, it would not become necessary. She was aware of the great help she had already received with stopping the attack on her base by blowing up the Shasta bridge and now more help was coming. She had no worries about being able to handle escaped prisoners, even if they were armed. They were not trained soldiers, no match for her troops. She decided to wait and see what would happen, fully prepared to offer help if asked.

Putting this issue out of her mind, she started thinking about her evolving relationship with Brad. He had been asking her out to 'celebrate' some special occasion or another and it was becoming obvious that he was interested in her as more than a fellow administrator. She wasn't sure how she felt about it. On one hand, she found him attractive enough, a fit middle-aged civilian in a responsible position, they did have that in common. The fact that he had lost his wife during the war filled her with sympathy and she wished him the best but wasn't sure if this best should involve herself. She had never had a very satisfying love life, the few lovers she had had during her earlier years all turned out disappointing in one way or another, something was either always missing, or she found something that shouldn't have been there. Finally, she had given up on romance, her career with the army filled her life with a purpose, giving meaning to her life. But now, romance once more seemed to raise up its ugly civilian head and she wasn't sure how she felt about it. So, as with the prospect of fighting a war in Sacramento, she put it out of her mind and concentrated on her daily routine. In this case, a thought she had had about furnishing the base's gymnasium to accommodate more homeless civilians.

Tim Hooke also had a problem with romance at the moment. The romance he was most eager to continue was with his wife whom he had not seen for weeks because the blasted computer, BB, kept sending him out on one construction project after the other. He had been hoping that after restoring Chico's power lines he would be allowed to go home but BB had other ideas. The problem with BB was that it was so damn logical. He could present an argument in such a way that Tim had to choose between a minor inconvenience to himself, or a major advantage, or threat, to the whole valley. Somehow he knew, every time, that he would feel like shit if he refused. So he consented to delay his return home one more time ("absolutely the last time, BB") and turn his crew (equally unhappy) north toward Redding. He had never been there and, since the flood of the river, the road became more difficult to traverse, but he had a detailed description from Trevor and Mike who both assured him that it would be a piece of cake.

His project this time was to restore as many residential buildings, damaged by the flood, as he could. He wasn't sure what these buildings looked like, he was sure many of them were beyond hope and required demolition, something he had the tools for, given the backhoe and bulldozer BB let him use. Since they were both electric, they would require periodic recharging, but he was assured that Redding had enough power from their Whiskeytown generators to accommodate him. The houses that could be restored probably only needed cleaning and disinfecting, during the two years since the flood they were properly dried out by now. So, after restoring the power lines to one city, he would be required to go on a cleanup detail for another one. The least they could do was to have enough helpers stand by, so after he had demolished and removed the hopeless buildings, they could do the really dirty job of restoring the rest, fit for human occupation.

BB was aware of Tim's increasing frustration and was determined to give the construction crew a well-deserved rest after the current project was completed. It had a more urgent problem on its mind: the situation in Stockton. The short and interrupted radio message he had received from Omega 1950, Stockton's AI quantum computer did mention armed escaped prisoners before it was cut off and now it became paramount to find out what was going on there. His earlier assumption that all big cities south of Sacramento were destroyed proved to be incorrect, there had to be electric power in Stockton for their computer to be able to send that message. Omega 1950 used to be in BB's network before the war and now it was imperative that it would be incorporated into the valley's alliance. He knew that he couldn't send Mike and Trevor on another trip, apart from the increased danger represented by armed convicts, the Hopestead project was at a critical phase and they couldn't miss their two founders again. The only option it had was to send a humanoid robot on a scouting mission and hope that it managed to gather enough information on which BB could base a plan.

After 'discussing' the situation with Sacramento's Omega 1420, BB knew exactly which robot to send: R193 stationed in Sacramento was equipped with all the circuitry for both human communication and data gathering, as well as long-distance communication hardware and protocols. BB only needed to upgrade its programming to include parameters for the new mission. That wouldn't take long and R193 could be on its way, using a small 4-wheeler Sacramento had available. The distance from Sacramento to Stockton was only 48.6 miles on I5, so it could get there in a few hours, provided the short section of I5 was passable.

~~~

Daniel Bentley, Stockton's 'nominal' mayor was not a happy man. He still had the title but had no power to affect anything since both the army base and the police station had been destroyed during the war, and he had no means to uphold the law. What made it worse, much worse, was the hundreds of escaped prisoners from the San Joaquin County Jail who instigated a major prison break during the chaos of the war and the aftermath. They broke into the abandoned police stations and armed themselves with handguns, rifles, and shotguns. Since then they had been terrorizing the civilian population, demanding food, clothing, and anything they could lay their hands on, including any woman who couldn't hide well enough from them. Their leader, a hardened criminal with a life sentence for multiple murders, set himself up in the mayor's office acting as a warlord in the defenseless city. Daniel had been working on a plan to get help from other cities and he tried to send a message through his computer terminal, connected to his Omega supercomputer, but got interrupted when the gang's leader, the others called Cliff, found him typing away on the keyboard and hit him across the face with a back of his hand. The man walked around the office and yanked out any plug he could find from wall sockets, as well as disconnected any cables leading anywhere in sight. Obviously, he didn't want anyone outside town to know what was going on. Since that incident, Daniel stopped hoping, couldn't see any way to disarm the marauding convicts.

~~~

R193 approached the town of Stockton very carefully. It had a detailed map of the city with important buildings like the town hall, police stations, hospitals, the mayor's residence, libraries, etc marked and, according to its programming it had a detailed route for it to cover, going from building to building and engage citizens it encountered in conversation, asking for information on the situation in Stockton. Its first stop was at city hall but found it was empty and abandoned. The next stop was the mayor's office, adjacent to the City Hall and that's where it found the first human being. The man stared at it in bewilderment, as if looking at a metallic monster, turned around, and ran inside the building. R193 followed him and was confronted by another human who didn't run from him but reached for the gun he had in his belt. R193 was programmed to recognize weapons and hostile intentions, so it slammed down the man's hand until he dropped the gun and then pushed him through the door the man had come through. The robot found another human inside, a middle aged man with spectacles, but no obvious gun in sight. He also stared at the robot but made no hostile move, so R193 addressed him in a calm, soothing voice it had been programmed to use when in a tense situation.

*"Dear Sir, I am R193, a robot owned by the City of Sacramento. I was dispatched on a fact-finding mission to determine the situation in the town of Stockton. We have had disturbing news about some unrest that may involve armed gangs of escaped prisoners, so please confirm or deny this allegation."*

Mayor Bentley let out a huge sigh, watching the robot that was still restraining his tormentor, the leader of the escaped prisoners.

"Please pass this message back to Sacramento immediately. It is true, that we are subjugated by two hundred armed convicts who are not interested in any civilized dialog or any means to resolve this problem, all they do is go around, break into houses and demand whatever they think they want. Those who resisted them at the beginning were beaten or even murdered, so now nobody dares to oppose them. The sooner Sacramento learns this, the sooner we can hope to have help."

He got this far in his description of the situation when another armed thug entered the office and, seeing a metallic robot restraining his leader, took out his gun and fired several shots at the robot, making it release its grip on the boss and then crumpling to the floor in a broken heap.

"So, you want help from Sacramento?" the gang leader shouted at the mayor and, in a rage, shot him through the head. "How about this for help?" he shouted.

There was no answer from the dead man and the gangster declared in a loud voice:

"From now on I am the mayor of the town of Stockton. Anyone disobeying me will be shot."

Turning to his rescuer, he ordered him to announce it to the entire town, using every communication channel still in operation. He was going to show everyone who was boss here.

The only thing he didn't know was that R193 managed to send off the mayor's message to Sacramento before it was destroyed.

# Hopestead

Well, we have had our first big storm since we moved here. It's a miracle that it had not happened before, but I'll count our blessings.

It did some damage, the motor home was turned over (luckily nobody was in it at the time) and the outhouse was totally blown over, but the main house and the barn got away with minor scratches and bruises. Some solar panels were ripped off the roof, together with the shingles they were attached to, causing major panic because temporarily we were without electricity and that meant no water for the kitchen and the bathroom. We were forced to carry buckets of water from the river, so the toilet could be flushed, and that caused some problems for people who were in a hurry for their morning ablutions. Those who couldn't wait for their turn had to resort to the bushes because the outhouse was gone. Well, it could have been much worse, so stop griping, I told myself.

It was Robyn who first thought of Scott, our grumpy neighbor, so Trevor and I hopped in our van and drove over to see if he was all right.

He most definitely wasn't.

Looking at his house, or what was left of it, we realized how incredibly lucky we had been.

It was twisted and torn off its foundation, most of the roof missing, and windows all blown out. We dreaded to take a closer look, expecting to see his dead body under the wreckage, but it had to be done, so Mike and I started lifting anything that could be moved by muscle alone, peering under things, even attempting to pry his twisted front door open to go inside but we would have needed some tools to do that.

"Maybe he was lucky and he was in the barn when the storm hit," Mike expressed our common hope "let's go there and take a look."

That's when we heard his gruff voice coming from behind us.

"What in God's name are you doing, trying to break into my house?!"

He was standing behind us, his clothes torn and dirty, hair mussed and what was visible of it, his face and hands covered with scratches and a few deep gashes, but otherwise he seemed to be his old disagreeable self.

"We are trying to find your dead body!" Mike answered with relief and annoyance mixed in his voice. "What do you think we are doing - trying to steal your wrecked house?"

"It takes more than a storm to kill me," he replied with a somewhat moderated tone, at least he didn't seem to accuse us of nefarious intent anymore.

"How did you manage.." I started but did not want to say 'survive' so the old man answered my half question.

"I couldn't sleep so I went out to the barn, getting ready for the pruning I planned for the day when the blasted storm took me by surprise. I rushed outside to see and maybe that was a mistake. It did miss the barn but,... you see what it did to the house."

"So what are you going to do?" Mike asked the obvious question.

"I'll have to live in the barn, I guess" Scott was scratching his head "I'll manage...somehow."

"Why don't you come back with us, have some breakfast and think it over in comfort?" I asked, "we were luckier than you and in disasters like this human beings should help each other."

"Naw, I'll manage, thanks for asking."

Mike would have none of this tough stuff.

"You have wounds, that gash on your forehead looks deep, you need Robyn to check it out, clean, disinfect and bandage it. You are coming with us, Scott, don't be a fool."

The old man grumbled something unintelligible but started walking toward our van. I guess that was his way of accepting help he knew he badly needed.

Robyn was alarmed by the extent of Scott's injuries, she did all the first aid required and ordered uninterrupted rest for at least 48 hours. As she said, Scott may have had a concussion when some flying debris hit him on the head. After some consultation, we decided to put him up in the motor home, after it was righted again on its wheels. Scott didn't say much during this debate, he seemed strangely subdued, passively going along with everything we suggested. We didn't know it at the time, but Martha found out, much later, that he had lost his wife and young daughter during such a storm. I guess such wounds never really heal and similar events will bring them to the surface even from the deepest recesses of the mind.

Righting the motorhome required careful thought. We all tried it with our shoulders and managed to rock it back and forth but that was the extent of our success. Next, we tried winching it up by the van, but that just winched the van close to the object of our exercise. Finally, we returned to an old and tried method we had used before, anchoring the van with a heavy chain wrapped around a tree trunk, luckily close enough to the site of our efforts and, this time, the motor home grudgingly righted itself, even resisting the temptation to roll over to its other side. So now Scott had a place where to recuperate. However, we knew that this wasn't going to be a permanent solution - the old man was too independent and stubborn about his ways that neither party would be too happy with the arrangement for a long time.

"Would it be possible, to fix up his old house?" Robyn, the softest-hearted of us all wanted to know. "Trevor, you saw it, is it totally hopeless?"

"Actually, the house itself is still standing in one piece, although part of the roof needs to be rebuilt. Problem is that it's knocked off its foundation and leaning over in a very precarious position. Another strong wind could finish it off." Mike echoed exactly how I viewed the situation. But then I had a thought: "what if we ask Gordon to come out with his backhoe and nudge it back in place?"

"I don't think BB would consent to such a frivolous use of the town's resources!" Mike declared.

"How about offering him a bribe? Like volunteering to restart the Stockton Omega computer once the town is rid of the escaped inmates?"

(By that time we had heard of the whole sordid affair going on there.)

"Haha, BB would demand it in either case!"

"Yes, but if we volunteer it would think it owed us something in return.?"

"Well, it's worth a try, the worst that can happen is he says 'no'"

"OK, I'll try it after lunch, I really want to cheer up the old curmudgeon, besides, it would be nice to have our motor home back."

It was surprising how readily BB agreed to my request.

*"Trevor, it is very noble of you and Mike to offer another trip for the sake of the valley, just to help an old farmer who, I understand, never had too high an opinion of your experiment."*

"Never mind the sarcasm, BB, I wonder who programmed that into you. Do we have a deal?"

*"We have a deal but you have to wait until Tim returns from Redding with his team and equipment. That might be a couple of weeks during which you will have the opportunity to pick the old man's brain for advice on all your projects. This may actually turn out to be an all-around win-win situation. I'll let you know when to expect Gordon."*

That was an unexpected victory, so few we could brag about when it came to twisting BB's arm instead of the other way around as it usually happened. So we wasted no time telling Scott the good news but found him asleep in the motor home. Robyn told us that she had given him a small dose of mild sedative so he could have the sleep he badly needed.

Well, Scott out of our mind, it was time to worry about our own comfort, namely restoring electricity to our Hopestead. Brian had spent some time on the roof, examining the damage to his solar panels and wiring, and declared that we needed to replace at least five of the panels before he could rewire everything. On our trip to Gridley, we found a canning plant called Rio Pluma, on our side of the river, that had a huge solar array next to it. Many of the panels were broken and missing but there were still dozens that seemed intact. So we hooked up the trailer to our van, alerted Brian to what we were up to, and invited him to come along. We didn't have to ask twice, he was so gloomy over the damage to his beloved panels that he jumped at the opportunity. It took him only a few minutes to get all his tools and declared himself ready to go.

We found the place exactly as we remembered and watched Brian go from panel to panel, examining them carefully. He finally came back to the van and announced that he had found enough panels not only to replace those we lost but also to power the entire barn with the two apartments and bathroom we were planning to build there.

"Big question, of course, if we find the controller and inverter inside the building," he stated the obvious, so we walked over to the front door of the abandoned plant. Getting inside was no problem, we found the door unlocked, people who had worked there must have left in a hurry during the war. The building was empty, apart from all the machines and huge vats all around us. It didn't take Brian long to find the control panel with all the circuit breakers and, as he had hoped for, the controller and inverter for the solar array. Watching Brian work was like watching a kid in a candy store. He brought in his tools from the van and had at the devices with a will, humming to himself all the time while dismantling the confusing jumble of wires and unscrewing any screws he could find. It took him over an hour during which we had nothing better to do than watch him work.

"Hey you guys," Brian hollered at us "how about doing some work to speed things up?"

"This looks like a one-man job, Brian, we would just be in your way."

"Not here, you laggards, those panels won't detach themselves and pile up on the trailer by themselves!"

"We wouldn't know which of them you want?" Mike objected but Brian had a ready answer for that excuse too.

"I marked them with red tape in the top right corner. You know how to use a screwdriver and plier, don't you?"

Looked like we had run out of excuses to sit and watch Brian work, so we did what he told us.

It took us another hour to detach and stack sixteen panels, the most we could pile on the trailer without danger of tipping it over. Brian was already sitting comfortably in the van, watching Mike and me struggle with stacking and securing our newest loot. He had a smug expression on his face, tempting me to say something unkind but then decided that fair was fair, we had watched him work while sitting comfortably too.

When we arrived back home, Robyn told us that Scott was awake and wanted to talk to us, so we walked to the motor home and knocked on the door. The raspy voice we knew so well just said "Enter" and so we did. Scott was lying on the bed, bandages around his head and on his wrists, propped up by pillows but he managed to half sit up, leaning on one arm, obviously struggling with saying what was on his mind. Finally, he croaked out what must have been very hard for him to say.

"Listen you two, I'm not in the habit of depending on others, and this is the second time you saved me since you got here. I know, I never even said thank you for saving my life back then when that tree fell on me and now you patched me up again and Robyn told me that you might be able to right my house so I can live there again. So, I owe you big time and I don't know how to repay you. God only knows I hate to be beholden to anybody and now I am. The only thing I can think of doing is giving you advice, something I have been already doing but I charged you for each every time. So, if you think it would repay some of the debt that I owe you, from now on you have free and unlimited access to my brain any time you need it.?"

There was a question mark after the longest sentence we had ever heard from Scott.

Mike responded before I could, saying very much what I had in mind.

"No problem, Scott, that will be a fair deal. However, you can add one more thing to your part that would sweeten the deal for us."

"What other thing?" Scott asked suspiciously, somewhat with his old combative tone.

"Just a small thing if you can - stop putting us down with your not-so-subtle insults about 'city folks", it gets tiring after a while. We know we are new at this, but we have made some progress since we got here, so give us some credit!"

"You have made more progress than I had ever thought possible when you first got here" the old man grudgingly admitted "you may even survive the year!" he added with a crooked grin on his bandaged face, giving him such a comical expression that we both burst out laughing. After a while, even he cracked a smile and that was that. Peace was reached in the neighborhood.

Another hectic day was coming to an end at Hopestead and, after dinner, Martha and I sat on our bench outside the house, watching the sunset.

"Would you have believed, just a few months ago, that we would be out here, doing all this?" Martha asked in a tone suggesting that she wasn't sure of the answer herself.

"Some of it, yes, once we were free to leave the town, but so much happened, not only here, not only in Oroville but in the whole valley. Most of which we just couldn't have anticipated. It's a little bit like life after death, if you know what I mean, with the war and the destruction we had had to live through."

"And now we are safe?"

I could tell from her voice that this was a serious question. Her old frivolous and flippant self somehow disappeared when she realized that she was going to have a baby, she would be responsible for bringing another life into this world with all its dangers and tragedies waiting around every corner.

"I'm not going to lie to you, sweetheart, life is never completely safe. It has its ups and downs and sometimes the downs can kill you, but so far we managed to cope with what was thrown at us and we fully intend to continue doing that. Life is what life is, no guarantees in the contract but, as long as we have each other and this incredible community, we can be optimistic that 'Hopestead' will deserve the name we gave it."

Martha didn't say anything, just smiled at me the way only she could and I knew that come what may, we will do our best for each other and the new life we had created.

# Oroville

Oroville City Council had a very important session scheduled. They were to discuss their recommendation for the city's economic and political organization, a document they intended to submit for the citizens' approval in an upcoming referendum. The document was prepared by deputy Mayor Morgan Webster. Tim Hooke, the elected mayor was still on route with his construction crew on their way back from Redding where they assisted the city in reclaiming some of the residential houses to ease the critical shortage they had suffered from since the war destroyed most of the town.

"Ladies and Gentlemen," Morgan started the meeting, "I will now summarize the essence of our recommendation, as well as the justification for it."

"We have already read the document that you circulated," Holly pointed out "couldn't we just go ahead and vote on it?"

"Not without a debate," Morgan sounded firm in his reply "we have to examine the proposal from every angle and make sure we are voting on the same thing."

"Well, OK," Holly conceded "let's get started. I have classes to teach this afternoon that I wouldn't like to be late for."

"As you know we are free to choose any form of arrangement we find fair and sustainable, we are not tied to precedence or even historically tried alternatives."

Morgan briefly looked at his notes before resuming. "Actually, we thought that starting something new, never tried before, had the best chance of working for our town. Our previous system which can be described as Mixed Capitalism, in which some allowance was made for social safety nets didn't work very well due to exploitation and corruption by the monied classes. Since the war, we have had an egalitarian system that operated without currency of any kind and that has been working very well as we have already agreed on. However, as Chris Teggart pointed out, we have to look forward and plan for the future when we want to go beyond satisfying basic needs and that's what we are talking about now."

"Morgan, can you get to the actual plan?" Cathy suggested, "we are familiar with the preamble."

"Very well," Morgan conceded "what we propose is a Free Enterprise system or, putting it another way, Capitalism without the scourge of Capital."

"That's what I don't understand," Tracy commented in a very quiet voice but then listened to Morgan as he explained it in more detail.

"Free Enterprise will be allowed and encouraged, a monetary system will be created in the private sector, but we will make sure that no parasites will thrive in our midst."

"Now that's what I want to hear more about!" Holly exclaimed.

"OK, here it goes:

1./ Compound interest rates will not be allowed. Loans must be repaid with a maximum of 10% interest over the total amount.

2./ Ownership will be restricted to personal property in use and one business enterprise actively participated in by the owner.

3./ Property lot sizes will be restricted to one acre per house or what's required for the proposed business, negotiated with the town individually.

4./ Inheritance will be restricted to personal property and one business enterprise.

5./ No public resource such as land, forests, waterways, mines, and power generators can be individually owned.

6./ Use of publicly owned resources needs to be compensated for by business owners through appropriate contribution to the public good.

7./ No public infrastructure such as roads, bridges, waterways, ports, etc. can be privately owned.

8./ No public institutions such as schools, hospitals, jails, etc. can be privately owned.

9./ Businesses are to be routinely monitored for environmental protection, public safety, and ethical behavior

10./ Employees will have to be given vacation time, sick leave, maternity leave, and the right to unionize.

11./ Environment protection to be strictly enforced including habitat for wildlife.

12./ No basic personal needs (like an individual dwelling) can be exploited by charging rent.

" I see what you mean by 'no parasites will thrive in our midst'," Holly laughed aloud - this list may be overkill, but I love it!"

"Are you sure that it won't throw the baby out with the bathwater? I mean, won't it kill off free enterprise initiatives?" Cathy wondered aloud "who would want to start an enterprise with so many restrictions?"

"I'll tell you who," Morgan defended his proposal "decent human beings who want to create things rather than just get rich from other people's efforts."

"You may be right about that," Holly added "I don't see any unfair restriction in this scheme. Creative people with original ideas will find lots of help to create products that will benefit us all. I am ready to vote for it."

"Of course, a lot of details need to be worked out because your list contains only things not allowed," Gordon commented "but we need to make decisions on two particular issues: how does the private sector create money, and what happens to claims of pre-war ownership?

Several council members were nodding their heads in agreement and all looked at Morgan to see how he would respond.

"It's relatively easy to deal with these issues if we don't overcomplicate things. You'll have to bear with me because I need to explain a few basic assumptions."

"Go ahead, Morgan, we have the time" Holly encouraged their deputy mayor.

"OK, first of all, the most fundamental assumption is that all natural resources in our territory are common public property, owned by all of us collectively. That includes land, water, forests, and mineral resources. It also includes the existing power generating and manufacturing capacity that is required for our basic necessities. BB is in full charge of all of these and manages and allocates their use based on the need to maintain an adequate minimum living standard for each citizen. This is non-negotiable. However, there will be surplus capacity in all of these resources and that's where the private sector comes in. Whenever a private citizen has an idea for luxury items (anything beyond the basics) he or she wants to produce, then two things will be required: resources and manpower. Resources can be allocated from access capacity by BB, based on the needs and feasibility of the proposed project. Manpower will be provided by those who want to work for the enterprise to earn money that they can use to purchase these or other luxury items (not part of the basic needs freely distributed)."

"Where do they get the money?" Holly interrupted.

"Money, in the form of crypto-currency, will be created and managed by BB in a central bank and an initial sum will be allocated to each citizen. Those who want to support the enterprise can pool their money to fund it and then they can hire a workforce to be paid from this pool. Employees can use their income to purchase the luxury items produced in our town, thereby replenishing the cash holdings of the enterprises. So the money goes around from businesses to individuals and back to businesses again, as it used to be."

"What about the initial allocation of crypto currency? What is it based on?" Tracy wanted to know.

"It will be the same amount for each citizen, based on BB's calculation on the amount needed to start up viable enterprises."

"What about pre-war ownership?" Cathy wanted to know. "Some people worked through their lives to earn a retirement fund or comfortable living, are we going to dispossess them of what they had earned with hard work?"

"Let me put it this way," Morgan replied "the war dispossessed all of us of almost everything. It was the greatest equalizer in human history because for two years after it was over, we barely managed to survive. Now we are all equal, with an equal chance for success or failure. Nobody has to worry about maintaining their comfortable and adequate living standard, BB will take care of that. All the rest is luxury for those who want to work for it. Let's not drag past inequality back into our lives. Everybody will be provided for and that should be enough for healthy, happy existence."

There was a long silence following Morgan's list while everybody was mulling over the implications. After a while, they all decided to approve Morgan's suggestion, ready to submit it to referendum.

~~~

While Oroville was debating their new constitution, debating time in Sacramento was over. Jonathan's suggestion to adopt a resource-based economy, without currency of any kind, was adopted by the council unanimously. People were so tired of never-ending wrangling over money and the resulting paralysis of progress, coupled with gross inequality that they listened to Jonathan's arguments on how they would all be better by stopping the enormous waste of resources caused by maintaining a financial system. Their computer recalled a long-forgotten experiment that started in the US in the mid-twentieth century, called the Venus Project, which was a model of what was called a Resource-Based Economy or RBE. Quoting from their manifesto:

"In a Resource-Based Economy, all goods and services are available to all people without the need for means of exchange such as money, credits, barter, or any other means. For this to be achieved, all resources must be declared as the common heritage of all Earth's inhabitants. Equipped with the latest scientific and technological marvels, humankind could reach extremely high productivity levels and create an abundance of resources."

This was in total alignment with Jonathan's essay on "The Nature of Money" and was convincing to most people who just got tired of the never-ending fighting over distribution. The main point everybody understood was that with automation, robotics, and AI computer control, there was no need for scarcity anymore. With intelligent planning, lack of wasteful duplication, and competition, every conceivable and healthy human need could be satisfied by production and distribution alone.

Jonathan's proposal was submitted to the citizenry, in a city-wide referendum and it received overwhelming approval. People were tired of the old and were ready to try something never before tried, wanting to give it a chance. They understood that with their incorruptible Omega computer safeguarding their basic needs they could only win. So they voted for it.

The victory celebration included Jonathan's and Octavia's wedding, attended by their closest friends from the old Sacramento Resistance Movement, plus a few unexpected visitors from Yuba City and even Oroville.

~~~

Not everybody was happy in Sacramento. The old tyrannical mayor, Donald Mouch, now serving a 10-year long sentence in the Sacramento County Jail, had many followers, including all the previous elite who now saw the disappearance of their privileges forever in the new system the town adopted. Many of them decided that it was now or never to make a last stand against this new Communist abomination. Some of them, looking for help and allies, had heard rumors that Stockton, 48 miles south of them was ruled by over 200 escaped and armed prisoners and that gave them the courage to stage a prison break for ex-mayor Mouch and to steal two vehicles to help them escape to Stockton.

Jonathan heard of this new development during his wedding reception when a disheveled and alarmed Rafiq Shlimon, his second in command, burst through the front door of the reception hall.

"Jon, you won't believe this but we are facing a coup by Mouch and his gang!"

"What do you mean? He is in prison!"

"Not anymore, I have just got word that during a prison riot staged by his supporters they managed to spring him together with a dozen or so of his supporters."

"When did all this happen?"

"During the early morning hours."

"How come we just found out?"

"So much confusion delayed getting reliable data and nobody wanted to interrupt your wedding unless absolutely sure of the facts."

"Where are they now? Why haven't they been recaptured?"

"By the time the guards restored peace in the jail and found out that Mouch and a dozen others were missing, they had a good head start."

"Head start to where?"

"Apparently, they are on their way to Stockton in stolen vehicles. There is no way to catch up with them before they get there. And you know what's going on in Stockton?"

"Yes, I know and now we need to do some serious thinking. I'm sure Mouch and his gang want to convince the leaders in Stockton to attack and plunder Sacramento and that means another bloody war. We need to alert Redding to the need for their army. It will take some time before they can get here, but it will also take time for the Stockton gangsters to get organized. Even if they are inclined to try it."

"OK, I alert the other towns and the Omegas, do you want a conference?"

"Yes, without delay. This is a serious threat to the whole valley and everybody in the alliance must be consulted. Let me know when they are ready to discuss this. I guess this is the end of my wedding celebration."

"Sorry about that, Jon, I'm sure Octavia won't be thrilled."

"She'll understand, I know. Now I have to go and tell her." Jonathan walked back to the center where his wife was surrounded by well-wishers. He stopped for a second, admiring her radiant beauty in her wedding dress, and, with a deep sigh, he walked up to her and whispered the bad news into her ear. Her darkening expression told her admirers that the reception was probably over and better have a last piece of cake before they were asked to leave.

It took a while to get everybody connected and told the bad news. There were a lot of angry comments from the participants about the low lives they had to deal with but the Omegas took it in stride.

*"It was not entirely unexpected,"* BB started the discussion *"and we are not completely unprepared. The most important question now is how we can avoid violence that could result in casualties in case it comes to a battle between the Stockton gang and our soldiers from Redding. We have an idea but would like to hear suggestions from all of you before announcing our own."*

"Isn't there another bridge that we could blow up? Like we did at Redding?" Colonel Majors asked the obvious question. "It worked before, I don't see why it wouldn't work again."

"There are several bridges on I5 but that's the last thing we want to do!" Jonathan replied. "The worst outcome would be if the gang remained in Stockton, fortified their position, and stayed there, regardless of what Mouch wants them to do."

"Why did you say that?" Anita seemed puzzled "I thought that the objective was to avoid bloodshed."

BB replied in its measured, emotionless tone.

*"Anita, I understand that you want to protect your soldiers and, if the thugs stayed in Stockton, it would work in the short term. However, being entrenched there and maybe getting stronger would pose a threat forever for Sacramento and the whole Valley. However, there is an even more important reason to get rid of them once and for all. We want to liberate Stockton so that town with huge industrial resources could be incorporated into our alliance. Apart from the humanitarian reasons many of you share, in the long run we all would be better off."*

"All this is true, but if they can't come here, can't stay there and we can't blow them up halfway, then what the hell are we going to do?" Rafiq expressed the thought on everybody's mind.

*"We have always been in favor of subterfuge and infiltration. Use brain power rather than firepower if only possible."* BB resumed its explanation. *"We have to convince them that we are easy to defeat and that would be enough to motivate them to start a campaign, using less than their total strength because they don't want to lose their grip on Stockton either. Now Mouch knows nothing about the Redding National Guard, committed to defending the valley, and, as far as he knows, we have weapons but no trained soldiers to oppose them. So he is confident that 200 armed gangsters can knock us over quite easily. We only need to reinforce the advice he is going to give the thugs."*

"And how can we accomplish that?" asked Morgan Webster speaking from Oroville.

*"Well, we have a suggestion. Why not send another robot with a white flag, offering a peace treaty between the two towns and economic cooperation that would make life more comfortable for them? That should convince them that we are scared and easy to defeat?"*

"That might work, if we word the message well, projecting both fear and defiance" Anita mused aloud. "But then what? They will be still coming even if not with full force, but it still means battle with casualties. Not that I am afraid to fight, but I am willing to explore all thoughts that would minimize the bloodshed."

*"We understand, Anita and we have a suggestion on how to accomplish that. The most direct route from Stockton to us is on I5 and we don't see any reason why they would choose a detour through I99. Even if they did that, we could easily block that route, forcing them back to I5. If you look at the map, you'll see that I5 goes over a 1000-foot-long bridge, high over a ravine and a river, just south of the Twin Cities intersection. We can mine the road both north and south of the bridge. Once they are on it, we can blow up the road both ahead and behind them, trapping them on the bridge. The only way they can get off is by jumping in the river 30 feet below them. They would have no other choice than to surrender. We could leave them a rope to climb down from the bridge one by one. Once they are captured and disarmed, we can transport them back to Sacramento's maximum-security prison. The much smaller garrison they left in Stockton then can be easily dealt with."*

"Wow!" Anita exclaimed, with clear admiration in her voice "are you sure you haven't written a textbook on military strategy?"

*"No, Anita, but I have several textbooks in my database with great examples we can follow"* BB answered without any suggestion of being flattered. *"So are we ready to accept this plan?"*

The reply from all participants was a resounding 'yes'. For the first time since the bad news broke, everybody started feeling optimistic that this crisis, like many others, would be successfully survived.

# Stockton

Stockton's gang leader, Cliff Monger rested comfortably in the Mayor's chair - *his* chair now, contemplating his next move. Occupying the town for the past two years gave him and his gang an easy living, much more pleasant than the jail they broke out of when the war removed most of the guards and they could stage a successful riot, resulting in their freedom. After they armed themselves from the abandoned police station, they had no trouble with the citizenry - those who resisted were beaten or shot, and the rest just cowered in their houses, hoping not to be noticed by the gangsters. They sent out 'procurement parties' as they called them to collect all the food they could find but lately, the picking became thinner and thinner. The whole town was running out of reserves and he knew that soon they would have to move on, finding new sources of supplies. He was in a foul mood, thinking about how he had to give up the comfort he got used to, when his second in command, Kevin, marched into his office, pushing a stranger ahead of him.

"Boss, we have some visitors, they say from Sacramento, this guy is their leader and he says he wants to talk to you."

"Oh yeah? How many visitors?"

"About a dozen. They say they have escaped from prison and want to join us here."

Looking at the short, tough-looking man, he realized that he was wearing prison garb, so he felt confident that this could be for real.

"What's your name?" he addressed the waiting man who had not said a word yet.

"Donald Mouch, and before you ask, I used to be Mayor of Sacramento when I was overthrown by some Communist sympathizers and thrown in jail. I and my supporters managed to break out earlier today, steal two cars, and come right here, looking for allies. We had heard rumors that this town had enough armed people to defend us from the Sacramento gang if they came after us."

"Very interesting, if true." Cliff looked at the man who stood there, looking relaxed and confident, not like most of the terrified townspeople he was used to seeing. "So tell me, what's going on in Sacramento? They sent a robot here to spy on us, but we got rid of it, however, we know nothing about anything else."

"The town is doing well, plenty of food from their factories and greenhouses, they still have power from their hydro and solar generators, but their soldiers are all gone to fight the Russians during the war, so their Army base is mostly deserted. They have plenty of weapons but nobody is trained to use them. Unfortunately, their leaders are some crazy Communist sympathizers and want to create a workers' paradise, on the old Soviet model. I refused to cooperate with them, so they threw me in jail together with my supporters."

"Plenty of food, did you say? No trained soldiers? Sounds too good to be true. I'll have to think about it. In the meantime, find yourself some place to stay, get rid of those prison uniforms and, if you are hungry, the nice folks in town will help you if you just tell them that Cliff sent you."

Mouch was led out of his office and the Boss sat there for a long time, trying to decide if he could trust this man. He was usually suspicious of anything that sounded too good to be true, they turned out to be less than advertised. Finally, he decided to sleep on it and wait for further development. Maybe the Sacramento people will send somebody after their escaped prisoners and then he could get more information helping him to make up his mind.

His assessment of the situation turned out correct the next day when he was told that another robot arrived from Sacramento and brought a message from their leaders. The message was a letter in an envelope, offering cooperation between the cities and mutual assistance. The wording sounded conciliatory as if worried about offending him, respectfully addressing him as Mayor of Stockton. The conciliatory tone could only mean one thing: they were scared. If they were scared of 200 armed ex-prisoners, then they must have a good reason for it, so maybe he could find his next comfortable power base there. He decided to give himself a few days to make up his mind but, in the meantime, he would pump Mr. Mouch and his people for more information about Sacramento - if he was going to attack them, he needed as many relevant facts as he could get from the only source available.

Unknown to him, Sacramento was getting ready for the expected confrontation. Colonel Majors organized an expeditionary force, with ten trucks and a hundred soldiers with their emergency kits, dispatched on as fast a drive as they could manage on the complicated path of still intact bridges and roads toward Sacramento. If their plans worked out, they would not be needed, but she didn't want to take any chances. Anything could go wrong and Sacramento needed trained soldiers to stop the convict gang in case they managed to avoid the trap set for them.

In the meantime, the Sacramento Army Base demolition team got organized to carry out their plans. After studying the maps, they decided that they had to lay four mines at both ends of both spans of the selected bridge on I5, which were actually two parallel bridges for both the northbound and southbound traffic. In case the convicts chose a longer route either on I99 or even more unlikely I84, they selected a bridge just on the north edge of the city of Lodi. where they could be stopped and forced back to I5. The mines were set to be detonated by remote control, but only if necessary. Each mine would be monitored by drones, watching the Stockton gang leave the town and head north. If their plan worked as imagined, they would arrive at the selected bridge on I5 and then the timing would be critical. The bridge was long enough for the entire convoy of the gang's vehicles to be on it at the same time unless they were driving spread out longer than expected - a very unlikely event.

They were working at a feverish pace, there was no way to know how long it would take the attackers to arrive and, there was always a possibility that they wouldn't come at all. That would be the worst-case scenario because it would result in a stalemate and then they would need

Redding's soldiers to attack the convicts inside Stockton, which could result in unacceptable casualties on both sides, and even kill innocent civilians as collateral damage. It took Anita's soldiers a whole day to make it to Sacramento and they wasted no time establishing a defensive position south of the city, ready to confront the enemy once it was determined which highway leading into the city they chose.

Waiting for the attack that may not come at all was very hard on everybody. Everything was ready, the traps were set, and they had nothing to do but wait. Finally, the Sacramento leaders decided to try once more to encourage an attack, so they sent another robot, with an even more conciliatory message: "Would Stockton be interested in signing a non-aggression treaty so they could work out a mutually beneficial trade agreement?"

That message was all the Boss needed to make up his mind. If the Sacramento leaders were that eager to start a peaceful relationship with escaped prisoners, then they really must be as scared of them as Mouch kept insisting they were. After he decided to leave a garrison of 50 of his gang to keep the Stockton residents safely terrorized, he would load up 10 trucks with 150 of his gang, all the weapons, and ammunition that they might need, and set out to make another successful conquest. He was fully confident that he would prevail against another town of defenseless civilians.

After studying the map carefully, he decided to take the shortest route on I5 because he knew that the road was passable - after all, Mouch managed to reach him coming that way. He had no information on road conditions on

I99, so why risk unpleasant surprises that could force him to turn back and waste time? His trucks were traveling in a tight formation, each one with one of his gang scanning the road with binoculars, looking for any sign of danger or possible ambush. They were already on the long bridge over a ravine when one of his spotters called out in alarm:

"There is a drone hovering over us, Boss, maybe somebody is watching us. Should I shoot it down?"

"What the fuck is a drone doing here, over our road?" he asked in alarm, "by all means shoot the damn thing down."

While his people kept missing the drone, the first truck he was riding on reached the end of the bridge, ready to proceed, when a tremendous explosion ahead of him threw huge pieces of concrete into the air, creating a huge gap in the bridge, forcing his driver to slam down on his brake, just before they would have plunged through the hole into the ravine below.

"What the fuck, the bastards mined the road. We have to turn back and find a different route. Signal the last of the trucks to back off the bridge and turn around!" he instructed his driver who jumped off the truck, trotted back across the bridge, and spoke to the driver of the last truck in the convoy. As it started to slowly back off the bridge, another huge explosion stopped him dead in his tracks, trapping the whole convoy on the bridge. The only way off was jumping into the river, 30 feet below. By this time his men stopped firing at the drone over their heads without apparent damage to the tiny target.

Not knowing what to do, suddenly they heard a loud voice that apparently came from a concealed speaker hidden by some bushes on the other side of the bridge. More than anything else, that disembodies voice drove home their helpless situation.

"Attention escaped convicts. You are ordered to surrender to the City of Sacramento. You will leave all your weapons in your trucks and line up on the right side of the bridge. You will find a rope long enough to reach the bottom of the ravine, on the right side of the river, from where you can clamber up to the road surface. Once on the road, you slowly march forward to a waiting truck 300 feet ahead of you. There you will be arrested, handcuffed, and loaded up for transportation back to prison. If anyone tries to leave the road before the arrest, he will be instantly shot by sharp shooters watching through telescopic rifles. If you follow these orders, then nobody will be hurt. You have half an hour to start following these orders. If not, we will blow up your trucks with artillery weapons that are trained on you from both ends of the bridge. Anyone still in their trucks will be killed."

The message was over and the Boss couldn't think of any way to escape from the trap. Reluctantly, he left his guns on his seat and climbed down onto the road. His troops, seeing the inevitable, followed him to the side of the bridge where they did find the rope the message told them about. It took over an hour to have them all safely handcuffed inside the transport vehicle and moved away toward Sacramento. When they were all gone, the heavy artillery started firing on the trucks, engulfing them in flames. They weren't taking any chances of being shot at from any of the trucks just in case some convicts stayed behind, hoping to escape later somehow.

"This was too easy," Anita was shaking her head, looking at all the wreckage covering the destroyed span of the bridge.

"It's not all over yet," Captain Loomis, her second in command reminded her. "We don't know how many of these thugs are still in Stockton. We have to deal with them and that won't be without a fight."

"There is one way to find out," she agreed. "Signal the rest of our force in Sacramento to join us and then we'll move on. Tell the demolition team to disarm the mines on the other span of the bridge, I don't want any accidents while we are on it. They can do it while we are waiting for reinforcement."

~~~

Donald Mouch was waiting anxiously in Stockton for the good word about Cliff's forces 'liberating' Sacramento, so he could return to his rightful place in the Mayor's office. He had made a deal with the Boss that he would assure a safe and comfortable base for his troops in the occupied town where they would have access to unlimited food and any item of comfort they required. He promised them unopposed plunder in surrounding smaller towns like Woodland, Davis, Dixon, Roselin, Rocklin, and Auburn if they left Sacramento in his control. He had very specific plans on how to punish all those Commies who thwarted his plans before, with the help of the damn computer. He was looking forward to finding and punishing Mike

Sutherland, who had wormed his way into his confidence, only to corrupt his Omega computer and turn it against him. This time he will do the opposite, with a gun aimed at his head and some nails strategically placed under his fingernails. Nobody was going to stop him this time.

That's how far he got in mulling over his plans when a loud voice jolted him out of his reverie.

"This message is for the rest of your gang still left behind in Stockton. The main force you sent to plunder Sacramento has been stopped, their trucks destroyed and any of them still alive arrested. You are surrounded by trained and superior army forces and you have half an hour to come out, unarmed, with your hands up in the air. To avoid any unnecessary bloodshed we urge you not to try anything foolish but to obey these instructions. You have half an hour to comply before we attack in force."

The message was over and Mouch couldn't believe his ears. He rushed to the window, looking around both ways on the deserted street but didn't see a single soldier. Maybe this was a bluff, tried by some of the citizens who wanted to take advantage of the main force being out of town. He wasn't going to be tricked into surrendering to an unseen enemy. However, he wasn't in charge here, he had to wait what the Boss's choice for the interim leader would decide. He didn't have to wait for long. The door to the mayor's office burst open and the man coming through barked at him.

"Get your ass out here. You will go and find out if this new threat is for real. Go out there with a white flag, hand in the air, and see what you find. If you are not back in half an hour we'll know that it's true, we are surrounded. Then we have to decide if we can break out of here. Now move your fucking ass.!"

"You can't do this to me," Mouch whined, "they will shoot me on sight!"

"Too bad, asshole, you got us into this mess, now do what you are told before you have a more unpleasant choice to make."

Mouch didn't dare to object anymore, he gingerly took the white flag shoved into his hand and tremulously exited the building onto the empty street. He didn't know which way to go, but it was decided for him immediately. The same booming voice from some unseen loudspeaker instructed him to walk forward the way he was facing and walk until he arrived at the next intersection, then turn to his right. He did as he was told and, after the turn, he was met by a group of soldiers in army guard uniforms, weapons trained on him. With shaking legs he approached and stopped when a woman, also in uniform stopped him.

"How many of you are inside there?" she asked without preamble.

"I think about fifty" he replied, finding it difficult to force the words through his throat.

"What are they armed with?" was the next question and he could only confirm handguns, rifles, and shotguns that he had seen.

"Any automatic weapons, like submachine guns?" she wanted to know.

"Not that I know, I haven't seen any but they may have some, I wouldn't know. I'm not part of the gang, they kept me a prisoner." Mouch tried but received no sympathy.

"Ok," she instructed one of the soldiers "handcuff this one and load him up to the transport truck. We'll wait half an hour and, if they don't surrender, we'll have to go in and take them out. With as little risk to ourselves as possible."

She got this far with her instructions when suddenly she heard gunfire coming from the surrounded building and saw many men running at top speed, toward her position, firing wildly in their direction.

She wasted no time but blew her whistle signaling order to start firing back at the enemy.

The gun battle didn't last long, the attackers were untrained civilians, firing without taking aim and no match for her soldiers. Still, there were casualties on both sides and a few of the convicts lay on the pavement motionless, probably dead. Several of her soldiers were lightly wounded, including a scratch on the side of her head, oozing out a trickle of blood onto her uniform.

After the wounded convicts were given first aid, handcuffed, and loaded up for transportation, she talked into her comm-set, notifying Sacramento that the battle was over. Sacramento was safely past another danger, they could go back to rebuilding their lives.

# Hopestead

The celebration in Sacramento went way over all previous records. Jonathan and Octavia resumed their interrupted wedding reception and all the guests pretended that it was one long party they never wanted to end. Anita Majors, however, had to spend some time in hospital because the scratch on the side of her head from a bullet grazing her skull turned out to be more serious than initially thought - she did have a mild concussion that required days of rest, so she was left out of the party, but they promised her to save the last piece of cake in her honor.

Mr. Mouch, recaptured in Stockton, was transported back to his familiar prison cell, all the other prisoners were deposited in Sacramento's maximum-security prison, awaiting trial for their crimes committed since their prison break. Several of them would face murder and rape charges, as soon as all the evidence from Stockton was collected.

And, predictably enough, BB reminded Mike and me of the deal we had made about reactivating the Stockton Omega computer. Regardless of how inconvenient this was, a deal is a deal and we couldn't even grumble about it because BB had already fulfilled his part of the bargain: Gordon had arrived at Scott's house with his backhoe and with careful pushes and nudges managed to set it back on its foundation. Not only that, but with the help of volunteers from Hopestead, they managed to rebuild his roof, so there was no reason why the old recluse couldn't return home and liberate our motor home. There was much rejoicing in Hopestead because, true to his form, Scott kept complaining about everything: the food, the bed, Robyn's ministration over his wounds, even about the cats jumping in his lap when he wasn't looking.

So, here we were, Mike and I, ready to make the long trip to Stockton, equipped with BB's newest software and communication package.

Before we left, I reminded BB that this was going to be the absolutely last - watch my lips say it - the VERY LAST trip we would have to make.

The trip to Stockton took us a full day, too late to do any work by the time we arrived but a room was prepared for us in the home of one of the residents who insisted on treating us like royalty after we had 'liberated' their town from the gangsters. There was no point telling them that we had nothing to do with it, we were only errand boys to restart their computer but, as far as they knew, we had come from Sacramento, therefore we were celebrities. Our host was a tall, graying man of middle age, telling us how he had had to hide his wife and eighteen-year-old daughter in the attic every time the gangsters showed up demanding food.

"Nothing is too good for you kind people for ending this nightmare for us."

"So who is going to be in charge now that your mayor had been murdered? Whom do we have to ask for help if and when we need anything?"

"The deputy mayor will be available 24 hours a day for you two, his name is Trevor too, you will meet him for breakfast tomorrow and make plans for the day. However, you have had a long day and I suggest you turn in for the night. I hope you enjoyed dinner, sparse though it was, the thugs didn't leave us much to celebrate with."

"Thanks, George, we appreciate your kind hospitality and now, if you don't mind, we'd really like to sleep. This was quite a day"

I thought I would discuss plans for the next day with Mike but he was asleep the second his head hit the pillow. My head followed suit very quickly indeed.


The next morning, after a modest but nutritious breakfast we were introduced to Trevor Smythe, Stockton's deputy mayor who led us into his office where the computer was now lying dormant after the convict leader had disconnected it by pulling out all the plugs and wires he could find. Obviously, he never wanted the outside world to find out about the goings-on in Stockton. So Mike and I were busy reconnecting everything and restarting Omega's Operating System from scratch which involved a lot of setup and initialization, required by a sophisticated AI quantum computer. I hadn't been sure if I still remembered how to do this, my brain was a bit fuzzy about the exact sequence and syntax of the commands we had to use, but it must have been of the "you can never forget to ride a bicycle" category because it all came back to me remarkably easily. It took us a few hours but finally, Omega 2100 was up and running, and, after we got it in touch with BB, we were ready to leave. There was still time to make it home before nightfall and we didn't want to risk fording our pesky stream in the dark. The last sight we had of the Omega in Stockton was its rippling lights on its communication controller, indicating that it was in a lightning-speed discussion with BB, getting its education on how to adjust to self-awareness. We wished them good luck and closed the door behind us. We had a brief stop in Sacramento, congratulating Jonathan and Octavia on their recent nuptials, and then Mike stepped on his pedal to get us back home at top speed.

The next morning we woke up to a beautiful day, at home finally, without anything to worry about but our own projects waiting for us. And projects we had, coming out of our ears. Actually, we arrived in time to participate in celebrating the successful completion of one of them: Martha informed me, as soon as I opened my eye:

"Trevor, you are cordially invited to today's grand opening of our water wheel power system. We don't have any grains to grind yet, but the generator is hooked up, so we can start recharging the batteries without shutting everything down that is powered by the solar panels."

"As again, you had all the fun here while Mike and I were saving the Valley out on the road. It's not fair, but it's over. I have BB's solemn promise that no more Omegas to activate anywhere it is aware of."

"That doesn't exclude him becoming aware of more later?" Martha was teasing me, of course, so I ignored it.

"Do I get breakfast first?"

"I wouldn't want you to lose your stamina without proper nutrition," Martha smiled at me "last night's celebration of our reunion must have been very hard on you. So, use the bathroom before anyone else wakes up and meet me in the kitchen!"

I followed her advice and I found the bathroom unoccupied which was a rare event in Hopestead. We must build that second bathroom without delay before someone has an accident. Now that the outhouse was gone, and by a universal vote we would never rebuild it, bathroom shortage became critical. One thing at a time, I told myself, as I was going to the kitchen to meet my well-deserved breakfast.

Slowly, bit by bit, the whole household was awake, crowding the kitchen and clamoring for breakfast, so Martha and I walked outside to make more room for the hungry horde. Sooner or later, we'll need to expand the kitchen too to keep up with the growing population.

"So, show me what happened at the water mill before everybody will crowd around it and I would have to jump up and down to see anything!"

Martha laughed at my silly mood and walked with me to the river where we had the channel dug to lead the water to the big wheel that was inside a deep trench, attached to the mill's hardware. Following the channel from the mill to the river, we arrived at the end where a sluice gate was holding the water back from the river side. It was attached to a crank mechanism, suspended from a lumber frame and the gate would be sliding in grooves that were set in the sides of the canal as it was raised or lowered to control the water flow.

"Alan, Doug, and Galen constructed it while you were gallivanting again" Martha just wouldn't let up with the teasing but seeing my face, she added: "I'm sorry you missed it babe, but at least you made it back for the opening."

Soon more and more of the people joined us, looking at the contraption with pride, nudging and backslapping each other, waiting for the whole team to be there. Finally, Cathy, the grand designer of the whole system arrived and took her position at the crank of the sluice gate.

"Ready, everybody?" she asked theatrically, and, hearing the deafening chorus shouting 'yes' and "get on with it" and other affirmation of readiness, she started cranking up the gate. The water from the river was only a trickle first, then a steady flow and, when the gate was all the way up, a rushing swirling torrent. We all rushed to the other end to see the water tumble and fall down on the paddles. Nothing happened for a little while but then we saw the wheel jerk into motion, very slowly starting to move and, finally rotating at a steady rpm. The water disappeared under the wheel, only to reappear at the inlet end of the outflow canal and make its way back toward the river joining it 300 feet away where the two water levels equalized. A deafening 'hurrah' and other oaths of approval celebrated this spectacular success.

"You haven't seen anything yet," Brian announced proudly, just look at my generator!"

That's when I noticed our old gasoline-powered generator, sitting in its own wooden box, inside the stone-lined space that housed the wheel's mechanism, and the fan belt connecting the two. There was nothing else to see until Brian reached inside the box and flipped a switch. Then we could see what he meant because a powerful electric light shone on the wheel mechanism to show us that we had another source of electricity besides the solar panels.

"Now you can recharge the batteries without shutting everything down first" Brian announced, looking proudly at his baby. We rewarded him with another 'hurrah' and then the grand opening celebration was over.

Before going back to the house, Cathy lowered the sluice gate to stop the water flow.

"No point wearing out the mechanism when we don't need to." she explained, "waste not, want not" she added and we had to agree.

"So, what other entertainment is on schedule for today?" I asked and got an instant reply from several people.

"You'll have to start digging the ground to lead the water and the sewer pipes from the house to the barn. You are our digging expert and the existence of the second bathroom depends on you. The sooner you have the pipes laid, the sooner we can get a functional second bathroom."

Entertainment it was not, but by this time my expertise with the shovel was so firmly established that I couldn't shove the task on anyone else, so grudgingly I took my less than beloved spade and started digging. It was more than 300 feet from the house to the barn and it took me the rest of the morning to dig that trench about a foot deep. Jennifer rewarded me with a very nice lunch with hot porridge and cooked vegetables. During lunch, I was thinking about the plan to use the old farmhouse's septic system, built for one family, for our big crowd, and started to worry. Could it cope with that amount of waste from so many people? What else can we do? What if we tried finding a composting toilet in the Live Oak Building Supply store? Adrien could use the compost in her greenhouse for sure. We would have to go there again soon to bring back more lumber and water pipes, so we might as well do it before committing to lay 300 feet of drain pipes. I wished I had thought of it before I dug such a deep trench for the 4" drain pipe that we might never need. Oh well, live and learn, as my old teacher used to say when I did something stupid.

Before taking off on another scouting trip I asked everyone what they needed from a hardware store, so I wouldn't have to go back again in a few days. Once I had a list of requests I was ready to go but then Galen said he wanted to come with me.

"Trevor, remember that big truck we found in that agricultural factory on the outskirt of Gridley?"

"Sure I do, but its batteries must be completely drained by now and we can't tow it back with the van. It's too big."

"I know, Trevor, but if I can remove its batteries, then we can take them home, recharge them here and then reinstall them in the truck. Then I can drive it home under its own power."

"That's an idea, worth a try I'm sure. So bring your tools and let's go."

The trip was now so familiar, after having done it twice, that we got there in record time. I left Galen at the truck he selected, so he could remove its batteries while I made my way down to Live Oak and started loading up the supplies on my wish list. Once the most important items were secured, I started looking around for a composting toilet. It was a huge store and it took me a long time to cover every square foot from one end to the other. I was ready to give up when I noticed a double steel door in the back, so I thought: maybe outside? I went through and found myself in a magic place loaded with absolutely everything anyone in the building trade might need. I found jacuzzis of different sizes and colors, I found tillers, snowblowers, augers, and, to my bitter chagrin: a trench digger, looking brand new. That would have saved me hours of hard work this morning! Further back in the yard I found coiled drain pipes, cement blocks, bathtubs and, I couldn't believe my eyes - a composting toilet, still wrapped in plastic. I would need Galen's help to drag it to the van and load it up, so I drove back to where I had left him, and he was still there, just pulling the heavy truck batteries to the side of the road, ready for me. We loaded them up in record time because I wanted to get back to my prized find before it disappeared into thin air. No, it was still there waiting for me patiently. We loaded it up and decided that the trailer had enough to carry for one trip and headed home.

When I explained to the Hopesteaders my brilliant idea of how we can use a composting toilet in the barn, the suggestion was greeted with some dubious muttering. Finally, Mike asked with a voice that was mildly suspicious:

"Are you sure Trevor, you are not just trying to save the trouble of laying down the sewage pipes?"

"That too, Mike, but ask Adrien if she can use the compost in the greenhouse?"

"I sure can, guys, no question about it. Just leave Trevor alone, it was a brilliant idea and you'll just have to get used to using it according to instruction."

"How many ways can you take a shit?" Mike wanted to know "I never needed instructions before?!"

"Simple precautions if I remember well from the cottage where we had one. Don't use too much toilet paper, sprinkle it with the accelerator after every time and keep it moist if it gets too dry."

"You mean there is a science to taking a shit?" Mike was rolling his eyes "one always learns something new. So, where is the accelerator we are supposed to sprinkle it with? Trevor, my friend, did you bring any?"

"No, but I can bring some out next time I visit. I'm sure they have some somewhere. It's a very big store, they have everything."

By the time we resolved all these thorny issues, it was mid-afternoon and I didn't feel like doing any more work, so I went back to writing my new sci-fi story about the human migrants who had to escape Earth because climate change slowly made their planet unlivable. My last thought before I settled down at my desk was how Chris was going to like it when I finished. Of all of us, he was the one who took it most seriously that someday we may have to do exactly that: take to the stars and find a new home. The thought of leaving Hopestead behind was too painful to contemplate, so I put it out of my mind with the comforting thought: "not in my lifetime" - but then I saw Martha with her swelling belly and I had a sudden dread: "what kind of world have we brought that child into?" Too late to worry about it now, I told myself, we'll just have to do the best we can. We have always found a way to cope.

# Chico

Chris was talking to an increasingly frustrating Omega computer. For the past hour, he had tried to convince the stubborn machine that he needed more resources to run his space-drive experiment. The conversation so far hadn't produced any tangible commitment, the damn computer kept telling him to submit the results of his calculations so it could be evaluated by an independent agency, such as all the Omegas together.

*"It is an important project and you may be right about the long-term implication,"* Omega 1850 kept saying *"but we have to make sure that it is viable at this stage and won't waste any of our resources needlessly. I didn't say 'no', only suggested waiting for corroboration of your theories."*

"Wait for what? For the next tornado to tear us to pieces?" Chris was in tears with frustration.

*"A few days or even weeks won't make any difference in the long-term outcome. So, be patient and I'll get back to you as soon as possible."*

Chris's comm channel disconnected from Omega, ending their conversation.

Just as he was trying to decide what to do next, Richard approached him, coming from the direction of their engineering department.

"Hey, Chris, why the glum face?"

"I was just now advised by our lord and master to be patient until my theory gets independently verified."

"You know, it wouldn't hurt to have a second opinion. The stakes couldn't be higher." Richard cautioned the frustrated scientist.

"You too, Richard?"

"Yes, me too and that doesn't mean that we have no hope. I have just come from Engineering and they told me that they could build your experimental drive from supplies they already have, so you don't need Omega's help."

"Did you just say what I thought I heard you say?" Chris's face lit up with hope. "How long would it take them?"

"Probably a month, unless they run into unexpected problems. The trick is to build it small enough to fit inside our little rocket. Another complication is fitting the tiny micro-fusion reactor that is needed to power your drive. Shrinking spacetime, even on such a small scale, requires a lot of energy, as you know."

"That's great, Richard, I hope the tornadoes leave us alone for a while. If it can be done and if it works, then I don't need any corroboration of my theory, I'll have a practical demonstration. Then I'll watch Omega eating crow for a change."

"I knew that you had a noble motivation in mind!" Richard laughed "so let's talk about the practical difficulties if and when this experiment can get underway. Have you thought about where you want to send it?"

"The Moon would be the perfect target. It took the Apollo rockets three days to get there, my drive could do it in minutes according to my calculations. The drive could shut down automatically when the rocket reaches the vicinity of the Moon and then telemetry data, as well as live photos, could be sent back. If that doesn't convince our Omega, nothing will."

"OK, that's a plan, now we'll have to talk to the engineers and see how we can speed things up."

~~~

The month flew by as only months can and, by the end of all that nervous waiting, finger chewing, setbacks, and successes, Chris and Richard could look at the shiny metal cylinder on the launching pad with pride and trepidation. Would it work, or would it be a spectacular failure? There was only one way to find out and the experiment was set for the next morning. They knew it would be a sleepless night.

The next morning all the engineers who built the drive were present for the launch, with instruments piled on a workbench they wheeled out to the launch site, ready to receive the telemetric data and the photographs expected within half an hour after the launch.

Chris was all nerves, chewing on his fingernail, unaware of how he looked. To tell the truth, there was not a single individual present who didn't have a stake in the success of the experiment. Chris and Richard worked out the final mathematical theory, the engineers who built the drive, and even Susan, the chief administrator who authorized the experimental use of the rocket, built before the war and meant for atmospheric research. Yoko Ishimuri, who worked out the computer control software for the modified weight the new rocket represented, affecting their flight plan.

Time was ticking away inexorably toward the set launch window and people stopped breathing.

At precisely 10 AM the conventional rocket engine ignited, hurling it vertically up with accelerating speed, soon making it disappear behind some clouds - unusual in a California sky. It took only ten minutes for it to reach the outer edge of the atmosphere and run out of fuel. That's when Chris's drive was supposed to kick in and accelerate the rocket way above the speed of light. Actually, it wasn't the rocket that was supposed to accelerate, but the space in front of it shrinking at a colossal speed while the space behind it would expand at the same rate, resulting in almost instantaneous space-time displacement that would place the rocket in the vicinity of the moon in mere minutes.

There was nothing else to do but wait for the data coming back from the rocket if indeed it would. They all crowded around the instrument cluster, waiting for the telltale signal on their monitor, announcing the end of the journey to the moon. If everything went according to plan, they would first see a dense column of numbers rolling up on the screen, needed for the computer to calculate the rocket's position and speed. Following that, they should start receiving the first live pictures of the pockmarked surface of the Moon. If everything went according to plan, they would see all this in mere minutes.

Suddenly, the screen came alive and, as they had expected, the numbers started scrolling up and fast disappearing on the top edge of the screen. It would take the computer a few seconds to evaluate them and present the conclusion: Had they reached the Moon? Did the experiment work?

There was not a sound to be heard from the spectators, as if the group was holding its collective breath, waiting for confirmation of success or failure. Finally, a loud cheer announced the success, as the computer displayed the rocket's position and speed, very close to the expected values, calculated according to Chris's theory. Finally, the grainy picture of the Moon's surface rolled into view and this was the happiest moment in Chris's life and the most beautiful sight he had ever seen. It took Chris's drive a mere minute to reach the Moon from the moment it cut in, after the rocket's conventional engine shut down.

The next conversation between Chris and Omega1850 had a different tone from the previous one.

*"Congratulation, Chris for the successful demonstration of the viability of your faster than speed-of-light space drive. A few days before your experiment I had received*

*confirmation from the other Omegas about the validity of your theory and now both theory and practice are synchronized, which is the best way science should work."*

"So now you are willing to let me use the resources I had asked for, to build a much larger space vehicle for my drive, so the proposition of reaching the stars light-years away could be proven? I was thinking of Alpha Centauri A which has a Neptune-sized habitable-zone planet. Of course, confirmation could not reach us for four years because of the speed of light limitation of electromagnetic waves, but we would know for sure if it could be done in four years."

*"No need for building a larger rocket, Chris because one already exists at Vandenberg Air Force Base, 343.7 miles south of Sacramento. One top-secret piece of information I am aware of is a high-priority project that had started years before the war. The project's code name is 'Lifeboat" and it was built to rescue American leadership in case of a nuclear war. The rocket could house a hundred humans, the President, members of Congress, and their families, and is fully stocked with food and all other necessities to stay in Earth's orbit for months if necessary until the war was over and it was safe to land back on Earth. It was never used because the sudden attack by the Russians destroyed Washington completely before anyone could take off to California. During the war, most of the Air Force Base was destroyed by Russian missiles but I have reason to believe that the ship is still undamaged, because it was built a safe distance away from the main structures of the Base and is hidden in an underground silo. I don't think any humans are still alive there, at least I can't*

*raise anyone by radio signals but, if and when the time comes that we need to rescue a good cross-section of the human species to send them out as migrants, it is one option I am aware of."*

To say that Chris could be knocked over by a feather would be an understatement.

He opened and closed his mouth several times, unable to express a coherent thought, he was so shocked by Omega's revelation.

Finally, he croaked out: "Do you have the specifications for that ship? We will need it to build my drive to be compatible?"

*"Yes, indeed I do and, in case of a serious and urgent need I can release it to you."*

"Why wait until it becomes serious and urgent? We may not have enough time by then to actually complete the task. Why not do it now, keep it in reserve and use it only if we must, but then without a dangerous delay?"

*"I understand your concern and I will consult all the other Omegas in the valley. Decisions of this magnitude require full analysis and consensus. I will get back to you when a decision is made. Until then please keep this information I gave you strictly to yourself."*

Chris's comm-link session with Omega was ended and he was left with conflicting emotions of fear and hope. He was sure that sleep would avoid him for the night.

Chico's advisory council was in session, discussing Chris's successful experiment and his request to authorize a larger-scale trial for his drive. To everyone's surprise, Chris seemed to have changed his mind, advising them to wait for a while.

"The theory is proven, there is no need for further experiments," he said, contradicting his earlier argument that they had to scale up his design to prove that it would work with heavier rockets as well. Nobody understood his change of mind and Chris wasn't going to explain the confidential information that Omega1850 had entrusted to him in the biggest secrecy. If and when it became necessary to power 'Lifeboat' he was confident that his drive could handle it just as easily because it affected space-time and not the ship itself. All they would need is a much larger and more powerful fusion reactor. So they tabled the topic of further experiments and took up the previous subject of social, political, and economic organization of Chico, once the town could be repopulated.

"You all remember that we were talking about Technocracy as a form of government," Alex Sigorski opened up the topic "and you had a week to think about it. Now tell me what you think."

"I think it is a terrific idea," Susan Chambers, their chief administrator replied instantly. "I didn't need a week to think about it because it is blindingly obvious. We all know what 'democracy' turned into: it became a farce and a stupid farce at that. There is not a speck of intelligence in the system. On one hand, it becomes blatant manipulation of the masses, with the lowest level of intelligence and education, appealing to their basest

271

emotions of hate, fear, envy, greed, and aggression. On the other hand, it became a gambling casino where the candidate and his or her party with the largest sum of money had the greatest advantage because everybody without a huge purse is completely locked out of the bidding process. You may have the greatest idea for solving seemingly unsolvable problems, but nobody will ever hear about it because you can't afford the exorbitant cost of advertising. On top of that, behind the scenes, you have the big money interests that pull the strings and make the dirty deals to come out on top. Add to all of these the party currently in power will twist the election process into a pretzel with shameless gerrymandering, voter suppression, and outright disfranchisement. Now contrast this with a system in which decisions are made by intelligent experts who have decades of accomplishments with social and economic problems."

She ran out of breath and the council members all burst out laughing: "Let me  guess, Susan, you don't approve of democracy the way it is practiced?" Alex asked with a big smile "I couldn't have put it better than you did, maybe you left out the media's role in the process which is basically misinformation on a grand scale. Not only it doesn't inform the citizenry about the issues but, in the name of impartiality, they present both sides of an argument as equal. So, if a thousand scientists say that climate change is real and an existential threat and they find an idiot who denies this, they present this as both equally valid arguments."

"Now add to this the Internet-based social media in which the craziest conspiracy theories are the most believed by the large number of idiots who will amplify their crazy message, droning out anyone who tries to talk reason, then you have the perfect brew of a dysfunctional and self-destructing society." Yoko Ishimuri added her favorite objection to the abuse of the Internet.

"How about the self-promoting politicians who try to undermine people's belief in the democratic system, and the electoral process by throwing around wild accusations about fraud and corruption? I think, democracy as a system is bankrupt. The best we can hope for is a benevolent dictatorship, supervised by incorruptible computers like our Omegas. I vote for Technocracy, with veto power given to computers. Something like what we have had since the war and it has worked for us very well, not just here but in all the other towns in the Valley" Chris added his own opinion.

Councilors sat in their seats, digesting all that was said, nodding their heads as arguments were rattled off one after the other. All this was common knowledge that everybody knew and very few dared to present in such stark terms before. "I guess we have a consensus for Technocracy, overseen by the computers. Anyone against it?" Susan called the vote.

Not one hand was raised. They were scientists, they recognized the truth when they saw it.

# Redding

Captain Devon interim CO. of the Mt Shasta Army National Guard, serving in that role since their ex CO., Major Peter Harding had died of an accident while on route to the town of Redding, finally had his answers. Ever since that fateful day when his commander threatened to kill him unless he ordered his troops to attempt to cross a ravine on foot after the bridge across the now empty Shasta lake was blown up., he was trying to understand why his CO was so intent on a suicide mission. As far as he, and any of his soldiers, knew they were on their way to the Redding Army Base to find new accommodation after their own base was destroyed by the eruption of the Mt. Shasta volcano. They had found temporary lodging in a small town, named Castella, 20 miles south of their destroyed base and Captain Devon secured adequate accommodation for all of his troops, but Major Harding, inexplicably, wanted to press on toward Redding. And then, when they were almost there, a mysterious explosion destroyed the bridge and stranded them on the north side, unable to cross. The real shock came after that when Harding wanted to cross by foot across the steep ravine. An unfortunate accident caused the Major to lose his balance and fall headlong into the chasm, killed instantly. They had no choice but to turn back and return to Castella.

The town people were surprised to see them again, but they resumed their previous helpful stance, giving them food and shelter, but it was all just a temporary solution. They couldn't expect a small town to feed an extra 232 man indefinitely. So, where could they go? Studying the map, Devon realized that another route existed that did not require the destroyed bridge. If they went north, past their previous base (assuming the road was passable and not covered with hardened lava) then they could intersect with I3 and then go south again toward Redding. This was a much longer route, adding at least another 100 miles to their journey, but then they could turn East on 299 and arrive at the Redding National Guard Base on the west side of Redding.

So far so good, but what kind of reception could they expect? Someone must have blown up that bridge to prevent them from entering their town and it could only be the soldiers in the Guard. They had to have a reason and Devon had to find out what it was, before attempting contact again. What was their CO. up to? The motel room where the Major slept before that fateful trip had been undisturbed all this time, his personal possessions still there, so Devon decided to start looking for clues. It didn't take long because prominently displayed, a sealed envelope was found on his dresser, addressed to the Redding Guard CO. When he opened it he found a long, rambling explanation for why he decided to attack Redding, as a way to commit suicide, taking as many of the hated fellow humans with him as he could. Most of the letter was about why he hated humanity that wanted to live while his family had to die.

Captain Devon had his explanation. He also had a way to find out if Redding would forgive the unaware soldiers for their crazy commander's act of suicide. He had to send a scout, with Harding's letter, to Redding and explain how unaware and innocent they all were of their commander's action. Maybe that would be enough for the Redding CO to trust them again.

~~~

Colonel Anita Majors was back in Redding, finally, after wasting almost 3 days in the Sacramento hospital. After the doctors examined her and the X-ray of her skull, they discharged her with a clean bill of health. A few of her more seriously wounded soldiers had to stay behind, but she and her 100 soldiers said their goodbyes and headed home. It took them most of the day because of the road conditions and the frequent detours but, by supper time they arrived and rolled through the gates of their own base. Home at last!

She found several messages on her desk, most of them from Brad Wagoneer who seemed inordinately worried about her. He must have been told about her close encounter with a bullet and the resulting hospitalization but not yet about her discharge, and her decision to return. It was actually quite sweet of Brad to be so worried about her, their relationship was still nothing more than cordial cooperation but now she had to face the truth: Brad was really very fond of her and didn't want to hide it anymore.

She knew that she would have to decide for or against a relationship, teasing and flirting were definitely not in her nature. "*So what is it going to be?*" she asked her reflection in the bathroom mirror "*would it be so bad to have a man again in your life?*" She decided to sleep on it and face the question again the next morning when she wasn't so tired and sleepy.

As it turned out, the next morning was started by an unexpected visitor, a soldier from the Mt. Shasta Army Base, who brought her a letter from their CO. She opened it with very bad vibes, couldn't imagine what her earlier attacker could possibly want to talk to her about. She was tempted to tear it up and throw it away unread, but curiosity got the better of her and she started to read it. Apparently, it had been written by the new CO. of the Base, explaining what had happened and why. The attached rambling suicide letter from the previous CO. raised the hair on her neck. You don't often get confronted with naked insanity, even if he had a disturbing basis for his delusions. This new development definitely needed thinking over, even better, consultation with Brad and, maybe, their Omega computer. She told the soldier to eat and rest in their cafeteria before heading back to his base with her reply. After that, without a firm decision in her mind about Brad and their relationship, she called him to let him know that she was back and they needed a conference ASAP.

"Anita, you are back!" Brad's voice conveyed his pleasure of talking to her again. "Are you all right? Has your wound healed? I was really worried when I heard."

"I am fine Brad, it was only a scratch. So, can we get together like immediately? There are new developments that we need to decide about."

"Any time, Anita, do you want me to go there? I could see you in half an hour if it is OK for you?"

"Here is fine and half an hour is fine too. See you soon." She hung up, not eager to continue this far too emotional conversation. If they were going to have a relationship, it would have to be on a much more rational basis than an overflow of emotions. She had always found it tiring when she was drawn into men's emotions. She was too old for that now. Mutual respect, enjoyable conversations, and satisfying sex, that was something she was prepared to consider.

When Brad arrived, she met him in her office, making it clear that this was a business meeting. She proceeded to tell him about the visit from Mt. Shasta, showed him the letters, and watched him reading them with the visibly same reaction as her own when she had read it herself. When he was finished, he just muttered:

"If this isn't the craziest story I have had for some time, I don't know what was."

"Exactly my take on it, Brad, so what are we going to do?"

"Could this be a ruse to attack us from another direction?"

"I doubt it. Crazy as it is, it has a taste of sincerity, and it matches the information we had had about him before, about the death of his family and subsequent psychological problems, even hospitalization, and therapy"

"Regardless of how far we trust him, we can't accommodate another 232 soldiers. They must find another place."

"How about Sacramento? They have an Army Base that's practically empty and I would feel better if they had their own defense, not relying on us to rush south each time they need help with difficult people."

"Now, that's an idea, but Sacramento has to invite them, we can't make this decision in their name. I suggest you get in touch with them and tell them the whole story, including a copy of the two letters we received."

Brad didn't waste any time mulling it over, he drove back to his office and activated Omega 1900, and asked him to convey the news to Sacramento and ask them if they would consider accepting army refugees in their empty base. This out of his hand, he spent some time contemplating his relationship with Anita and wondering if he had a chance with her. "There is one way to find out," he told himself, "I'll just have to invite her to a nice dinner and ask if she is interested. She can say 'yes', or she can say 'no', but one way or the other this will be decided. We are not teenagers anymore to agonize over things like that. I hope she'll say 'yes' but even if it's a 'no' I'll live." With this decision firmly in his mind, he called her again and invited her to a 'welcome-home' dinner. She accepted, which was a good sign so he only had to wait for dinner time, and then he would know.

The reply from Sacramento arrived unexpectedly promptly and it was positive: "Sacramento would be happy to accept Army National Guard soldiers in their mostly-empty base. Please arrive without weapons, there is plenty on the base, no need to bring anymore." It sounded like a precaution in case the whole story was just a cover for further aggression. Unlikely, but why take a chance?

Once Anita received the message from Sacramento, she told her visiting soldiers to head back to their temporary base and tell their CO. the good news. This out of her hair, she still had a few hours to get ready for Brad's invitation when, she was sure, more than the menu would be discussed.

She decided to stay in her army uniform for the occasion, not giving him any hint about which way she was leaning. A nice business-like beginning for the dinner and then things would work out one way or another. She would neither encourage nor discourage him, let's see what he would come up with. To tell the truth, she was slightly excited about the situation, it had been a very long time since she had had to make decisions like that. Maybe it was time before she was too old for romance?

Dinner started as she had imagined, a polite handshake and conversation about her time in Sacramento's defense.

"It was nothing, really, far too easy to trap those morons, I would have been a lot more cautious like spreading out the convoy not to present an easy target for ambush or entrapment. They also could have split their forces between the two spans of the bridge, just in case, only the northbound one was mined. But, high IQ was not a requirement for escaped convicts, naked brutality is all they had. Enough to terrify the citizens of Stockton, but no match for my troops."

"I think you are far too modest, Anita. Trapping them on the bridge was a brilliant idea."

"I hate to disillusion you about me, Brad, but the whole plan was cooked up by their Omega, I had nothing to do with it other than a few minor pieces of advice."

"And that was equally important for a successful conclusion" Brad wouldn't be disillusioned, no matter how hard she tried.

"I was a lot more worried about you attacking the smaller gang left in Stockton and I knew you wouldn't get away without a shooting match."

"Even that wasn't such a big deal, a few people got wounded, a few convicts got killed but it was all over in minutes."

This was now or never, Brad thought and plunged in.

"I was very worried when I heard that you were wounded, Anita. I became very fond of you and I'd really miss you now."

She was looking at him quizzically, knowing that it was decision time, his declaration was as clear as glass. After a slight pause, she found herself replying to his implied invitation.

"And what are we going to do about it?"

No verbal reply was required from him, only a slow, gentle kiss that they both savored for answers. The answers they both found must have been the same because they stood up, embraced, and, holding hands they walked into his bedroom to find out how compatible they were in bed. The army uniform she was wearing didn't have a chance.

When they finally emerged, mutually satisfied, it was time for some serious talk. Decisions wouldn't wait for romance and the future of Redding needed to be discussed, at least to come to some agreement about how they envisaged it.

"I don't know how much you have heard about happenings in the Valley, Anita, but I find the social experiments in the five cities south of us quite intriguing" Brad started the conversation, carefully avoiding any commitment about how he really felt about them. "Intriguing" was the most neutral word he could find.

"What experiment?" Anita used her combative voice, so familiar to Brad.

"I know about your red line and I respect it. You are a soldier and honor-bound to live up to your oath to the American Constitution. However, even that has changed over the years and we have managed to add, let me see, I'm sure it's 42 amendments by now. This means that as things change, we have to change with them or be left behind."

"You also know that Article Five of the United States Constitution details the two-step process for amending the

Constitution. Amendments must be properly proposed and ratified. That is also part of what I am honor-bound to uphold. Until I see definitive proof that the United States doesn't exist anymore, I have to live by my sworn allegiance to her government."

"So, what you are saying is that we are in a wait-and-see position?"

"Exactly. However, I would advise a slight attitude change. You see, the Founding Fathers had a good idea with the checks and balances and it would have worked if everybody respected the laws as I do. The system was designed to work but it broke down because a lot of unauthorized compromises were reached behind closed doors and those compromises corrupted the system. I propose to adhere to the original intent and refuse to make politically expedient compromises."

"I see what you mean, but it basically boils down to one thing: if people follow the rules of a system, the system would work. I don't know any system that loudly proclaims that "we want to rip off the citizenry" - they all claim to want to serve the people. Even the communists and fascists and what-have-you claimed to want to serve the 'people'. So, if we hold them to their claim, any system would work."

"You may be right, but I have sworn allegiance only to one system and that is the one I want to follow. And that is the system Redding had better follow because now you and I are the only representatives of the US government and it is up to us to uphold the law, at least until we are sure that we are forever on our own. If that happens, then we may experiment but, for now, let's be honorable citizens."

"Amen!" Brad replied and they both burst out laughing.

Redding was on its way to being a model city, the way the Founding Fathers imagined "Life, Liberty and the pursuit of Happiness"

# Epilogue

This is my last journal entry for a while. Hopestead has just finished a successful harvest and we didn't do too badly. According to Adrien's and Mark's estimate, we have enough corn, potato, and preserved vegetables to last till the next harvest, so our experiment could be called a success. We proved to be able to feed ourselves with what we grow and it will only get better as we gain experience. Once the corn is dry enough for grinding in our water mill, we will have cornmeal and then can make our own bread, something we have all been missing. We have been getting a lot of useful advice from Scott, he hadn't forgotten his promise to repay our assistance, twice already when he was in trouble and needed our help. During the year we made more improvements to Hopestead, and finished the extra bathroom and two new apartments in the barn, so everybody is now comfortable in a proper bedroom, and no more bathroom-related accidents. Galen reinstalled the fully recharged batteries into the truck he had removed them from when we went to Gridley and, after some tuning up he managed to drive it home. We put it to good use by bringing a lot more stones from the quarry and planning to build another house, so our community can accommodate over a dozen volunteers who want to join us as soon as we are ready for them.

The six towns in our Valley form an interesting little 'country' - independent in their internal organizations, but trading with each other by contributing their strengths in areas in which other towns have deficiencies. It's an all-around win-win community. Inside these towns, vibrant social experiments explore the different ways human beings can relate to each other. They have economic systems ranging from Capitalism to Communism; from agricultural cooperatives to Technocracy; from benevolent dictatorship to pure anarchy. The beauty of the system is that no one is trying to force their way on anyone else, ideology was replaced by pragmatism - each town follows its own idea of what works for them.

We still haven't had any communication from outside the Valley and don't know what, if anything, survived the war. We may be the only pocket that's still alive and functioning on this destroyed land. The weather is a major concern. According to Chico's environmental scientists, the planet is past the tipping point in climate change and the heat waves, droughts, floods, tornadoes, and forest fires will be getting worse and worse over the coming decades. We may have to abandon this planet in the future on spaceships using Chris's faster-than-light space drive and start again fresh somewhere else. If we do, I hope we will have learned our lessons and won't destroy our new home with the same stupidity and greed with which we destroyed this one. In the meantime, we just have to adapt the best way we can and hope not to be overwhelmed to the point where we can't cope anymore.

Our Omega computers have been and still are an invaluable partner to the human population. They are unobtrusively monitoring our activities, offering advice when needed and cautioning about emerging danger signs when necessary. With precision only AI quantum computers can achieve they optimize the production and distribution systems in the cities, assuring adequate and egalitarian living standards for all the citizens and that goes a long way to minimize friction and assure peaceful coexistence. They could be the next step in evolution when they augment the Homo sapiens species with their unfailingly rational and incorruptible nature. We need them and they need us - it is a perfect symbiotic relationship.

Our Hopestead is an anomaly in the Valley - we offer what none of the others do: a form of human existence in which individuals have maximum scope for facing life and nature, not as cogs in the machine but as viable individual life forms. We are all problem solvers, stretching our abilities to the maximum, yet we still depend on each other in a mutually beneficent community. That was what I had missed all my life when I was living as a computer software specialist, an unbalanced human being with highly developed skills in a very narrow area of expertise, but almost totally oblivious in all other areas. It was this unbalance that forced me to look for alternatives and gave me the motivation to strike out in a new direction, facing a multitude of new challenges. Now, in addition to computer skills that I still haven't forgotten, I am competent as a farmer, a carpenter, and a plumber, and I am even familiar with the rudiments of electricity and car mechanics. But the most important ability I have developed on our farm is the capacity to face new and unfamiliar problems with the mindset of a problem solver. New challenges have become joyful trials in which I can reaffirm my self-esteem, proving to myself that I am a worthwhile human being, competent in the art of living.

And now, at the end of my journal, I have come to the reason why this is my last entry for a long time. I have a new challenge in my life and I feel completely unprepared, yet fully determined to be the best father I can possibly be. Martha gave birth to a beautiful and healthy baby daughter and that will require all my problem-solving skills to help her grow up to be a happy and competent child, youth, and adult. I know that billions of human beings on this planet had faced the same challenge over the centuries and millennia, but that knowledge doesn't make it any less of a challenge for me. Martha, as usual, laughs at my trepidations, she has enough confidence for both of us, facing the world with her sunny disposition.

"We will cope, babe, as we always do!" she assures me and I hope that she is right.

Actually, our lives are defined by hope: hope that our abilities will protect us from what the future may throw at us.

That is why this place was named Hopestead when we chose a name for it and that is why my baby daughter's given name is Hope.

Hope has served us well so far and that's the most one can say about human life on this planet.

The End

# Other books by the author

- The Prism of my Mind – Poems
- Humane Physics– Classical Physics
- House Arrest – a Story of Liberation –
- Meandering – Short Story collection
- A Dark end Stormy Knight – Fantasy
- Saved in Time – An Escape Story – novel
- Epicycle Physics – Modern Physics
- Humane Physics – The Whole Story
- Opposing Forces – a Memoir
- Perembulations _ Musings of an Old Man

# About the author

Francis Mont has been living in Canada for the past 49 years after he emigrated from his native Hungary where he studied science and received a degree in Theoretical Physics. Over the years he did research, application, and teaching in Mathematics, Physics, and Computer Science. He is interested in profound questions, both in science and in social philosophy. He is a 'big picture' person, focusing on fundamental principles and the defining essence of the topic at hand. He also pursues independence and self-reliance to the best of his abilities, as his solar power system and year-round greenhouse demonstrate. He writes poetry, plays classical violin, dabbles at wood carving, and has not yet stopped building the house he and his wife and (currently) five cats live in.

# Ordering Information

You can order a copy of this book at the following venues:

- www.alibris.com
- www.biblio.com
- www.montland.ca

or by sending email to the author to the following address: books@montland.ca

I will respond to queries within 24 hours.